JUDI McCOY

ONE NIGHT
WITH A
Goddess

AVON BOOKS
An Imprint of HarperCollinsPublishers

This is a work of fiction. Names, characters, places, and incidents are products of the author's imagination or are used fictitiously and are not to be construed as real. Any resemblance to actual events, locales, organizations, or persons, living or dead, is entirely coincidental.

AVON BOOKS
An Imprint of HarperCollins*Publishers*
10 East 53rd Street
New York, New York 10022-5299

Copyright © 2007 by Judi McCoy
ISBN: 978-0-06-077460-8
ISBN-10: 0-06-077460-6
www.avonromance.com

First Avon Books paperback printing: May 2007

Avon Trademark Reg. U.S. Pat. Off. and in Other Countries, Marca Registrada, Hecho en U.S.A.
HarperCollins® is a registered trademark of HarperCollins Publishers.

Printed in the U.S.A.

10 9 8 7 6 5 4 3 2 1

"So, what are we going to do?"

"Do?"

"About this . . ." His palms slid from her bottom to her lower back. "I assume you feel it, too?"

"There is no attraction. It's simply—" Her gaze linked with his. "—hormones."

Matt drew away, still grinning. "Probably, considering you started driving me crazy the moment I saw you. For some reason I find impossible to fathom, you've worked your way under my skin."

His fingers caressed her nape, encircling the curve of her throat. "Are you really going to leave soon?"

"Absolutely." Though the thought filled Chloe with regret.

He leaned forward. His skin scorched hers, burning through the gossamer of her chiton, melting her flesh. No mortal man, and certainly no citizen of Mount Olympus, had ever made her feel this lost yet found, this weak yet powerful . . .

This needy for love.

By Judi McCoy

ONE NIGHT WITH A GODDESS
ALMOST A GODDESS
WANTED: ONE SEXY NIGHT
WANTED: ONE SPECIAL KISS
WANTED: ONE PERFECT MAN

To Renee and Brandon.
May your life together
be filled with love and laughter,
always and forever a honeymoon.

Prologue

Blah, blah, blah.

Chloe rolled her eyes at the sound of the high and mighty words spewing from the mouth of the highest and mightiest of all deities, Zeus, the great father god, head honcho, and CEO of Mount Olympus.

Zeus had been ranting for a good ten minutes, calling up thunder and lightning as he scolded her, Kyra, and Zoë, the last muses taken to task in his once-a-century performance review. He'd already impressed upon them their bottom-of-the-heap status and was now into the reward and punishment stage of his pronouncement.

Biting her lower lip to keep from screaming, Chloe waited for the next series of threats. Zeus raised his bony hand. "I fathered a dozen muses, but you three have been completely ignored by the legend books. And why? Because you're slackers, do-nothings who care more about gossip and good times than inspiring mortals in the field I chose for you." He looked down his nose, appraising them one by one. "You have two choices. First, you may stay on Mount Olympus and accept a loss of status. Instead of flirting the day away, you can muck out the stables, toil in the kitchen, or work in the dairy. There are any number of chores that will allow you to earn your keep.

"The second offer is more challenging, therefore of greater risk and eventually of more value. Each of you may go to earth and take a final stab at fulfilling your destiny, which means doing something that nobly inspires mankind. If you succeed, you may return here and live forever in splendor—no more performance reviews—just frolic and fun. But if you fail . . ." He leaned forward. "You will remain on earth and live as a mortal until your dying day."

Kyra tugged her sisters into a huddle and whispered, "What he's offering is impossible."

"Handmaiden to Hera the Harridan is *impossible*," moaned Zoë. "The other choice threatens our very existence."

Chloe narrowed her eyes. "I have no intention of pulling udders or shoveling horse droppings until the end of forever. We are demigoddesses, created to inspire. What else can we do?"

"Is that all?" Zoë, the most pragmatic of the trio, asked their father.

"Well, there is one more thing." Zeus stroked his snowy beard and gave a flinty grin. "Falling in love with a mortal is forbidden. Dally if you must, but keep your mind strictly on the work at hand so I know you're taking this seriously. Dire consequences await you if you return here more impassioned by a mortal than by your job."

"Fall in love? Not bloody likely," said Zoë, more to herself than her sisters.

"It'll never happen," muttered Chloe, fixing her gaze on Kyra. "Will it, sister dear?"

Kyra shrugged and Chloe rolled her eyes. Just what she needed, to be stuck on earth with two siblings who were high on intelligence and humor, but big fat zeros in the diva game. A true goddess could dally with dozens of mortals and never fall in love. All she had to do was stick to the rules—Chloe's rules, that is. Too bad neither of her sisters knew how to command respect or establish themselves as true demigoddesses like she did.

Tired of her father's growling voice, Chloe tossed her head. A single word stood out as he sounded his last threatening sentence, trying her patience and stretching her nerves taut.

Computer.

"Wh-What?" Chloe sputtered.

"I said, you'll need to learn the use of one of those." He jerked a thumb over his shoulder, indicating the modern marvel sitting on his desk. "So we can stay in touch."

Chloe jutted her chin. "Why can't we use Hermes?"

"That boy hasn't taken wing since the day I installed the telephones. He's in charge of networking the system. I'll allow you a day to become proficient, so we may communicate via the Internet."

Each of her demigoddess sisters had been reassigned and, to her knowledge, not one had been given these ridiculous orders or threats. Up to her curly tresses with his pompous demands, she stomped her foot. "That's not fair. The others don't have to—"

Zeus shot to his feet and lifted his arms. Thunder shook the clouds around them as lightning speared the sky. "Silence!"

Without warning, a gust of wind swept Chloe skyward. Floating, swaying, cresting on waves of cool dry air, she glanced left and right and saw the same thing happen to Kyra and Zoë. Would she ever learn to keep her opinions to herself?

Darkness overtook her as she spiraled downward. Like a lone leaf tossing in the wind, unable to control her destination, she was falling . . . falling . . . falling . . .

Chapter 1

A suburb of northern Chicago

"I now pronounce you man and wife," Judge Haywood Armbruster solemnly intoned. "You may kiss the bride."

Chloe Degodessa watched with a practiced eye as the happy couple stood at the rear of the main chapel. She was there to assist the bride and groom in the orderly arrangement of their receiving line. She'd worked on this sumptuous affair with the bride and her mother for the past ten months. She knew to the second the timing of the line, when the couple should head to the reception, and the exact minute they'd be announced as Mr. and Mrs. George Howard Allen. She'd even memorized the honeymoon itinerary for their trip to Barbados.

The organist played the exit march, and she

steered the attendants in place as they came through the wide oak doors, ending with the bride and groom. Flashing what she hoped was a brilliant smile, she took George's hand in her left hand and Francine's in her right and gave them the identical, Mount Olympus inspired, congratulatory message she'd given every person with whom she'd dealt professionally since her arrival on earth.

"I wish you both every happiness."

"Thanks, Chloe. You've been an angel," said Francine, her porcelain cheeks blushing the way only a new bride's could. "How do I look?"

"Radiant. And very, very happy." Chloe rushed to the doors, which had been closed when the couple departed the chapel, and flung them open. Stepping back to allow the guests their first chance to wish Francine and George well, she grinned at Isabelle Castleberry, who'd been observing quietly from a corner of the vestibule.

"You feeling all right?" asked Chloe when she reached Miss Belle's side. "Where's your coat? And why aren't you wearing those lamb's wool-lined boots I gave you for Christmas?"

"I feel fine, child," Miss Belle answered, leaning on her polished mahogany cane. "Stop fussing and carry on as if I'm not here. You're doing a wonderful job."

Chloe gave Miss Belle's gnarled fingers a squeeze, then took a final glance at the line's progress and nodded to one of the assistants hired to work weekends. "No more than fifteen minutes,

Leah, then escort the bridal party to the limo. And make sure Freddy takes Miss Belle home as soon as the chapel is cleared. I don't want her working alongside the clean-up crew like she used to." After slipping on her full-length mink coat, she headed for a side door. "I'm on my way to the reception."

Bracing for the blustery air, she secured the top button of her lustrous Blackglama, struck out into the cold, and trotted swiftly down the winding path that led to Castleberry Hall about a hundred yards away. A family owned property, the estate's grounds and outbuildings were situated on Lake Shore Drive, directly across from Lake Michigan, where at this moment the wind was more a gale than a breeze.

She guessed the temperature to be ten degrees above zero and the wind chill factor at about five below, practically a warm spell for January. The crippling winter weather had been twice as debilitating, actually freezing her lips together, when she'd taken her maiden walk here after arriving from Mount Olympus. Though Zeus had sent her to an interesting city, he'd fallen miles short in the area of climate control.

She scoped out the macadam drive, free of snow and ice thanks to a diligent ground crew, and noted the meticulously cleared parking lot. Everything was ticking like a Swiss watch, which meant the staff was finally taking her seriously.

Making a final check of the grand ballroom

was her next order of business. Striding through the main dining room, she assessed the pink and purple table linens, colorful wedding favors, and multicolored centerpieces, then stopped by the buffet holding a magnificent four-tiered chocolate cake frosted in white and decorated in candy pink lilies, purple marzipan orchids, and pale lavender butter cream roses. Try as she might, she hadn't been able to dissuade the bride from using colors more appropriate for a twelve-year-old girl's bat mitzvah than a tasteful society wedding, but the Castleberry was known for always giving the customer her heart's desire.

Even with the garish hues, the celebration would go off without a hitch. Each table of ten was assigned a personal waiter or waitress who would see to the guests' needs and serve the food family-style. In that way, the rack of lamb, grilled vegetables, rice pilaf, braided herb bread, and sides of minted aioli gravy, champagne mustard, and béarnaise sauce would be parceled out in an orderly manner.

Waving to the bandleader, who was putting the musicians through a rousing warm-up, she continued to the kitchen, drawn by the enticing aromas wafting in the air. The delectable smells assaulted her senses as she entered through the swinging doors and took stock of hundreds of canapés arranged on elegant silver trays that lined the shelves, ready to be passed the moment the guests arrived.

In the central area of the kitchen apprentice chefs and assistants worked at plating the salad course, while others toiled over the course to follow.

Chloe stopped at Clark Parrott's side. Clark, owner and head chef of Queer Food for the Straight Dude, was the hall's main caterer. Clients were allowed to use anyone they chose to furnish the edibles for their affair, so she'd often had to deal with other, sometimes temperamental chefs, but the gay and very savvy young man was so easy to work with, his company was the only one Castleberry Hall recommended.

Right now he was putting the finishing touches on his signature dish. "Smells like food fit for the gods," she said, grinning at her personal pun. If only Clark knew how close to the mark her comment had landed.

"Hey, sweetie," said the caterer as he covered the last lamb riblet in a puffy white sleeve. "How was the wedding?"

"Beautiful, as usual. So far, the bride and groom are thrilled with the way we've managed the event."

"Well, bully for you." Clark raised his hands like a surgeon preparing to operate. "Holly, Diego, get over here with those vegetable platters. It's time to add the garnish." He clapped, and a half-dozen assistants rushed to do his bidding. After giving a final perusal, he waggled his fingers in a shooing motion. "Hurry, to the warming ovens." Then he turned, rested his backside against the counter, and heaved a breath. "Almost finished."

"You've done a remarkable job," said Chloe, propping herself next to him. "The guests should be here in about five minutes, and we're right on schedule."

Clark tossed her a naughty grin. "I'm free after the reception. Want to go clubbing when we're through?"

"To Ride 'em Cowboy? I don't think so."

"Aw, come on. You might meet another yummy straight guy."

Chloe raised a brow. "I've already decided that James Parcells will be my one and only questionable conquest. I'm still not certain that story he gave about going to a gay bar just to 'see how the other half lives' was the total truth."

"Miss Belle said you had a date last night. If it wasn't the possibly confused Mr. Parcells, who was it?"

Chloe grimaced at the memory of her second encounter with the buff-bodied Bryce Cummings, owner of a big ego and a few completely unremarkable body parts. The man had been so full of himself, she swore he'd watched his technique in the mirror while they had sex. Before leaving his apartment, she dropped a good-bye note on his dresser, positive she would refuse any of his future calls. She had to deal with several more events before she was summoned home, which left her little time to dally with him or any other mortal.

"Just a guy I met, but he's off the radar screen. I'm done with men for a while." The warning bell shrilled from the lobby, signaling the bridal party's arrival. "Got to run. I'll check with you later."

"Ta-ta," Clark chirped, already flitting to another section of the kitchen.

Chloe hung her mink coat on a hook in a closet outside the grand ballroom and smoothed her cream-colored, body-hugging silk sheath. Peeking into the salon, she observed the event greeter passing coats to an attendant who handed the guests tickets for their garments' retrieval. Then the greeter found the guests' names on a seating chart and gave them directions to the gift table and their places.

She wandered the room, aiding couples in search of their seats, doing whatever she could to speed the process. When the line trickled to a halt, she made her way to the wedding party's private room to check on the bride and groom and their attendants.

"I will not sit at the same table as that . . . that . . . hound dog," Chloe heard as she opened the door to the ladies' lounge.

One of the bridesmaids, Patty somebody-or-other, was pouting up a storm. "Francine knew he'd taken advantage of me at Lisa and Carl's wedding, and she purposely forgot to tell me he was one of the ushers. I hate that man."

Just thank your lucky stars you didn't get him for your escort, Chloe almost reminded the girl.

"Now, Patty, there are hound dogs in every pack. A woman's got to be smart enough to choose the best of the lot, have fun, and move on, just the way they do," quipped Chloe. "There's no rule that says you have to sit next to Gary," she added, taking a stab at the usher's name. "But you do have to act like an adult and share the table. I'm sure you wouldn't want to be remembered for ruining your best friend's wedding."

Patty narrowed her eyes as one of the other attendants concurred with Chloe. After a few more words of encouragement, the catastrophe was avoided, and Chloe moved them in line for the march out. Then she stuck her head around the corner and signaled the band, which segued into the happy couple's chosen song.

"Ms. Degodessa?"

She turned and bumped into Eugene Whitlock, father of the bride. "Yes?"

Beaming a smile, he handed her an envelope. "The wife and I gave Miss Belle the payment for this shindig, but we wanted you to have this personally."

"Oh, no, I can't accept—"

"You can and you will," said Eugene. "You've done a marvelous job, seen to everything needed to make our little girl happy on her big day. If not for your easygoing manner and attention to detail, she might be sobbing right about now, like we've seen a couple of her friends do on their wedding days."

Chloe realized it was fruitless to try and return the money, so she tucked it in her pocket and promised herself it would go with the others she sometimes received. "Well, thank you, then. I enjoyed working with you and Mrs. Whitlock, and Francine too."

"Oops, there's my cue," he answered when the band played the lead-in to a sentimental ballad. "Got to dance with my baby one last time before I let her go." Blinking teary eyes, he rubbed his nose. "Thanks again. And don't be surprised if Castleberry Hall's business triples in the next two years. I'm advising all my friends to have their daughters' weddings here."

Chloe leaned against a wall as he walked away, still fascinated by the sentiment mortals placed on certain festivities. This was the forty-eighth wedding she'd been responsible for since her arrival. Too bad she'd be gone in a few weeks, because she was going to miss Castleberry Hall and the career she'd carved here.

Then again, if Zeus deemed that she'd failed in her quest, earth and Castleberry Hall would be, for her, a better place in which to toil than the stables, chicken coops, or cow pastures of Olympus. Not that she was planning on failure, of course, but one never knew how the father god would react if he deemed she'd fallen short of her quota.

Closing her eyes, she recalled the afternoon she'd arrived here. A performance review every hundred years was hard to swallow, especially when the person in question hadn't had that successful a century. All the muses had been reassigned, but she, Kyra, and Zoë had gotten the brunt of Zeus's wrath.

When she'd awakened in her high-rise apartment and checked the elegantly furnished rooms, she'd found a closet full of designer clothes, including the expensive Blackglama, a bathroom stocked with the best hair care products and makeup, and a Chanel handbag on the kitchen table. The tote was filled with everything a girl needed to exist in a busy city, including pepper spray, several thousand dollars in cash, an American Express card, and a paid-in-full year's lease on the apartment.

After exploring her building, she'd slipped on the mink and walked the city. The next morning, she'd stared out her high-rise window and spotted an idyllic scene: a wedding party scurrying into limos on parklike grounds a half mile in the distance. Since Zeus's criticism had focused specifically on the rising divorce rate and many unhappy marriages, she was thrilled to learn the site was a privately owned facility that planned and hosted special events such as baby and bridal showers, retirement luncheons, sweet sixteens, even postwake parties.

But the Castleberry specialized in weddings.

Chloe had knocked on the doors of a stately home and been ushered inside. There, she'd met

Isabelle Castleberry, known as Miss Belle to everyone in the greater metropolitan area. After a quick introduction, the eighty-three-year-old woman had confided that she was searching for an assistant, and Chloe jumped to offer her services.

Luckily, Miss Belle didn't ask for references or past experience. She was waiting for the perfect person to walk through the door, hired Chloe on the spot, and insisted she move into a set of double rooms on the second floor of the manor.

The Muse of Happiness had taken the entire encounter as a sign and promptly agreed.

In the past months, Chloe had assisted at close to one hundred events, until Miss Belle felt she was ready to handle things on her own. Because her special handshakes were sure to inspire happiness for the long haul, she had high hopes for a successful and triumphant return to Mount Olympus.

She was a muse, created to inspire. As a daughter of the mighty Zeus, she could not fail.

Dr. Matthew Castleberry arrived at O'Hare Airport in a foul mood. Sporting a beard and dressed in fatigues, he'd spent several days at an army outpost waiting for a plane heading out of Ituri. After arriving in Beirut, he'd been held up for two days while government toadies ironed out a glitch in his paperwork, then he'd flown to Paris, where he waited for a jet to Chicago. Since both stops had been short on amenities, he was certain he resembled a bison and smelled even worse.

The past couple of years had been filled with abject misery interspersed with moments of incredible joy. He'd achieved every goal he'd set for himself as a member of Médecins Sans Frontières, better know in the states as Doctors Without Borders, but he'd paid a hefty price in the bargain. Right now, his goal was to surprise his grandmother and spend the next few months figuring out what he wanted to do with his life.

"Yoo-hoo, Matt, over here!"

He'd just dragged two duffel bags from the Customs gate when he heard the demanding female singsong. Raising his head, he spotted his ex-fiancée, Suzanne Armbruster, her limo driver at her side, making a beeline in his direction.

"Matt, darling." Suzanne tottered on sling-back stilettos as she rushed toward him and planted a polite kiss on his mouth. They'd last met about six months ago in London, where he had told her he was breaking off their engagement. Obviously, Suzanne had forgotten the small but vital detail.

He guessed that someone—probably her well-connected father—had found out about his month-early return and informed his only child just to be on the safe side. Even a pussycat like Judge Haywood Armbruster was smart enough to realize it was unwise to piss off a daughter like Suzanne.

Drawing back, she captured his hands in hers and gazed into his eyes. "Why didn't you tell me you were coming home? It was embarrassing finding out from Daddy."

Matt pulled from her iron-clad grip. "My travel plans changed from day to day, and I wanted to surprise Gram. Besides, since we're no longer an item, I didn't feel it was necessary." He cocked a brow. "Your father didn't give the news to Belle, did he?"

"Of course not," Suzanne said, tucking her arm in the crook of his elbow. She nodded to Bales, the judge's faithful driver, and the man immediately lifted the duffel bags and followed them out the airport door toward the line of waiting limousines.

Matt shivered in the biting wind, happy to be rid of the near stifling heat and humidity of Africa. Though Chicago was usually mired in snow, freezing wind, and unpredictable weather from October through April, it was still good to be back on American soil.

He opened the limo door while Bales loaded the luggage in the trunk. "I've been worried about my grandmother. Have you seen her lately?"

"No, but it wasn't for lack of trying. She came to the manor on Christmas Eve, but we had a full house. You know the judge and his holiday parties."

She slid across the buttery black leather, a toned thigh covered in sheer red escaping from under the cover of her ankle-length mink. Annoyance rose in Matt's chest, tamping down his curiosity. What in the hell was she wearing? "Keeping tabs on Grandma Belle was the one thing I asked you to do for me when we said good-bye in London. I didn't think it would be that much trouble."

Suzanne thrust out her lower lip as she settled into a far corner. "Don't be angry. I called her a half-dozen times after I got home from England, and several more between Thanksgiving and Christmas. She never returned my calls."

Which meant Suzanne hadn't told Belle of their split.

"Her assistant always had an excuse as to why she wasn't available," she added. "Damned woman."

"Assistant?"

"Someone named Chloe. Apparently, she's become Miss Belle's second-in-command. I went to Castleberry Hall once, but a gofer told me she and Miss Belle were in town meeting with suppliers. When your grandmother didn't respond to the note I left, I figured she'd rather be with her assistant than me, so I stopped trying."

Matt vaguely remembered Belle writing to inform him of a woman she'd hired to help with the bookings and party details. He didn't recall her name or the fact that she was screening phone calls. His grandmother had to be sicker than she'd let on to willingly give away control of her family empire. Or had it been taken from her?

"So you haven't met the woman? You don't know if she's young, old, intelligent, or possibly a con artist?"

"I haven't, but Daddy has. He says she seems honest, she's doing a competent job, and Belle adores her. Besides, your grandmother is too smart to be conned by anyone. Now, close your eyes, I have a surprise for you."

"I'm really not in the mood for games, Suzanne. I just want to get to the Hall."

Instead of answering, she stretched out her leg and tapped the toe of her shoe on the seat in front of her. The smoked-glass partition rose, cocooning them in the spacious rear seat. With a secretive smile playing on her lips, she shifted to her knees and slipped the mink off her shoulders, exposing a model-thin body clothed in nothing but a tiny red bikini bottom and red thigh-high stockings.

"Welcome home."

Matt took in Suzanne's small but perfect breasts and pale pink nipples, her flat stomach and boyish hips. He rested his head on the seat as she plastered herself to his chest and began kissing him in earnest. Oddly enough, he felt not the slightest twitch from behind his zipper, which made no sense, seeing as how he'd been celibate for the past six months.

"Bales has orders to drive around town until I give the signal for him to stop. He knows to follow my—" She wrinkled her nose and sniffed. Rearing away, she covered the bottom half of her face with a hand. "What is that disgusting smell?"

Matt pressed a button on the door handle, and a bar complete with ice, crystal tumblers, and bottles of liquor slid silently into view from a compartment on the back of the front passenger seat. He filled a glass with frozen cubes, then poured three fingers of brandy. In the confines of this small space, the five—or was it six?—days he'd spent since last taking a bath were finally making themselves known.

"Me, I'd imagine," he answered after taking a drink.

Her honey-brown eyes opened wide. "You?"

"Have you bothered to really look at me, Suzanne? I haven't shaved or been near a shower in close to a week, and I've worn these clothes since I left the hospital. I'm lucky I managed to find decent water to brush my teeth." He finished the drink in a long swallow. "And I didn't think you'd be here to welcome me home, considering we agreed to end our engagement six months ago."

"I never agreed to anything. You weren't conscious of what you said back then. Daddy told me that anyone who had to spend time in the darkest recesses of the Congo would lose all reason, and that's probably what happened to you," she said, her hand still covering her nose. "Nothing we discussed then made sense, so I decided to give you another chance."

Matt stared at his feet, still encased in combat boots. It had taken him a while to figure out that Suzanne was a woman who never took no for an answer, especially when it might be detrimental to her social standing. "I don't want another chance, Suzanne. I'm not the right man for you, and it's time you accepted it. I wrote you a dozen letters before you insisted we set up a meeting in London, where I told you how I felt in person. Wasn't that enough?"

"Not when you sounded so off-kilter and depressed. All that talk about children with machete or burn wounds, the war, the pestilence. It made me want to gag."

"Yeah, I'd imagine it would gag anyone who lived in an ivory tower with a wait staff and limo driver to take care of them." He poured a second drink and downed it in one gulp. "It really ruined the last two years of my life."

Suzanne rearranged her coat to cover her body and huddled in the corner. "Don't be such a class snob. I can't help the way I was raised. I begged you not to go. You had everything a person could want here: a supportive family, a well-known name, respect from the community, even a promising career as a surgeon. But you decided to throw it all away and—"

"I didn't throw anything away. I merely put my

life on hold for a while because of all the advantages you just listed. I wanted to give something back for having been gifted with a great family, decent work ethic, and the brains to become a doctor. I thought you understood, but apparently—"

"I do," she said, placing her fingers on his shoulder. "At least, I want to." She sighed. "Try to see it from my point of view. I'm engaged—"

Matt eyed his ring, still on the fourth finger of her left hand. "Excuse me, but unless you met another guy and that's his rock you're wearing, you are not engaged. I said you could keep the diamond, but I didn't say you could wear it as if nothing had changed."

"I'm wearing it because I want to work this out," she said with a huff. "I didn't tell anyone except the judge about the breakup, and he promised he wouldn't breathe a word to Belle because he agrees with me. You're going to come to your senses and change your mind. And when you do, I'll be ready to accept your apology and announce the wedding date."

"You can't be serious."

"I most certainly am. In fact, Ron Lassiter called last week to ask if I knew when you'd be home. He's still holding a position in his practice for you and thought I might have an idea as to whether you'd decided to take it." She pulled the mink tighter against her chest. "It was humiliating having to tell him I wasn't privy to your plans."

"You aren't privy to my plans because we aren't

going to be married, not now, not in a year, not ever." Matt had made an effort to be patient, but exhaustion, worry, and two glasses of brandy had dulled his brain. He leaned forward and rapped on the partition. "Bales, drive to Castleberry Hall," he said when the window slid down a few inches.

The partition glided into place.

"Fine." Suzanne ran her fingers through her light brown hair. "Daddy's at the Hall officiating a wedding. If he's still on the grounds, maybe he can get you to listen to reason." The warmth in her tone was only a tad above the outside temperature.

Crossing his arms, Matt leaned back and closed his eyes. "We can talk until we're blue, but nothing is going to change."

Chapter 2

Chloe tiptoed down the central staircase, crossed the foyer, and turned the lock on the mahogany-paneled door. Thank the gods, Miss Belle had gone to bed without protest. The Allen-Whitlock wedding reception had finished an hour ago, and though Chloe had ordered the elderly woman home, Miss Belle had attended the function as if she were an invited guest. After Chloe had given final instructions to the clean-up crew, she'd personally escorted Miss Belle home and seen to it she retired in comfort.

Isabelle Castleberry had been nothing but kind to her since she'd arrived, first hiring her for a job that enabled her to fulfill Zeus's order to inspire, then by bestowing her trust. As the days passed, she had come to rely on Miss Belle almost as much as the woman depended on her.

Zeus had sired the muses with Mnemosyne, a minor goddess, and the infidelity had so enraged Hera she'd denied the girls interaction with their mother. Chloe and the others had matured without a woman's guidance, which caused them to hold a special place in their hearts for any female with a motherly nature, and Isabelle Castleberry did more than fill the bill.

Of late, Miss Belle had given her an inordinate amount of responsibility, until it seemed to Chloe as if she were running the business single-handedly. Not that she minded the work of arranging weddings, coordinating corporate functions, planning christenings and family gatherings. She'd decided the job was perfect for her in many ways, most important of which was inspiring happiness in whomever she met.

Brushing a tear from her eye at the tender thoughts, she sighed. Feeling gratitude toward a mortal was ridiculous. She was a demigoddess, intelligent, exceptional in face and figure, and made to inspire, not a sentimental sap who cried at the drop of a hat. Mankind should be grateful for her existence. If not for the muses, there would be no poetry, no music, no order or beauty in their world.

She heard a car door slam and peeked out a front parlor window just as Judge Armbruster's limo pulled away. Then she spotted a hulking shape trudging up the steps of the stately home, unwieldy baggage in tow. Before she could gather

her senses, a key turned in the lock and the door swung open, allowing the freezing Lake Michigan wind to whistle through the foyer.

She stared as the large man dropped his bags. Who the heck was this guy, and how had he gotten a key to the Castleberry mansion?

Tapping a toe, she folded her arms and waited for the intruder to notice her. After glancing to his right, the man turned left, and Chloe inhaled a gasp. With his shaggy hair and beard, camouflage pants and bulky jacket, the interloper could have been an escapee from a military compound.

He also looked vaguely familiar.

"Who are—"

"What are you—?"

She blew out a breath. "I'm Chloe Degodessa, and I work here. Who are you?"

The hulk took her in from top to bottom, his whiskey-colored eyes causing her to quiver from the inside out.

"I'm Matthew Castleberry. This is my home."

Oh, crap. Just what she didn't need. She'd hoped to finish her mission here without interference. From the way Miss Belle described her grandson, that would now be impossible.

"Do you have identification?" she asked, well aware the house key should have been enough. But how did she know he hadn't stolen it from the real Matthew Castleberry or had one made? In the back of her mind she recalled the photo she'd seen on Miss Belle's nightstand. If she tried hard enough, she could match this hair-covered giant to the picture, but just barely. "A birth certificate or driver's license?"

Matt inspected the unfamiliar woman's sinfully long legs, flaring hips, and shapely breasts encased in a form-fitting and expensive-looking sheath studded in sparkling rhinestones. Sweet Jesus and Mother Mary, *this* distrusting angel had to be the person who had his grandmother in a stranglehold.

At first glance she reminded him of Marilyn Monroe or a more coherent and intelligent Anna Nicole Smith; then he took better inventory and realized her beauty was one hundred percent natural. Her huge baby blue eyes resembled those of a terrified doe, but her challenging expression was all business. She stood her ground, giving him time to examine her lush lips, delicate nose, and upswept smoky lashes.

"Miss Belle's grandson is a member of Doctors Without Borders. He's in Africa and not scheduled to come home for another month."

"Well, guess again, honey, 'cause he's home and he's dead tired. Now, if you'll excuse me, I'm going to my room. We can sort things out in the morning."

She stepped in front of him, blocking his way. "Don't force me to call Security."

He gazed at the ceiling, then took his passport from his jacket pocket, flipped it open, and waited while the lady inspected his picture, then him.

"Oh."

"Yep. Oh." Matt hoisted the duffels over his shoulders and shuffled to the staircase, trying to ignore her tantalizing scent. Honey? Flowers? Hell, it had been so long since he'd smelled anything other than disinfectant and the rancid stench of death, he wouldn't recognize a pleasant odor if it hit him with a two by four.

Halfway up the steps he realized that Chloe Degodessa was hot on his heels. "Trust me, I remember the way," he said, striving for calm.

"I'm sure you do. It's just that I . . . that is, Miss Belle . . . I'm staying in your rooms."

Matt made a left at the top of the stairs. This was the first he'd heard about the woman moving in, but he'd handle it tomorrow. Right now all he wanted was the king-sized bed he'd bought when he graduated college.

"Not a problem. The house has six other bedrooms. I'm sure you can find one to your liking."

"But—"

He juggled a duffel, opened the door, and strode inside, where the bags slid off his shoulders and landed with a dull thud on the sitting room carpet. Then he took a long hard look at the room. Things seemed the same, yet different. He walked to the floor-to-ceiling bookcases covering the wall next to the fireplace. Perusing the shelves, he found that the middle row of tomes he'd lovingly acquired through college, med school, and his residency had been replaced by books of a more historical bent: *Ancient Greek Architecture, A Day in the Life of a God, Classical Statues of the First Century*.

Instead of his color-coded drawings of various sections of the human anatomy, the walls were covered with poster-sized photos of tropical islands floating in azure blue waters, majestic mountains looming over grassy plains, and scenes of both modern and ruined temples.

A quick glance at the vacant spot next to the fireplace had him fisting his hands. "What the hell did you do with Elvis?"

"Elvis?"

Matt walked to the point in question, almost tripping over a pair of pink, satin-heeled shoes with a cluster of feathers decorating the arch. "Naked guy, about five-foot-ten with a big goofy grin on his jaw."

"That disgusting bag of bones had a name?"

He raised a brow. "Hell yes, it had a name. Elvis was a gift from my dad, right before—" He ran his fingers through his hair in order to keep from shaking her. "Elvis was a gag gift for my graduation from high school."

"He's in the cellar along with the rest of your stuff. I didn't throw anything away."

"Well whoop-de-doo." He continued to appraise the sitting area, then, without giving her a chance to say more, stomped through the archway and entered the bedroom.

This, he told himself with a shake of his head,

was the real epicenter of the disaster. Cosmetics, perfume bottles, brushes, and hair paraphernalia covered the top of his antique mirrored dresser from one end to the other. His highboy doors were askew, revealing sweaters in every color of the rainbow. A dozen pairs of shoes were heaped haphazardly next to a chair draped with bras, stockings, and other colorful bits of satin and lace.

His closet door stood open, giving him a clear view of the dresses, skirts, slacks, and blouses hanging from the rod. A shelf ran the upper length of the wall, and on it sat more shoes, more sweaters, and more clothing. How in the world could a woman own so many shoes or wear so much . . . stuff?

He frowned when he saw the pink satin quilt and dozen frilly pillows lining the headboard. When he'd left, the bed had been covered with a warm and serviceable brown corduroy spread and two matching pillows.

"Wait, don't tell me." He jammed his hands in his fatigue pockets. "Bergdorf's exploded, and this is the fallout zone."

His nemesis pushed from the archway, where she'd struck a nonchalant pose, and strutted to his side. "I planned to have the rooms professionally cleaned when I moved out before I—before you arrived."

"Don't bother," he answered, trying not to snarl. "Just cart your junk to the guest room next door."

"Junk?"

"That's J-U-N-Q-U-E, so don't get your knickers in a twist."

"Now?"

"Now would be good."

"But it's after midnight."

"No kidding."

Instead of getting the lead out, she gave him a sly grin. Plopping her curvaceous butt on *his* king-sized mattress, she smiled. "Make me."

Matt raised his eyes to the ceiling. Right now there was nothing he'd like better than to take up the challenge, carry her to a different bedroom, turn her over his knee, get his hands on her bottom and—

The tempting scenario shot straight to his dead zone—namely, the area behind his zipper. How was it that his penis had slept through his ex-fiancée's risqué offer in the limo but seemed remarkably wide-awake since he'd laid eyes on his grandmother's recalcitrant assistant?

Good going, Castleberry, he chided himself. He was acting as if he was fifteen again, giving in to raging hormones like he was rounding second base and heading for third.

"Look, Chloe—"

Stretching her dynamite legs over the coverlet, she crossed them at the ankles and inspected her fingernails. "That's Ms. Degodessa to you."

Matt knew when he was licked. Heaving a sigh, he traced a path back to the sitting area and slung his bags on his shoulders.

"Where are you going?"

His rapidly rising dead zone reacted to her husky voice as if he'd taken a dose of No-Doz. "To the nearest bedroom. Lucky for you, I'm too tired to fight."

She scampered to face him, her hands on her hips. "I don't want Miss Belle to find out we argued. She's getting too old to be upset."

His stomach flipped a somersault. "Is something wrong with Gram, something I'm not supposed to know about?"

She quickly shook her head. "I don't think so, though she did see a doctor this week."

"Who, what was his name?"

"Kelsey, Katz, Kevlar? I can't remember."

He mulled the names over in his mind as he edged past her to the door. When he'd left town two years ago, there'd been one Katz doing oncology and three Kelseys practicing in specialties ranging from anesthesiology to podiatry. And he didn't recall a Kevlar.

"Do you know the doctor's area of expertise?"

"Sorry, no. But when I asked her if anything was wrong, she assured me it was just a general checkup."

A possibility, though it still worried him. "Okay, well . . . I guess we can talk about it in the morning."

Chloe Degodessa didn't slap a hand over her nose as she closed the door, but she did sniff her disapproval. "Breakfast is at eight, and it wouldn't hurt to shower before you come downstairs."

Chloe opened her eyes to brilliant sunshine streaming through the windows of her bedroom. Deciding to take advantage of the moment, she stretched out on the huge mattress. Any second now she expected Dr. Hairy and Disgruntled to bang on her door and demand she move her things. The big jerk.

Matthew Castleberry's arrival had been more a shock than a surprise, as no one was expecting him for at least another month. Chloe was a bit annoyed that the blasted man had returned early, but Miss Belle was certain to be overjoyed. Women in their eighties, even those as spontaneous and cheerful as her employer, got their thrills where they could.

She gave Matt Castleberry a point for appearing genuinely concerned about his grandmother. She had yet to meet a mortal who thought more of his fellow humans than he did of himself, which was the way people described Matt. As a member of Doctors Without Borders, the local media had labeled their hometown boy one of the few good guys on the planet; someone children and adults should admire, a man politicians would do well to emulate, and a humanitarian beyond compare.

The city council had even given him an award, which he'd promptly rejected. But that hadn't stopped Miss Belle from attending the luncheon ceremony, accepting the plaque in his name, and hanging it in a place of honor behind her desk in Castleberry Hall's sales office. Aside from last night's unpleasant encounter, Chloe hadn't had a single experience with the man, though Miss Belle bragged about her only grandson as if he were Linus Pauling, Mother Teresa, and Albert Einstein rolled into one.

All she knew for certain was that Matthew Castleberry had the personality of a dyed-in-the-wool grouch, and smelled more like a hobo who'd drowned his sorrows in a bottle of sour wine than a man who deserved to be on a pedestal.

She checked the clock on her nightstand and noted it was almost eight. After slipping from bed, she hopped into the shower, changed into a pair of navy slacks and a white cashmere sweater, and thrust her feet into a pair of bright red pumps. Then she ran a brush through her hair, anchored it on top of her head with a plastic clip, and headed to breakfast.

"Hey, gorgeous." Clark Parrott sat at the table, reading the morning paper. Castleberry Hall was his second home, especially when he was catering back-to-back functions during the week. Miss Belle loved his company, and Chloe had grown to enjoy him as well. Clark could dish about fashion, men, and sex as well or better than any of her sisters.

She poured coffee from the sideboard server,

another plus when the chef was in residence, because he did all the cooking. "Have you seen our new arrival?"

"Haven't seen a soul since I woke up, except for Ruby. She's nursing a cold, so I told her to stay in bed." He propped his chin on his fist. "Who's here?"

"His Royal Highness, Dr. Matthew Castleberry," said Chloe, picking through Clark's breakfast offering, a tray of warm croissants drizzled with rich dark chocolate.

Clark slapped a palm on the table. "Get out."

"How well do you know him?"

"Miss Belle and I only got close after I bailed her out of a jam with a bridal shower about eighteen months ago. The heroic Dr. C and I have never met, but I've heard plenty."

Curious, Chloe hunkered down over her croissant. "Like what?"

"He's engaged to Judge Armbruster's daughter, and she's pretty much a bitch on wheels. My money says they'll break it off within the month."

Chloe had only spoken to Suzanne Armbruster on the phone, and none of their conversations had been pleasant. It was hard to imagine Matt Castleberry putting up with her haughty and demeaning manner. "The judge is such a sweetheart. How did he end up with the daughter from Hade—ah, hell?"

"They say her mother ran off with the gardener when Suzanne was about six, so the judge spoiled his only child rotten to compensate for her loss. Seems she always gets her way. Everyone was in shock when Matt joined Doctors Without Borders, because Suzanne had been telling anyone who'd listen they were going to be married and Matt was going to partner in some exclusive surgical practice that she had arranged." He batted his lashes in innocence. "Or so I've heard."

"Just who do you get your information from?" asked Chloe. She suspected Clark had a tendency to speculate when he didn't have all the facts, but nine times out of ten whatever he reported turned out to be true.

"From whomever I can, of course. You should know by now that I'm shameless when it comes to gossip." He folded the paper and set it aside. "So, is he as saintly as they say?"

"Hardly. And he didn't act like the kind of man who'd take orders from a woman."

Clark gave her a wink. "Let me guess, instead of falling at your feet as do most mortals, he was less than charmed when he found out you'd commandeered his room."

"He demanded I move out, so I guess I'll get to it today." Chloe took a dainty bite of her croissant. "Or not."

Matt took that moment to walk into the dining room, go straight to the sideboard, and pour a cup of coffee. "Take your time about relocating. I decided that I might have been a little . . . impatient last night."

Though his sandy brown hair was still on the long side, Chloe noted that his army surplus wardrobe had been replaced by snug faded jeans and a white shirt, over which he'd slipped a hunter green sweater that showed off his broad shoulders, tight buns, and long legs.

She was prepared to cut the affable-looking man she remembered from Miss Belle's picture a break and give him a true welcome home smile, when he turned—and her jaw dropped.

"I'm going to take a tray to Gram and surprise her," he continued, as if he hadn't seen Chloe's gaping mouth or heard Clark's sharp intake of breath. "I guess you figured out by now I'm Miss Belle's grandson," he said to the caterer, holding out his hand. "You must be Clark, the faithful chef."

"Um, yeah, that would be me," said Clark, accepting the friendly offer. "Why don't you sit and enjoy your coffee while I fix the tray. Then you can carry it to your grandmother."

"Great, thanks."

Chloe tried not to stare, but it was difficult. Matt Castleberry's face, which could only be considered ordinary on its best day, was lined with fatigue and several frightening scars, as if he'd been in a knife fight and lost the battle big-time. She hadn't noticed the damage last night, because of his beard, but now that he'd shaved . . .

"Do I look that bad?" Matt asked, resting his forearms on the table.

"I'm sorry," said Chloe, lowering her gaze. "I didn't mean to stare, but—what happened to you?"

"It's a long story. The wounds are still healing, so I'm hoping they'll look better in a couple of weeks. If not, I plan to see a plastic surgeon."

"Did it—were you—injured anywhere else?"

"In the ribs, but that's healing too." He sipped his coffee, then added more cream. "How badly do you think it will frighten Belle?"

Chloe wasn't sure how to answer. The scars had scared the crap out of her, but now that she'd had a chance to study them, she decided they gave him a rakish, sort of piratical appeal. "She'll be so happy to see you, I doubt it will matter."

"I thought about writing to tell her, but I didn't want to worry her. From your expression, I guess I should have gone with my first instinct."

Clark pushed through the kitchen door carrying a tray with a budded red rose in a vase, a cozy-covered teapot, and other service items. After setting two croissants on a plate, he said, "It's all yours."

"Thanks, I appreciate it." Matt collected the tray and took off for the foyer.

Matt carried the breakfast tray up the winding staircase and down the corridor that led to his grandmother's rooms. The house was huge, but he didn't mind the walk. He'd run these halls as a child, cursed them as a teenager, and grown to

love them as a man. The first Matthew Castleberry, his great-grandfather, had built the manor
for his bride, and it was tradition that the patri-
arch of the family, and his wife and children, reside there until something happened that made it
inconvenient or impossible to stay.

As a boy, he'd occupied the nursery, which had
been closed for the past thirty years, and moved
to a good-sized bedroom on the north side of the
house when he started first grade. His parents had
died right after he graduated high school, and
once he'd left for college, Miss Belle had taken the
liberty of installing him in his parents' old rooms,
which he used whenever he came home.

It really wasn't a big deal that Chloe Degodessa
now inhabited the rooms, but it would have been
nice if someone had asked his permission or
warned him beforehand. Then again, he'd arrived
a month ahead of schedule, and Chloe did say
she'd planned to move out before his return, so he
probably shouldn't be such a whiner.

Compared to the remaining items on his plate,
the loss of his personal space was insignificant.
First, he had to check on his grandmother's
health. She hadn't complained of anything in particular, but she had hinted in several of her letters
that she wasn't feeling as spry or energetic as she
used to. Though the complaint was normal for a
person of her age, he had an inkling there was
something Miss Belle wasn't telling him, and it
was his duty to find out what that was.

Second, came his future. The two years he'd spent in Ituri had left him drained and scarred, mentally as well as physically. He'd taken an oath to do no harm, which he'd upheld to the best of his ability, but he was no longer certain he could be trusted to keep his vow. Disease, poverty, and death had turned him into a disillusioned and bitter man. And though his grandmother had never said so, he knew that Castleberry Hall would fade away if he wasn't here to take the helm. Could he keep the family business intact and be a competent doctor at the same time?

Then there was Suzanne. The moment he'd spotted her marching toward him in the airport, he'd been certain that breaking their engagement was the right thing to do. Two years ago, when he'd proposed with her father's blessing, everyone, including Suzanne, had agreed she'd make the ideal doctor's wife. Then he'd told her about his decision to join Doctors Without Borders. She'd said okay, but her approval was short on sincerity, and things had gone downhill in the months he was gone. When they met in London, he knew they had to split. Especially since there'd been no sighs of longing or cries of misery from either of them at their being apart. And definitely no tremors of desire.

Then there was Chloe Degodessa.

Beside the fact that she'd brought out one dilly of a response from his dead zone, he had no idea what to make of her. Was she here simply to perform a job, or did she have some nefarious scheme in mind, maybe a way to embezzle funds or get Miss Belle to sign over the business to her?

He needed to investigate his suspicions without upsetting his grandmother . . . or letting Ms. Degodessa know the full potency of her electrifying presence.

He set the tray on the sideboard outside Belle's door and smoothed his hair. It needed a good cut, and he probably should have left the beard until he figured a way to cover his scars, but it was too late now. He'd never been able to hide anything from his grandmother, so he'd just have to suck up whatever she had to say and move on.

Inhaling a breath for courage, he tapped the door.

"Ruby? Is that you?" asked a firm yet fragile-sounding voice. "I thought I told you to stay in bed this morning. I'm not the one with a cold, and I can certainly get my own—"

The door swung open and Miss Belle put her hand on her chest. Tears filled her eyes, then she smiled.

"Oh, my word. Matthew."

He ignored the tray, stepped into the room and gathered her in his arms, lifting his grandmother from the floor with the force of his embrace. Awash in memories of how she'd cared for him after he'd lost his parents, he swallowed hard at the feel of her birdlike body.

By the time he set her down, she was crying in

earnest, and he was almost too choked to speak. He helped her to a chair and brought over the box of tissues from her nightstand. "I'm sorry. I know I should have warned you I was on my way, but I wanted it to be a surprise." He offered her a tissue. "I guess it wasn't such a bright idea."

Belle snatched the tissue, removed her thick, wire-rimmed glasses, and dabbed at her eyes while she stared, drinking him in. Then, as if struggling to speak, she opened and closed her mouth. Reaching out, she traced the scar on his right cheek with a trembling finger.

"What happened to your beautiful face?" she whispered.

He smiled at the compliment, knowing full well he had a mug only a grandmother would find beautiful. But he'd have to tell her the truth because he hadn't come up with a clever lie. "Late one night, there was an altercation in the hospital. The local troops captured a group of rebels and brought a pair of them in for treatment."

"To the children's center?"

"We were the closest infirmary." Hell, they'd been the *only* infirmary for miles. "The men were shackled, but I had to operate on one of them to remove a bullet from his shoulder. When I finished, the soldiers strapped him to a bed."

"Good," Miss Belle spat out, her expression ferocious. "No less than he deserved, I'm sure."

"Three hours later, when I checked on my patient, he'd somehow gotten loose and found a scalpel. He had a little girl in his arms and threatened to kill her if I didn't give him a gun, ammunition, medicine, anything he could use as barter or bring back to camp."

Belle clasped both his hands, as if anchoring him to her. "And then what?"

"I did as he asked. Made a bundle of whatever we had, which was antibiotics, gauze, just medicinal stuff. When I passed it to him, he set the child down to pick up the spoils. That's when I jumped him. Unfortunately, he got in a few licks with the scalpel before I disarmed him."

"Oh, my lord, you could have been killed."

Then and there Matt decided he'd been smart not to tell her of the wound he still nursed in his side. "But I wasn't."

"So they sent you home."

"I only had a few more weeks, so when the director asked if I wanted early leave, I said yes. I missed my grandma."

Belle exhaled a weary sigh, then seemed to draw strength from within. Her chocolate brown eyes brightened and she stood. "I want to spend the next twenty-four hours just looking at you. Let's go downstairs, sit in the parlor, and talk the day away, like we used to do when you came home from college."

"I brought you a breakfast tray. Your caterer prepared it instead of Ruby."

"Clark's a dear. I didn't realize he'd stayed overnight, but I'm not as involved in the scheduling as I used to be. Chloe takes care of most of it now."

"We need to discuss that, Gram."

"About Clark staying over? Why, it's a convenience for the both of us. His condo is forty miles south of here, and you know how bad traffic can be. I believe there are two events he's preparing for this week, and it's so much easier if he—"

"Not the caterer, Gram. Ms. Degodessa."

"Chloe?" His grandmother reseated her glasses. "Then you've met?"

"Last night."

"She'd planned to move to a different room before you were due home. I just couldn't see giving her one of the smaller bedrooms when your suite was sitting empty and she had so many clothes."

So many clothes? Hah! Now there was an understatement. "It's not about the room."

"I'm sure she'll move out, if you ask her." His grandmother grabbed her cane and started out the door. "Come along, and bring the tray. We'll eat in the dining room, where it's nice and bright. I'll tell you all about the wonderful things Chloe's done for Castleberry Hall."

Chapter 3

"Brr," said Clark when Matt left the room. "Something tells me he's not the warm sweet boy Miss Belle remembers." He refilled his cup and brought it to the table. "What do you suppose happened to his face?"

"Something he doesn't want to talk about," said Chloe. "But it must have to do with his time in Africa."

"Well, duh." Clark propped an elbow on the place mat and rested his chin on his fist. "I know that. Question is—what?"

Chloe read the papers and watched the news. She was well aware of the unrest and terror in the world. It was one of the reasons the gods rarely strayed from their mountaintop paradise. Many of them thought it amusing to see mortals maiming and killing each other for something as trivial as property or a personal belief, but they refused to get caught in the middle of it. "Live and let live" was their motto, or at least it had been for a while. Once mortals decided the gods were a myth and not a reality, Zeus decreed earth off limits to all but a small group of Mount Olympus's citizens. He and Hera, sometimes a minor deity Zeus chose to reward, and of course the muses, who had been created specifically to inspire mortals, were among those few.

The father god still expected them to inspire, in hopes they could steer humans to a better way, but she, Kyra, and Zoë hadn't had much success over the centuries; which was why they were here now.

These days, when any of the other gods wanted to visit, they had to fill out a permission slip, then flatter, coerce, and downright lie to Zeus to be allowed to leave Olympus. Perhaps if she and her sisters inspired enough good fortune, happiness, and fashion sense, the road from Mount Olympus to earth would become better traveled

Clark tapped his spoon on the side of his coffee cup. "You're off on another one of your daydreams. Did you hear what I asked?"

"Yes, and I suggest you speak to the man yourself. He was rude and short-tempered with me last night. I don't think he likes me." *And I certainly don't care much for him.* "What's on schedule for today? The cake for the baby shower, or are you going to try out a new sandwich filling for the Optimists' luncheon?"

"I plan to do both. After I get the cake in the oven, I'll start the fillings. I'll work in the house kitchen today . . . just to keep up with the inside gossip."

"I doubt the doctor is going to approve of that. He seems very suspicious."

"Of you, maybe, but I didn't get that vibe," said Clark in a haughty tone. "After all, I'm not in competition for his grandmother's favors."

Chloe squared her shoulders. "That's ridiculous. I'm Miss Belle's employee, as anyone with half a brain can see."

"Then maybe the man has less than half a brain."

"You're the one with no brain. Where do you come up with these ideas?"

"Observation, my darling girl, and a world of experience dealing with people who can't accept someone simply for who they are. I've fought more prejudice in my lifetime than you'll ever have to contend with."

Chloe snorted. "Puh-leez. How would you feel if you were continually referred to as a dumb blonde or treated like a—a bimbo every time you voiced an opinion or—"

"I'll take being treated as a dumb blonde over being called an abomination any day, my dear bimbo, and don't you forget it." He struck a girly pose, curtsied, and trotted from the room.

Oh, bother, now I've hurt his feelings. Chloe felt smaller than a gnat. She'd forgotten how little tolerance some humans had for anyone who didn't fit their ideal. Sighing, she told herself she'd give Clark a chance to cool down, then apologize.

"Here, now," scolded Miss Belle, striding into the room at a goodly pace for a woman using a cane. "Enough of that. I heard the two of you arguing from the stairway."

"Sorry." Hoping to reanchor the strands that had come undone in the argument, Chloe undid the clip holding her hair in place. "I'm leaving. I have work to do, and I'm sure you and your grandson have a lot to talk over."

"But I thought we could tell Matthew about all the changes we've made and the great strides Castleberry Hall has taken. Most of the ideas were yours, you know."

"Yes, Ms. Degodessa," said Matt. Placing the tray on the sideboard, he stood behind his grandmother. "I'd love to hear about all the things you've done for the *betterment* of my family's business."

Chloe took in his scarred face with its so obviously fake nice-guy grin. Lucky for him Miss Belle was here, or she'd pick up one of those croissants and smash it on his big shaggy head. "There's plenty of time for that," she said instead, with a smile as phony as his. "I'm working in the office today, so you can come in whenever it's convenient."

Miss Belle nodded. "After lunch might be good. I'm going to check on Ruby. You two have a nice chat while I'm gone."

Chloe waited until the woman left, then she stood. "I have to get to work."

"I'll just bet you do," said Matt, biting into a croissant.

Chloe smacked her hands on her hips. "What's that supposed to mean?"

"Let's just say I'm watching you. In the next week, I plan to learn more about the inner workings of Castleberry Hall than I have in the past thirty-three years."

He licked the chocolate off his fingers, and Chloe's stomach did a funny little flip. Not enough breakfast, she told herself. Choosing a pastry, she set it on her plate. Then she gave him a too sweet smile and tossed a final comment over her shoulder as she left the room. "Good, because I'm looking forward to teaching you everything I know."

Matt sipped his coffee as Chloe Degodessa flounced from the room, her generous hips swaying and her head high. His dead zone had started twitching the moment she'd undone that clippy thing and her white-blond hair tumbled to her shoulders in glorious disarray. Between the wiggle of her butt and the seductive way she filled out a simple sweater and slacks, he was grateful to be sitting down. What would his grandmother think?

It was obvious from the snappy comebacks Ms. Degodessa kept tossing his way that the woman was a lot smarter than she appeared. Though Miss Belle had been taken in by her baby blue eyes and innocent look, he wasn't falling for it. He'd find out exactly who she was, where she'd worked previously, and anything else he could in the next few days. Then he'd tackle Castleberry Hall's books to make certain she hadn't been dipping into the profits. Before he decided what to do with his own life, he'd see to it his grandmother and her livelihood were safe and protected.

The door from the kitchen swung open and Belle tottered in, leaning heavily on her cane. "Ruby was sound asleep, so I didn't wake her, and Clark is hard at work, so we can talk." She poured tea from her tray on the sideboard, brought it to the table, and glanced around the room. "Did Chloe leave?"

"She said she had a lot of things to do in the office," he answered, focusing on his croissant.

"Oh, dear. I can't tell you how often I've asked her not to work so hard, but she simply refuses to listen. Once a reception's scheduled, any one of the crew can handle it, but she insists on overseeing the entire affair."

"How much are you paying her, if you don't mind my asking?"

"Mind? Why goodness, no." Belle returned to the sideboard to retrieve her pastry, then took a seat. "This business will be yours someday. You're entitled to know everything I know."

Matt raised his eyebrows when she mentioned a sum that would barely keep some women in lipstick, let alone the feminine frou-frous and shoes he'd seen cluttering his room last night. "That's not very much. When did you become such a tightwad?"

"I am not a tightwad," Miss Belle countered in a wounded tone. "When I agreed to hire Chloe, she said she'd work for minimum wage until we were certain she could do the job. After I saw how wonderful she was, I offered her double the salary with benefits, but she refused. Kept insisting all she needed was room and board and a little spending money. One day I gave her a check with a generous raise, but she refused to cash it." Belle frowned. "I wish she'd let me compensate her for all the help she's been."

"I'm sure Chloe will think of something," Matt said. *If she hasn't already pilfered the family silver.* He rested his elbows on the table and pretended to read while his grandmother finished her first croissant and reached for a second. Comforted by her hearty appetite, he folded the paper and set it aside. "So, how have you been feeling?"

"Me? Fine. Why?"

"No reason. Have you been to a doctor lately?"

Belle placed her teacup in its saucer and pursed her lips. "I saw Dr. Kellam last week for a checkup."

"Why did you switch doctors, and how did you find this one?" he asked, intending to get the entire story.

"He's Ruby's doctor, and she's been so pleased with him that I decided to see him as well. We make appointments together to keep each other company."

"What's his specialty?"

"If you must know, he's a heart specialist with an emphasis on geriatrics." She dabbed her mouth with a napkin and tossed it on her empty plate. "That means he takes care of the old, the doddering, and the infirm."

Matt rolled his eyes. "I know what it means. And I never thought for a minute that you or Ruby were doddering or infirm—but heart problems?"

"Hah!" She frowned. "You probably think we're ready for toe tags. And my heart is perfectly fine."

"Glad to hear it. As for age, you are getting up there. I haven't seen you in a long while, and I've been worried about you—"

"Well, you needn't be." She crossed her arms in defiance. "Dr. Kellam says I have a good ten years left, maybe more. You're aware we come from a long line of ancestors who have lived well into their nineties."

"Yes, but—"

"Is this about your parents? Because a car wreck doesn't count," she continued, tapping a finger on the table. "When one is considering one's lifeline, dying from accidental causes should not enter the equation."

"Take it easy," Matt said, reaching for her hand. "I don't mean to upset you."

"Well, you did, and you are still." She sniffed. "I'd rather talk about you. I have so many questions to ask about your months in Ituri, but more importantly, I want to discuss your future."

"What about my future?"

"Suzanne for one. Are you still planning to marry her?"

Matt had held off telling his grandmother about the breakup because he wasn't sure how she'd take it. Now that she'd asked him directly, he couldn't avoid a response. "No."

Belle grabbed her chest, and Matt rose from his seat. This was exactly what he didn't want to happen. "Shall I call your doctor? Get your pills? What kind of medication are you taking?"

"Hallelujah," she shot back, raising the hand from her chest to overhead. "It's about time you realized the two of you aren't right for each other."

"Not right for—since when?"

"Since the day you started dating. The girl is spoiled and selfish. Even her father agrees, but it's too late to do a thing about it. Personally, I don't like that she keeps telling everyone what you're going to do when you're back, as if she's mapped it all out for you." She pushed her glasses up her nose. "When did you break it off?"

"We broke it off in London."

"Six months ago? Well, thank you so much for letting me know."

Matt recalled Suzanne's insistent attitude in the limo. "I thought you liked Suzanne, and I didn't want to upset you."

"I like her well enough, when she keeps her distance. Was this a mutual decision?"

"Not exactly. She didn't think I had my head on straight when I told her it was over, so she kept it to herself, only told the judge." He heaved a breath. "She's hoping I'll reconsider."

Belle *tsked*. "That is so typical of her."

"Typical?"

"I've known Suzanne since she was an infant. She never could accept rejection, especially after her mother left."

"You know, if you'd gone to lunch with her you might have found out, but Suzanne told me you refused her calls."

Miss Belle had the decency to blush. "I told whoever answered the phone to give her that message. All she's ever talked with me about is the house she wants to build once you're married. She had no intention of living here and carrying on the Hall's traditions."

"We've already addressed this issue, Gram. You know it's going to be difficult for me to keep the Castleberry and a practice going at the same time."

She raised her shoulders. "I know, and I don't

expect you to, it's just that I hate the idea of—oh, never mind."

He ran a hand through his hair. "Why the hell didn't you tell me how you felt about Suzanne three years ago, when we started dating?"

"Because I assumed you would see the error of your ways. You were so involved in joining Doctors Without Borders, I thought when you arrived in Africa and got away from the girl, you'd realize you didn't miss her."

Matt focused on his crumb-filled plate. That was exactly what had happened. Too bad he hadn't written Belle with the news, because they wouldn't be having this conversation if he had. Still, when his grandmother was right, it made him feel as if he were ten years old again and she'd instinctively known he'd had detention or gotten a bad grade.

Raising his gaze, he said calmly, "What do you think I should do about my future?"

"I think you should do whatever is right for you."

"Then I will." *When I figure out what it is.*

"Good." Miss Belle took a sip of her tea. "Well?"

"Well what?"

"Please tell me you won't change your mind where Suzanne is concerned."

He laughed at her tenacity. "I won't, but I'm going to let her break the news to everyone."

"That's very nice of you," Belle said, squeezing

his fingers. "Now, let's go see Chloe. I can't wait for you to hear about all she's done for this place."

The Castleberry business center was located in the wing to the right of the grand foyer. Years ago Miss Belle's husband had closed off the largest of the two parlors and its attached sunroom and turned them into offices. The second Chloe heard the tap-tap-tap of a cane, she reached for the latest letter from Party Palaces Corporation and attempted to look busy. If Miss Belle was alone, she'd show her their third offer, if not . . .

"Do you have a moment?" the older woman asked, standing at the door.

When Chloe glanced up and found Matt looming behind her employer with a suspicious glint in his eye, she folded the letter and slipped it in the folder she used to collect all of PPC's correspondence. "For you, I always have time." *But who said anything about Dr. Disgruntled?*

Matt dragged a pair of antique Chippendale chairs from a corner, helped his grandmother get settled, and took a seat.

"Would you be so kind as to pass me both of our brochures?" Miss Belle asked Chloe.

She did as requested, and the older woman handed one to her grandson and immediately began describing the advertising campaign Chloe had launched her second month on the job.

"The old material was terribly out of date," Belle said after a few minutes of singing the campaign's praises. "It was Chloe's idea to modernize the type font, focus on our amenities, and use current pictures for the wedding brochure. We ran a commercial on the radio, and thanks to Chloe, got a spot on a local television station doing a wedding special."

Matt stared pointedly at Chloe. "Really. How did she manage that?"

"She was dating the anchorman—what was his name . . . ?"

"Peter Thomas," said Chloe. The guy had been drop dead gorgeous, and like most of her mortal paramours, had talked about nothing but himself.

Belle chuckled. "Ah, yes. The man with two first names." She grinned at Matt. "It was our private joke. I'd sometimes ask her about the 'man with two first names' and we'd giggle like children." She turned to Chloe. "Whatever happened to Mr. Thomas?"

"I met Phil McAllister," Chloe answered, her voice as flat as McAllister's crew cut. "The Blackhawk's new goalie."

"Oh, yes." Miss Belle tapped a finger to her chin. "Did I tell you he wasn't good enough for you?"

Chloe nodded. "I dropped him at your suggestion, remember?"

"Pity. He was a nice boy, but—"

Matt loudly cleared his throat. "Can we get back on track. You were talking about the brochure."

"Right. Chloe even wrote the slogan."

" 'Castleberry Hall promises a lifetime of happiness.' " Matt's upper lip curled. "How positively . . . syrupy."

Belle frowned. "It might be syrupy, but it's proven to be very catchy. Our wedding and reception bookings increased by ten percent the first month after the brochures went out. I believe we're operating about twenty percent above last year's sales. Isn't that right, Chloe?"

"Twenty-one, but who's counting?" *Take that, you big jerk.* "And the corporate business is up by about the same percentage."

"Is that so?" Matt chose a second brochure, one designed with a more professional appeal, and turned to the back page. " 'Happiness is holding your event at Castleberry Hall'? Sounds too flip to lure a corporate venture."

"Every meeting planner who comes here loves it," chimed Miss Belle.

"Isn't it premature of us to guarantee happiness with each wedding?" Matt said. "After all, we have no control over the bride and groom's relationship. If a couple ends up getting divorced, they might even find a way to sue Castleberry Hall for false advertising."

"Nonsense," said Miss Belle. "Besides being pessimistic, that's a very depressing attitude."

"Maybe so, but it could happen."

"That makes about as much sense as saying an

ostrich has wings, so it should be able to fly," said Chloe, tired of his negativity.

Belle tittered a laugh as she continued to list Chloe's accomplishments, describing the Castle-berry's new pricing schedule, more flexible contract terms, and changes in what they would and would not supply. Then, like a sailboat running out of wind, she slowed to a near stop. "My, just listen to me, going on and on as if I enjoy the sound of my own voice."

Matt glanced at Chloe, who was biting her lower lip in—could it be?—concern. "How about if I escort you upstairs so you can take a break?"

"I think that might be a good idea." Rising to her feet, Miss Belle grabbed her cane while Matt took her other elbow and led her into the foyer. "I'm perfectly capable of walking by myself," she grumbled.

"I know you are, but I like holding onto you," he replied. "It reminds me of when I was a kid, and you held my hand while we strolled the Lincoln Park Zoo. We used to go there at least twice a month so Mom and Dad could have some time to themselves."

"I remember. I'll never forget the day you asked me what they did while we were at the zoo. The question took me completely by surprise."

Matt clasped her more firmly as they climbed the stairs. "And I'll never forget your answer."

"Oh, and what was that?"

"You said they were 'home, monkeying around.' Then you laughed, and I laughed too, because I thought it was a pun on the zoo. For years I saw them in my mind swinging from the chandeliers and eating bananas like a pair of deranged chimpanzees."

"You did not," she exclaimed. When she saw him smiling, she wrinkled her nose. "You are a naughty boy."

They finished the trek in silence. When they reached her room, he led her to the bed. "You going to be all right?"

Miss Belle slipped off her shoes and eased backward onto the mattress while Matt hoisted her thin legs onto the bed. "I'll be fine. I'm just going to close my eyes for a few minutes. You go downstairs and let Chloe tell you about the remodeling upgrades we had done. She dated the contractor, so we got a good deal on the work."

"Sounds to me as if Chloe's dated just about every man in Chicago."

"Not every man, but I'm sure she'll get around to them all eventually. She's a beautiful young woman, both inside and out."

Matt tiptoed from the bedroom, closed the door, and retraced his steps, relieved his grandmother wouldn't be there to hear him question her assistant. He had to agree that Chloe was beautiful on the outside, but the quality of her inner attributes had yet to be decided. When he arrived at the office door, Chloe was engrossed in a telephone conversation.

"I'm busy . . . No, I can't make lunch either." She frowned. "I thought we already discussed it. I'm simply not comfortable dating you."

Another man begging for acknowledgment, Matt thought in annoyance. Maybe his grandmother was right. Someday, Chloe Degodessa *would* get to every guy in Chicago.

Still oblivious to his presence, Chloe tipped back in her chair and set her heels on the desk. "I don't know how much longer I'll be here, so no. And please don't call me again."

She leaned forward, slammed the receiver in the holder, and sighed. When Matt cleared his throat, Chloe whipped up her head and her chair tilted even farther back. She threw him a murderous glare, and the next thing Matt knew, her bright red pumps were waving in the air.

Biting the inside of his cheek, he raced around the desk and found her scrambling to stand. "You okay?"

He offered his hand, and she slapped it away. Then she pulled down her sweater and brushed off her slacks. "I don't need a doctor, if that's what you're asking."

Matt raised his palms in surrender and took a step of retreat, still fighting laughter. "Fine. Call an ambulance if anything's broken."

"Nothing's broken but my pride," she admitted,

righting the chair. Then she reseated herself and placed her laced fingers on the blotter. "You don't approve of me, do you?" she asked before he could gather his thoughts.

"I've already apologized for the way I treated you last night. I'm sorry I jumped to conclusions."

"But—"

"I'm suspicious of anyone who does all Miss Belle says you do for such a ludicrous salary."

Chloe exhaled a breath. "Why does it always come down to money with you mortals?"

"Us mortals?"

"You know—men. Why is a race for the almighty dollar behind everything you do?"

Matt recalled the hundreds of *almighty* dollars he'd spent on his education and how he'd used up almost the entire trust fund his parents had left him to get through medical school. Belle had offered to support him financially, of course, but he wasn't about to drain the family business and jeopardize his grandmother's retirement.

"It's Gram's cash flow I'm concerned about, not mine. She's devoted her life to Castleberry Hall; it's all she has."

"So you're going to give up your career and run it for her when she can no longer carry out her duties?"

Matt stuffed his hands in his pockets. He'd thought about the problem a hundred times over the past two years, and it irked him that Baby

Blue Eyes could almost read his mind. "Let me worry about my grandmother and the Castleberry. Besides, didn't I just hear you say you wouldn't be here much longer? How do you think Belle's going to feel when you give her that bit of news?"

"I'll tell Miss Belle—and only Miss Belle— about my plans when I'm ready."

"If you aren't going to be here much longer, you owe it to her to give two weeks notice."

Chloe rose to her feet, arched a brow, and bowed mockingly. "Yes, your majesty. Shall I fetch the appointment book, your majesty? Or perhaps you'd rather I just licked your boots." The phone rang and she smiled as she sashayed from the room. "You want to be in charge, Castleberry, the job is all yours."

Chapter 4

Chloe stormed through the dining room and pushed against the kitchen's swinging door at the exact moment someone tried to make his way into the dining room. When she shoved, he shoved back, and she stepped aside. A second later Clark forged through the now free exit and stumbled past her with a tray of sandwiches in his hands. Toppling forward, he righted himself just as Chloe snatched a sandwich off the tray and trotted into the kitchen.

"The Keystone Kops have nothing on us," he commented as he followed her. Seeing her frown, he added, "I was bringing these out for lunch, but I guess that won't be necessary."

"I like eating in here," said Chloe, munching on the triangle-shaped delicacy. "This is great. What is it?"

"A little idea I whipped up, curried chicken with cashews and grapes."

She gazed at the platter, picked up a second sandwich made with pumpernickel, and took a bite. "This one's okay too. But not as tasty as the chicken."

"Roast beef hash in a horseradish dressing, with a dollop of pickle relish to brighten the flavor." He raised the tray high. "I have a third, shrimp and avocado with roasted peppers, but I don't want to hear you complain if you gain weight."

"That will never happen," she said as she stood and nabbed the shrimp salad. As with all the citizens of Mount Olympus, she never gained or lost an ounce, no matter what she ate. Though her figure was called plus-size here on earth, she'd always received compliments about her generous curves from the mortals she dated.

"Is your meeting over?" asked Clark while pouring her a sparkling lemonade to go with the sandwiches.

"I wouldn't call it a meeting." She took a swallow of the cold drink. "Miss Belle gushed and the good doctor grumped. In between, he threw daggers at me with every glare. I think he'd accuse me of stealing Castleberry funds if he thought he could make it stick."

"That doesn't sound right. What does Belle say?"

"She keeps pushing us together, hoping we'll get along, but I don't think that will happen."

"Too bad, especially seeing as you're without a man right now."

The outrageous statement caused Chloe to inhale, which in turn sent a swallow of lemonade up her nose. Tears sprang to her eyes as she coughed and tried to catch her breath.

Clark passed her a tissue. "There there, calm down. I didn't mean to make you choke."

"Then don't spout ridiculous comments," she squeaked. She blew her nose and her breathing returned to normal, enabling her to scowl. "There isn't a chance in Hade—hell that Matt Castleberry and I will ever so much as go out for dinner, even as coworkers. He caught me telling Bryce I'd be leaving soon, and he was not amused."

Clark pulled a stool to the massive island and sat next to her. "Then you're still thinking of quitting?"

"I have to. When Miss Belle finally accepts the fact that her grandson has no intention of running this place, she's going to be forced to take the PPC offer, and it stands to reason they'll want to put their own manager in charge. I'm going to leave before I'm fired."

In truth, she had planned to give notice to Miss Belle after the coming weekend and move back to the apartment Zeus had given her. She'd wait there in comfort until he summoned her home, where she intended to be met by a humbly contrite chief god and her also triumphant sisters.

"It's going to break Miss Belle's heart," Clark

warned. "Both she and Ruby have grown fond of you, and I believe the feeling is mutual."

"I care about them as much as I care about my own mother." *If I'd had one I could count on.* "But I don't see another ending to this saga. Miss Belle's too old to continue running the business, and her grandson has a fulfilling and potentially lucrative career for which he's worked hard. I may not care for his bossy attitude, but I will give him credit for what he's accomplished with his life. It's best if Belle sells out to the Party Palace Corporation and uses the millions to retire. She and Ruby can move to a senior citizens' home and live the remainder of their days in style."

Clark slumped forward and rested his chin in his hands. "Bummer."

"Double bummer." She sighed. "It's the safest thing for Miss Belle's health, and Ruby's. How old is she now . . . ?"

"I'm seventy-six, since you're wondering."

Chloe and Clark jumped at the sound of a woman's cold-clogged voice. "Ruby. I thought you were going to stay in bed until your fever broke," said Chloe.

"I was and it did." She hobbled into the kitchen carrying her breakfast tray, slammed it on the island, and regarded them with a grimace. "I heard every word you two just said. What in the name of Satan is going on around here?"

Chloe took a sip of lemonade. She'd been hoping Miss Belle would tell Ruby about the takeover offer before the woman found out on her own, and now the worst had happened. "Castleberry Hall has a buyer."

"Since when is the Castleberry for sale?"

"It's not, but we've been getting offers via mail." Chloe slid her gaze to Clark. "Lucrative offers."

"Why didn't someone tell me?"

"Because Miss Belle has no intention of selling."

Ruby hoisted her ample frame onto a stool. "Does Matthew know?"

"So far, no," admitted Chloe. "And Miss Belle wants it to stay that way."

"Hah! He's one of the smartest men I know. He's going to figure it out on his own, if you don't tell him. And right soon, if I know Matt," Ruby warned with a shake of her head. She knotted her wrinkled hands on the island. "There'll be hell to pay if he thinks you're pulling the wool over his eyes."

Jeesh, another person accusing her of a dastardly deed. How come she was always the accused? "Hey, don't make it my fault. I'm only doing what Belle wants."

Ruby gave a toothless grin, telegraphing the fact that she'd forgotten her false teeth . . . again. "In his eyes, his grandmother can do no wrong. Since you're the next logical person to blame, I wouldn't wait for the other shoe to drop. I'd tell him myself."

* * *

Matt sat at Chloe's desk and hung up the phone. He'd left Dr. Kellam a message asking him to call Castleberry Hall to discuss his grandmother's condition. He wanted to know the status of Miss Belle's health straight from the doctor's mouth. And he'd get the lowdown on Ruby too.

While waiting, he decided to inspect the Hall's financial records. It couldn't be that hard to decipher a profit and loss statement or get a handle on the bottom line. He opened a drawer and found a neatly organized row of hanging files. Choosing the one marked DEWEY AND HOWE, Castleberry's accounting firm, he retrieved the paperwork. Fifteen minutes later Matt knew for certain the business had finished the previous year well in the black. Income had been up, expenses were down, even with a larger advertising budget, and Miss Belle had added a fat chunk of change to her retirement fund.

Though the figures weren't as high as Chloe and his grandmother had bragged, they were impressive. The Castleberry had always made a profit, but never in the mid-six-figure range. The positive result supported Miss Belle's claim that the institution's success was due in part, if not entirely, to Chloe Degodessa.

It also dispelled a lot of the suspicions he had of the argumentative assistant.

After returning the file to its folder, Matt searched for Chloe's employment application. Just one more check, he told himself, and he'd get off his soapbox where the delectable Ms. Degodessa was concerned, and let her do her job in peace. He needed a good long rest, and he had to get a handle on his grandmother's health and his future.

Though still confused about the direction he wanted to go in his career, he was darned sure he didn't want what Suzanne had arranged for him: partnership in an elite surgical practice that made tons of money. The tragedies he'd witnessed in the Congo had worn him out, both mentally and physically, yet instinct told him he should be of service to his fellow man. He might be Belle's sole heir, but he wasn't about to sponge off the Castleberry. With a little research, he could probably find a clinic that paid a nominal fee to their doctors. There, he could give physicals or take throat cultures, anything that didn't tax his brain or his stamina, until he made some decisions.

Feeling more secure with his thoughts, Matt continued to search the files. He found employment applications for the ground crew, bartenders, waiters and waitresses, and most of the lesser positions needed to keep the business running. He even found a list of caterers with remarks made in a neat, flowing script he assumed was Chloe's, assessing the pros and cons of each food supplier.

But he didn't locate a single sheet of paper that gave a clue to his grandmother's assistant.

Puzzled, he meandered from the office in search of lunch. When he arrived in the kitchen, he was greeted by Clark and a teary-eyed Ruby.

"It's about time you came to see me, young man," said Ruby, swiping her damp cheeks as she smiled. "I couldn't believe it when Belle said you were home." She peered at his face. "Holy Hannah, what the heck happened to you?"

Matt gave the rotund, gray-haired housekeeper a hug. "It's great to see you too. And it's a long story, but I'm fine."

"Looks like you had a battle with a lawn mower, and the mower won." She drew back and touched his face. "Does it hurt?"

"Less and less each day. How are you doing?"

"I'm managing." She gummed a grin. "You hungry?"

Ruby Simpson had been seeing to Miss Belle's welfare since right after his parents' deaths, and done it in a humorous, down-home manner that was hers alone. She'd managed all the cooking and cleaning until about five years ago, when her arthritis had made the work difficult. Then his grandmother had hired a cleaning service, while she and Ruby shared kitchen duty. With no family to care for her, Ruby had become more of a sisterly companion to Belle than an employee. If anyone knew Castleberry Hall's secrets, it was Ruby.

"Starving." He stepped to the stove. "What smells so good?"

"Soup," said Clark, stirring a pot on the six-burner range. "It's the first course for tomorrow's lunch meeting of the Optimists Club."

Matt accepted a bowl filled with creamy broth.

"I thought they met downtown at the Palmer House. Since when did they move their get-togethers to the Hall?"

"Since Chloe had a sit-down with the current president and his committee," Ruby interjected. "That girl talked them into signing a year's commitment for monthly meetings along with Clark's services. I swear, she could charm the feathers off a rooster if she put her mind to it."

"So Gram's told me," he said, hesitating to mention that roosters were male, like all of Chloe's conquests. Then he tried the soup. "Hmm. Not bad. I recognize the taste of crab and shrimp, but what's this green stuff floating around with the corn kernels?"

"Spinach," said Clark. "Though it's the sherry and a dash of cayenne that make it special."

"Never can use too much sherry," added Ruby, slurping up her own serving. When finished, she said to Matt, "Come see me after my nap, and we'll have a jabber. I've missed you, boy."

"Yes, ma'am." Matt waited until she walked away before turning to Clark. "Ruby hasn't changed a bit. I see she still refuses to wear her dentures."

"She treats them like her heirloom pearls, brings them out for company then stores them away for the next special occasion," said Clark with a laugh. "And since there's not much entertaining at the house these days, it's a rarity." He lowered the heat on the burner, removed two large bowls from the refrigerator, and brought them to the island.

Matt noted the three rectangular layers of cake cooling on racks at one end of the work space. "What's that for?"

"A bridal shower, tomorrow night in the smallest reception room. The wedding's booked here too, thanks to Chloe."

Chloe again, thought Matt, smiling inside when he recalled her not-so-delicate slide from grace behind her desk. "Why especially to her?"

"She dated the bride's brother and convinced him to talk his sister into coming by for a quote."

Matt bristled. How the hell many men had been bitten by Chloe's love bug, anyway? From the sound of it, she'd dated just about every single guy in a fifty mile radius.

"The Hall didn't come in with the lowest bid, but after a bit of sweet-talking, the bride and her mother were hooked." He slathered the bottom layer of cake with a concoction that resembled chocolate but smelled of raspberries. "She even convinced them to try my food, which is how I got the catering contract."

"Maybe we should start calling her the wedding goddess," Matt muttered. *Or the love goddess,* he added silently. "Does the woman have any flaws?"

"Sure." Clark stacked the second layer on top of the first. "Besides a shoe fetish, she has a temper when it suits her, and a weakness for champagne and strawberries, eaten either together or separately. If there's any bubbly left over after an event, I slip her an open bottle just to see what she'll do next. One glass and she's tipsy, but give her two and she's downright silly. By that time she needs to unwind, so it doesn't matter."

"I take it you think she's good for Castleberry Hall?"

"The best. Thanks to her, Miss Belle's been able to slow down to a crawl, and so has Ruby. I don't know where the girl finds the energy, but she's a dynamo." He placed the top layer on the cake, dipped into the second bowl, and began to carefully spread snow-white icing over the entire creation. "She carried a tray to Belle's room about fifteen minutes ago. Probably still there, if you're interested."

"Thanks," Matt answered as he brought his empty bowl to the sink. "I think I'll see if I can join the conversation."

"I mean it, Chloe. Castleberry Hall has been family owned and run for the past seventy-five years, and it's going to stay that way. I do not want you to mention Party Palaces or their offer to Matt." Miss Belle leaned back on her pillows. "He might push me into selling, and I hate fighting with him."

Chloe removed her employer's lunch tray, set it on the credenza outside her room, and returned to Belle's bedside. "All right, I promise not to tell your grandson about the gigantic dollar amount Party Palaces is willing to pay for the Castleberry, but I think you're being foolish. I don't mean to sound fatalistic, but he's the one who'll inherit this place when you . . . in a few more years. And since he's not involved in the business, he'll probably sell it anyway." She placed her hands on her hips as she finished the lecture. "If you accept this latest offer, you can enjoy a comfortable retirement until . . . then."

Miss Belle's disapproving *tsk* echoed off the room's high ceiling. "You can say the words die and death in front of me, Chloe. I know I'm not immortal. I've had a wonderful life with a darling husband, God rest his soul, surrounded by my family and those who love me, and there's nothing more rewarding in this entire world than that." She straightened her shoulders, as if firming her resolve. "But I refuse to sit on a shelf for the next ten years. I want my final days to be filled with the things I enjoy most, the things I'm doing now. Besides, thanks to you, I am more comfortable."

"I need to talk to you about that," said Chloe, though the older woman's words gave her pause. Maybe this was the right moment to give Belle her notice. Quitting would practically force Belle into retirement, which was the smartest decision she could make, given her age and her health.

"It's about time you asked for a raise," pronounced Miss Belle, incorrectly guessing where her assistant was headed. "How about double your current salary? Or triple, though it still won't be what you're worth."

"This isn't about money." Chloe took a seat, hoping to soften the news of her leaving. "I love working here, but I can't continue to—"

"Is this a private party?" asked Matt, sticking his head through the doorway. "Or is anyone invited?"

"Come in, come in," said Belle. "I was just about to hear Chloe's answer to my offer of a raise. Now that you're here, maybe you can convince her to accept triple her current salary."

"Triple?" The scars on Matt's suddenly pale face stood out as clearly as a major highway on a road map. "I agree she's been working for too little, but before we discuss a raise I'd like to ask her a question."

Instead of your usual dozen? thought Chloe. "And that is?"

He raised a brow. "Your application wasn't in the employment file. Maybe you could point me in the right direction so I could look it over."

"Chloe didn't fill out an application," Belle answered. Crossing her arms, her expression turned defiant. "And she's worked out so well, I don't see that she needs to."

Before Matt could respond, the downstairs phone rang. Chloe gave silent thanks for the interruption as she rose to answer it. The sooner she left, the sooner she could avoid this dangerous conversation. Just then a buzzer sounded, and she punched a button on the intercom mounted next to the wall phone.

"Yes?"

"It's . . . you know," said Clark in a hushed tone that hissed into the room. "I told him someone would be right with him."

"I'll take it in my office, just give me a minute." She turned to Matt and Belle. *You know* could only be the main buyer from Party Palaces, and Jeremy Jadwin was the last person Belle would want her grandson to hear about. "I'm needed downstairs," she said, hoping the older woman could read her mind.

"I'm counting on you to take care of it, dear," said Miss Belle, as if she understood.

"You two have a good talk. I'll see you later."

Chloe straightened and headed for the stairway, mentally preparing another list of arguments as to why the Castleberry would not be sold. Protecting Belle from unhappiness was the least she could do for the woman before returning to Olympus, and she would do so with every fiber of her being.

Chapter 5

Matt sat in the chair vacated by Chloe and took his grandmother's hand. "Feeling better now that you've had a decent lunch?"

"I was feeling fine before I came up here, just a bit tired," she answered, snatching her hand away.

He rested his elbows on his knees and gave her a teasing grin. "Then why are you in such a grumpy mood?"

"I'm not in a grumpy mood—I'm pissed off," she grumbled. "There's a difference."

"Ooo-kay. How about you tell me why?"

"You already know the reason why."

"I do?" he asked in an amused tone.

"Stop trying my patience. *You* are the problem."

"Me?" Matt tried for an innocent expression, but doubted he could fool his grandmother. "What did I do?"

"You know perfectly well what you did." She closed her eyes and leaned back against the pillows. "I want you to leave Chloe alone. Stop badgering her about her past or fussing over the way she carries out her duties. And stop talking to her as if you'd caught her embezzling funds."

"Who said I was doing all that?"

Miss Belle gave a wounded sniff. "No one had to say. Your barbed comments concerning her employment application, or lack thereof, spoke volumes. It was an insult to me as well as Chloe."

"I'm just watching out for the best interest of you and the Castleberry," he countered. "And how did I insult *you?*"

"Your question made it sound as if I were an idiot, hiring someone without getting their employment history or checking their references."

"My point exactly. You *didn't* get any references. How did you know she could be trusted, let alone do a competent job?"

"How did I . . . ? Listen to me, Matthew Castleberry, I've been judging character since before you were born, and I've never once been wrong."

Matt continued his quest to make Belle see reason. "What about the gardener you let go when I was in high school? The one with the nasty habit of sleeping in the toolshed instead of working on the grounds?"

"Hired by your father."

"And the hostess you fired? The one who helped herself to the leftover booze in the liquor closet?"

"Ruby had a good feeling about her, not me."

"And the parking valet who was caught taking customer's cars for joy rides?"

"Oh, all right, so I made a mistake. But the young man seemed so earnest."

"Just like Chloe."

Belle humphed as she poked a finger in his direction. "Mind your own beeswax. Unless, of course, you plan to make Castleberry Hall your new line of work."

"Are you telling me I have to commit to taking over the company in order to ask questions, check the books, approve the staff, or do anything else I deem necessary to protect this place?"

Matt regretted the statement the moment it left his lips. His grandmother had just thrown down the gauntlet, and thanks to his boisterous concerns, he'd been too preoccupied to see it coming. Now that she'd laid out the challenge, he knew what was coming. And he had to accept it or look like a total fool.

"That's exactly what I'm saying."

Score one for the little old lady, he thought with a silent groan. On the other hand, taking a vacation from medicine would buy him some time to cogitate on his life and reacquaint himself with his grandmother. And his heritage.

"All right."

Belle's eyebrows shot to her hairline. "What do you mean, all right?"

"I agree to get involved in the running of Castleberry Hall."

"You'll do no such thing," she answered, frowning. "You're a doctor, not a party host. It would be a complete waste of your superior education, never mind your talent."

"I have yet to decide what I plan to do with my life, so why not? Managing this place was good enough for you and my parents, why can't I give it a try?" He gentled his voice, hoping to break the tension that had risen between them. "Besides, I have to let my face heal, otherwise I'm going to frighten away all my patients."

Tears sparkled behind Belle's Coke-bottle lenses. "How dare you be so superficial! No one chooses a doctor for his appearance. They pick one because they want a caring person who tells them what's wrong physically and offers suggestions on how to become well. Oftentimes, all they need is a kind word or gesture and they're back to their old selves."

"My patients don't swim in the adult pool of reason, Gram. Most of them are no higher than my kneecap, let alone old enough to have a driver's license. It's important they feel safe and comfortable around me, not terrified."

"As well they should. But you must know by now that children are much more forgiving of a person's looks. You resemble your great-grandfather, and though he didn't turn heads, he was admired and respected. He was lucky enough to find a woman who loved him not for his physical appearance or his name, but for his exemplary personality and intelligence," she lectured. "Unlike Suzanne."

"Suzanne is history, so there's no need to keep throwing her into the conversation."

"Then let's stick to the issue."

"I thought we were."

"Fine. I don't believe you have negative feelings about medicine due to those scars, because they can be taken care of by any competent professional. It's your skill as a pediatric surgeon you're doubting, and that is just plain silly."

Matt felt the weight of the world settle on his shoulders. "I'm not sure I can do what I trained for anymore."

"What do you mean?"

He didn't want to dwell on the past two years, but the ugly thoughts bubbled to the surface before he could stop them. "I witnessed just about every atrocity known to man in Africa, and it made me . . . second-guess myself and my profession. Right now, I don't think I'm capable of handling anything more life-threatening than a paper cut."

His grandmother held her palm to her chest. "I don't believe what I'm hearing. You cannot be serious."

He hung his head. "I can't believe I said it. It's just that I'm confused and very tired." If he told his grandmother about the nightmares that had plagued him since shortly after he'd arrived in Ituri, she'd sit by his bedside all night just to keep the demons at bay.

"Doctors Without Borders tried to warn us, but it was worse than I ever imagined it could be. The famine, the heat, the cruelty of men fighting their own brothers and sisters." He felt the tears well but couldn't stop his tirade. "The brutality foisted on the children, sometimes by their own people, was . . . unconscionable."

He held his emotions in check as he recounted the tale that continued to haunt him. "My first day there, I had to operate on a boy no more than six years old who'd had his legs chopped off by a machete. The little guy died from blood loss before I finished the surgery."

"Oh, Matthew. My dear, sweet Matthew."

"I . . . it was horrendous." He didn't bother telling his grandmother that the child's pained yet resigned face stalked his dreams, both day and night.

Belle sat up and leaned forward. Falling into his arms, she whispered, "Instead of dwelling on that boy, why not think about all of those you saved?"

"I do think of them, and the conditions I returned them to after their surgery. The poverty and filth . . . do you know how long their life expectancy is, even after my heroic efforts? Many of the girls die in childbirth at the age of twelve, and don't forget the ones who are brutalized. And boys who wouldn't be old enough to drive in this country are commandeered for the army. They're lucky if they see their eighteenth birthday."

Belle swiped at a tear. "I had no idea it was so bad. You never let on. Your letters were always so positive, so full of promise."

He cradled her, as he'd done to so many sobbing women this past twenty-three months. "Yeah, well, I'd probably have gone crazy if I'd dwelled on the truth while I was there. Now that I'm home, I remember it with more clarity." After sitting her back on the bed, Matt stared at his entwined fingers, too embarrassed to meet her eyes. "I'm a coward, Gram. I don't think I can go back to surgery. Especially if I have to operate on children."

"Chicago is not Ituri. We have some of the most well-equipped hospitals in the country here, with every modern gadget and medicine known to man. The conditions aren't the same, none of it is."

Matt was aware of all that she said, because he'd already been over it a thousand times in his mind. But he'd still have to contend with the gang violence, drive-by shootings, and sexual abuse that killed so many innocent children almost daily, not to mention the tragedies of birth defects and debilitating illnesses.

The fear that cut into his heart was one he had yet to speak out loud, but his grandmother deserved the truth. "It's not just the uncertainty of an operation's outcome, Gram." He heaved in a breath. "I don't know if I'm still capable of practicing medicine of any kind."

Chloe stood in the closet off the main kitchen of the reception building, checking the condition of the table linens, and seeing to the less important tasks that needed doing at the start and completion of every event. The job was usually done by the wait staff supervisor, but after her weekly tug of war with the smooth-sounding and altogether too insistent Mr. Jadwin, she'd left to escape Matt Castleberry and his questions.

Since the wedding they were hosting this weekend was under control, and the Optimists' lunch meeting wouldn't take place until tomorrow afternoon, she had to do something that would keep her away from his prying eyes.

After tagging two tablecloths for the recycle bin, she inspected napkins and found several she could add to the pile. The company from which they bought their linens would have to be contacted in order to replace the worn pieces. She might as well meet with them before she left, and ask for new color samples to show prospective customers. Now that the Castleberry was on the A list, she wanted it to remain there, which meant keeping current with the trends of fashion and design.

Finished with the chore, she turned the knob

on the closet door, but it refused to budge. After several tries she put a bit of shoulder muscle into it and managed to tug it open. A few days ago Leah had mentioned the door was a problem, but Dr. Disgruntled had shown up before she had a chance to call a locksmith or inform maintenance.

After adding that to her list, she headed into the smallest of the Hall's four dining rooms and sat at one of the round tables. Dropping her clipboard, she sighed. Though facts and figures on contracts were a staple in this job, she really did enjoy handling the day-to-day facets, including simple tasks like inspecting the linen supply or checking the glassware for cracks and chips.

But it was the people with whom she worked that kept her in thrall. Instead of the uptight and occasionally foolish mortals Zeus so often complained about, the Castleberry staff was kind and fun-loving, more like a family than a group of coworkers . . . sometimes even more of a family than her eleven sisters and dozens of cousin gods.

She was positive she'd inspired enough happiness on earth to meet her father's stringent challenge, but who knew what idiotic quotas or constraints Zeus would put on her numbers? When she achieved eternal glory, she planned to laze the days away with Kyra and Zoë, because she was sure they too would prevail. Hera and the others could jump in the River Styx if they didn't like it, and it wouldn't bother her one whit.

She imagined the reaction of the other muses when the trio returned to Olympus in triumph. Terpsichore, who had always been jealous of her beauty, would ignore their success. Erato might compose a poem to make up for the fact that modern men and women rarely read poetry. Melpomene and Polyhymnia would whine because they hadn't gotten a chance to improve their own performance ratings, and the rest would look down their noses at the trio because they'd finally proven themselves worthy of the history books.

Chloe was so much of an optimist she could have been a charter member of the group coming to the Castleberry for lunch tomorrow. If the worst happened, and she was ordered to the kitchens or pigsty, she might still be able to find a way to escape, sneak back to earth, and live here with Ruby and Belle. Residing with them would be several rungs up the ladder from slopping hogs or plucking chickens, and Zeus would never think to look for her in a retirement village.

She felt a true sense of accomplishment in the many improvements she'd made to Castleberry Hall. Thanks to her, the respected but somewhat dowdy institution had become the "in" place to host all manner of events. Besides helping an aging woman salvage her pride, she'd inspired hundreds of mortals to achieve happiness.

Then there were the fripperies of the modern world: sling-back pumps, perfume, dresses of silk and satin, strappy open-toed sandals with super high heels, strawberries and champagne, knee-high suede boots with pointy toes, frilly lingerie, sleek and sporty cars with divine smelling leather interiors, satin pumps covered in rhinestones and bows . . .

And how could she forget the men?

She absolutely basked in the compliments she received from them, loved their silly attempts at coercing her into a date, preened when they praised her flowing tresses or lush figure. The stupefied grins they wore when she graced them with a bit of attention were priceless. She'd dallied with a dozen men since arriving on earth, and she could easily have taken a dozen others to her bed if she'd had the time.

A vision of Matt Castleberry flashed in Chloe's mind, and she quickly pushed it away. An ordinary looking mortal such as the doctor was definitely not her type, even if he was a godlike humanitarian. As the most beautiful of the muses, it was right and fitting that she attract the most handsome of men, and the doctor fell miles short of that requirement.

Besides, interacting with only the most attractive males was the safest way to avoid Zeus's stupid condition of not falling in love. No sane woman, be they goddess or mortal, wanted to spend the rest of her days with a self-absorbed guy who cared more about his looks than he did about them. Men of that ilk were a snap to leave, because they never complained when their lovers stopped answering their e-mails or taking their phone calls. They were too busy either soothing their own wounded egos or searching for their next adoring conquest.

Weary of worrying about her fate, she concentrated on her job. Thanks to Miss Belle's interfering grandson, she'd forgotten to check her messages on the office computer this morning. She imagined there would be a half-dozen inane notes from Zeus, and responding to them had to be her next priority.

Much as she liked it on earth, Mount Olympus was her home; the place she was born to be.

Chapter 6

TO: Cdegodessa@CastleberryHall.com
FROM: Topgod@mounto.org
SUBJECT: Final push for success

Be aware, your trial period on earth is coming
to an end. Your repeated refusal to send weekly
updates and reports may be held against you,
as might your revolving door policy concerning
mortal men. NOW would be a good time to take
things seriously. Remember, I am watching.

Sincerely,
Zeus
Your father (and still Top God)

P.S. Have a nice day ☺

Chloe inhaled sharply. What in Hades did the old fart think she'd been up to? He knew she had a job here—he'd practically arranged it! And he had to know how all-consuming and nerve-wracking said job was if he'd been watching.

As for her "revolving door policy with men," if memory served, she, Zoë, and Kyra had been given permission to dally with mortals, as long as they didn't fall in love. Okay, so she'd done a lot of dallying.

Big deal!

Zeus should be grateful she'd even bothered to learn how to use this mind-boggling and mentally inferior plastic box of nuts and bolts. It had taken all of her concentration to become accustomed to the stupid piece of electronic junk. Clark, Belle, even Ruby had given her lessons. She'd become quite proficient for someone who'd positively balked at the mere idea of a computer, never mind being expected to submit reports and answer e-mails.

Chloe stuck her tongue out at the monitor and hit the exit tab. She'd answer Zeus when she was good and ready, and not before. He might be top god, but she was top muse, and she would not be controlled by threats or intimidation. She spun around in her desk chair, careful not to do another fanny drop just in case Dr. Disgruntled was lurking behind the corner. Flipping open a file, she went over the details of tomorrow's lunch gig.

This would be the second meeting the Optimists held at Castleberry Hall, and she wanted everything to take place without a hitch. Besides getting them to sponsor the Birthday Party, acquiring a raft of new bookings for Miss Belle was the least she could do in the way of a thank-you before she returned to Mount Olympus.

While studying the contract, the hairs on the nape of her neck stood on end. As she raised her head, Matt's stare struck her like a thunderbolt. She cut her eyes to the paperwork, telling herself the warm squiggly rush zinging through her veins was nothing more than concern over the success of the luncheon . . . or maybe the furnace had just turned on.

It certainly wasn't any type of attraction to the pesky man who seemed to fill the entire doorway with his presence.

"You got a minute?"

She propped her chin on a hand and shrugged.

"I think we need to talk."

No kidding!

Matt shuffled to a chair and straddled it, giving her a clear view of his crotch. The zing did a little cha-cha from her stomach to her corresponding body part. Uh-oh.

"If this isn't a good time—"

"It's fine. I don't have an appointment with a client until after dinner."

"It's about your nonexistent employment application."

"I suppose you want me to fill one out?"

"It's too late for that, but I do hope you can provide a couple of references. A person or two you worked with before you came here."

"Let me guess. You're going to call and pester them with questions? Like, did I steal money or have a poor attendance record?" She grew angry just thinking about him prying into a past she didn't have. "Or did I screw up their business so completely they had to close their doors?"

"Did you?"

Chloe rolled her eyes. "Why, yes. When I finished with Apex Pool Cleaning, Car Repair, and Electrolysis, they were broke and ready for the funny farm. The owners hightailed it to Bolivia, never to be seen or heard from again."

Matt raised his hands as if he were being robbed at gun point. "Okay, okay, I get the picture." He curled up a corner of his mouth, and the scars on his cheeks morphed into half-moons. "I guess I'd be just as prickly if my integrity was in doubt."

"I'm glad you're finally seeing this from my perspective," said Chloe.

"Now why don't you try and see it from mine? I've been away for two years. When I return, you're in residence, in my old rooms no less, and my elderly grandmother has practically turned her company over to you."

"Your point would be . . . ?"

He raised a brow. "You're kidding, right?"

The man was as bad as Zeus, always thinking

the worst of her. "Trust me, I only want what's best for your grandmother and this business, nothing more."

"I can see that. What I don't understand is why."

Because the top god from Mount Olympus sent me here. That answer wouldn't fly, but it might make him smile. And he'd done very little of that since his arrival.

Just then the phone rang. "Castleberry Hall," said Chloe. "We care about your happiness."

"It's Dr. Lloyd Kellam, returning Dr. Matthew Castleberry's call."

"One moment, please." She passed the phone across the desk. "It's Dr. Kellam. Feel free to use the office. I have things to discuss with Clark."

Chloe sauntered from the room as Matt raised the receiver to his ear. Damn if the view from the rear wasn't almost as good as the view from the front. He sighed. He'd come to inform Ms. Degodessa that he was now in charge, but their verbal sparring had shoved everything right out of his mind. When he realized the doctor was waiting, he shook his head.

"Dr. Kellam, thanks for getting back to me."

"I assume this is about your grandmother?" the doctor asked in a friendly tone.

"Isabelle Castleberry. I've been out of town, but I'm home now, and I'm a little worried. She seems . . ." *Old, frail, not her usual self.* ". . . tired, lacking vitality. I know she's getting up in age, but—"

"Isabelle has a few health concerns, but they're nothing out of the ordinary for a woman of eighty-three. A weak heart is one of them, but she's on medication and doing better."

A weak heart? He should have known better than believe Belle and her *perfectly fine* pronouncement. "I've been away—"

"I know. I think all of Chicago has been aware of your location for the past two years. Your grandmother is proud of you. As a member of the medical community, I have to say you're very much admired."

Matt's gaze rested on a plaque he'd been given by the city's Chamber of Commerce that Belle had accepted in his stead, even after he'd told her not to. If they only knew how tarnished the golden boy truly was . . .

He turned the conversation back to his grandmother and was given the names of the medication she was taking. Then he asked about Ruby.

"What is your relationship to Ms. Simpson?"

"To my knowledge, we're the only family she has, at least the only family I know of."

"I'm not comfortable discussing Ms. Simpson with someone to whom she isn't related, especially in light of the new HEPA laws. If she gives me permission, I'll be happy to tell you whatever you want to know."

Matt had to respect Dr. Kellam's request. There was the matter of doctor-patient confidentiality to be considered, not to mention the privacy law. He made a mental note to talk to Ruby, then told the physician he'd be in touch.

He leaned back in the desk chair. Now that he knew the type of meds Belle was on, he'd check them out. There were a lot of new compounds on the market, while he had used basic medicines to repair the horrors of jungle warfare. He could find out about her prescriptions by calling the drug company or looking them up online.

It was only his first day home and he was exhausted, which was probably the reason the nightmare he'd suffered on and off for the past eighteen months hadn't haunted him last night. But he was fairly certain the reprieve would soon be over. He'd thought about taking a sleeping aid when they started but hadn't been able to down that type of medication in Ituri, because he never knew when someone would wake him for surgery. If the nightmare returned, he'd try something over-the-counter before getting a prescription for himself.

The buzzer signaled that they had a visitor, then a swath of cold air brushed over him as the door opened. Chloe's client wasn't expected until after dinner, but it could be a walk-in who wanted to check the facility. Might as well dive in, he told himself as he stood. He had to meet and greet customers if he planned to help with the business.

Just as he moved beyond the desk, Suzanne swept through the French doors and circled around to embrace him. Then she drew back. Her eyes widened and her cheeks paled as she stared.

"What happened to your face?" she finally asked. "Why didn't you tell me you'd been injured?"

"It wasn't serious—just a skirmish in Ituri. It's nothing time and a trip to a plastic surgeon won't cure."

"Oh, well—"

"Why are you here, Suzanne?"

"I thought—I mean I wanted to—that is—are you up to going out to dinner?" Her eyes darted from his scars to the desk, as if the sight of him made her ill. "I'll understand if you say no, of course."

He'd suspected that once Suzanne saw his face, she wouldn't want to appear with him in public, and her actions only proved it. "I'm beat, but thanks for asking."

She slipped out of her mink, draped it across the back of a chair, and took a seat, her gaze focused firmly on his. "Are you in pain? How long will it take until you're more . . . um . . . normal?"

"I'm normal now, just battle-scarred. Plus, I'm still trying to get in sync with this time zone and reacquaint myself with Belle and the Castleberry." He eased into the desk chair, rested his elbows on the blotter, and read the disgust in her eyes. Since he'd already ended their engagement, he wasn't sure why she was there. "Is there something I can do for you?"

"How did you get them?"

"There was a situation at the hospital." He met her stare head on, waiting until she finished studying him before asking again, "Suzanne, why are you here?"

"I told you. I thought that maybe we could go to dinner and . . . talk. But I see that won't work."

"We're no longer a couple, so no, it wouldn't work," he agreed, knowing damn well she was referring to his disfigurement.

"I thought that maybe, once you returned home and were in a better place, you would reconsider your decision to end our engagement."

But now that you've seen my face . . . "I have no intention of reconsidering anything. In fact, I think it's best if we steer clear of each other for a while."

She wrinkled her nose, as if smelling something sour. "That will be impossible. Daddy performs dozens of weddings here, and we travel in the same social circles. If we call attention to the fact that we're avoiding each other, there'll be gossip, innuendo . . . people will think it odd."

He folded his hands on the blotter. "People frequently break engagements. It's better than getting married and divorcing after a few months, don't you agree?"

"Does Miss Belle know about this?" she asked, changing tactics.

The fact that Suzanne had brought up their standing in society, his mental stability, and now his grandmother, but had not once mentioned the L word, spoke volumes. "She's been told."

"And what did she have to say?"

"She believes it's my life, so it's my decision, just as she feels about all my endeavors."

"I see." Suzanne stood and tossed the mink over her shoulders. "There's going to be a ton of speculation once word gets out. What do I say when someone asks?"

Her lack of concern for anything but public opinion was the final straw. "Tell them whatever works for you. Since you've been wearing the ring, I'd take it off and see what develops. When your friends notice, say you ended it because I'm a jerk, or I returned with an ego the size of Lake Michigan. Take out an ad in the society pages, if you want, accusing me of infidelity. It's all up to you." He rose to his feet and stepped around the desk. "Just get the word out."

She twisted the two-carat, emerald-cut diamond surrounded in channel-set baguettes from her finger and dropped it on the blotter.

"I told you to keep the ring, and I meant it."

She shrugged into the mink, her face void of expression. "That's very generous, but no thank you."

In an effort to offer a true good-bye, Matt

moved from behind the desk and tried to clasp her hands, but she took a step of retreat. After a final inspection of his face, she marched from the room.

Chloe slipped into her favorite powder-blue satin nightgown and let it fall softly to the top of her toes. Then she brushed her hair until it gleamed, walked to the sitting room and took a seat on the sofa in front of the roaring fire. Digging through her purse, she found her cell phone and set it on the coffee table. It was past eleven. If Kyra didn't reach her soon, she was going to initiate the three-party call herself.

While waiting, she thought about the past few hours. Dinner had been quiet, even with Clark in attendance. She'd gotten the feeling something wasn't right with Matt Castleberry but couldn't put her finger on it. Though he'd encouraged Ruby and Belle to talk, and reacted positively to Clark's quirky repartee, he'd seemed preoccupied, almost as if he was there physically but his mind was on another plane.

Whenever Clark asked him about his time in Africa, Matt had responded politely, but his terse explanations suggested the topic made him uncomfortable. She'd chalked it up to his grueling return trip and whatever had scarred his face, figuring he would be more animated once he was fully rested, but Miss Belle's concerned expression made her worry.

When her appointment arrived, Chloe had excused herself and met with the bride-to-be and her parents in the sales office. After going over what they anticipated in the way of a wedding and reception, she gave them a tour of Castleberry Hall and the chapel, and returned to the office to discuss pricing and a standard contract for the happy event, which they could read at their leisure.

With the wedding scheduled for eighteen months in the future, she was saddened by the fact that she wouldn't be there to see the task done correctly, but she was certain Party Palaces, or whoever was in charge, would do an adequate job.

The phone rang, and she picked up immediately. "I thought you might have forgotten us."

"Not a chance," Kyra answered.

A few seconds later all three muses were on the line. "So, how is everyone. Anything new?" Chloe asked.

Kyra and Zoë were strangely silent, so Chloe dived in with her latest experience with Bryce. "Thank goodness he's the last guy I'll have to deal with, since we'll be leaving soon."

"I'm sure Miss Belle is thrilled with your revolving door policy where men are concerned," said Zoë with a snort. "You are shameless. How many has it been?"

Revolving door policy? Where had she heard that before?

"Twelve, but who's counting? And Miss Belle thinks a woman should sample a bushel of fruit before she picks a favorite orchard. It's not my fault mortal men are so easy."

"For a senior citizen, Miss Belle sounds like a very progressive woman."

"She is. And I really do care about the mortals I've been with. There isn't a single god I'd take to my bed after seeing so many good-looking men down here."

Chloe loved voicing the shallow statements, though only Kyra and Zoë would know for certain she was joking.

"May I remind you," said Kyra, "that it might blow your chance at glory if Zeus finds out you've been playing around instead of doing your job. Have you been keeping track of the happiness you've inspired?"

This conversation was fast turning into a frustrating copy of her father's e-mail. "If you'll remember, Zeus gave his permission for us to mess around with mortals." She sighed. "And I've done all I could in the way of inspiration. Each and every time we have a wedding, a baby or bridal shower, or a christening or birthday party, I wish them eternal happiness. I've said those words over three hundred fifty times."

"That's more than once a day. Do you really get that much business?" asked Kyra.

"I told you, I've turned the place into a rousing success. Now, enough about me. Zoë, what's going on with you?"

"What about me?"

"Any new men . . . or new problems?"

"Not a one. The women at Suited for Change are inspired by my suggestions, the window dressing job is a success, and I just took on a new project."

"Is the guy cute?" Chloe asked, reinforcing her own private rule. It was so much easier to stay detached if the man was good-looking and empty-headed . . . more the blond bimbo type she always seemed to be compared to here on earth.

"Who said it involved a guy?"

"I could tell by the sound of your voice, silly, and it might do you good to have a final fling before you leave. We all should."

"Don't preach to me about a final fling. Kyra hasn't had any. She's the muse we need to worry about."

Kyra didn't say a word, which had Chloe concerned. "Hey, sis, you still on the line?"

"I'm here."

"Is there something you don't want to tell us?"

"It's just been a couple of interesting days."

"Define interesting," said Zoë.

Kyra proceeded to explain her current working relationship with a man. When Chloe asked her to give a rating using the kiss-o-meter, she cringed at Kyra's response. "A twelve! You can't be serious."

"I am, but I can handle it."

"Just don't let Zeus hear you," advised Zoë. "You know how much he'll enjoy thinking up a punishment if you fall in love with the guy."

"Shh," warned Chloe, glancing around her room. "He could be listening to our conversation as we speak."

"He could, and since there isn't a thing we could do about it, it isn't worth the worry," said Zoë.

"I, for one, am counting the days until we're recalled," said Kyra. "It's going to be very rewarding when Zeus announces our triumph and gives us our due."

"That's the spirit," Zoë encouraged "It will be so satisfying to see him humbled."

"And don't forget Hera," Chloe added. "The witch."

"I think you've got the first letter in that last word wrong," said Zoë with a chuckle. "I believe it should start with a capital B."

They shared a laugh, then said good-bye, and Chloe disconnected the call. Hooking her phone to the charger, she couldn't help but wonder if Kyra and Zoë had told her everything concerning their relationships with mortals. Men could be such problems, and rarely were they worth the trouble they put women through. That old earth adage—can't live with them, can't live without them—was so true.

She walked through her bedroom and into the bathroom that she'd realized only minutes ago she shared with Matt. After turning the lock on his side of the room, she again noted the razor, shaving cream, and other masculine toiletry items arranged neatly in a corner of the counter. A man's bathrobe hung on the door that led to the adjoining bedroom, and a precisely arranged towel and face cloth took up space on a drying rod.

She'd had no idea where he disappeared to last night, and now she knew. As long as he didn't invade her shower time, it would be easy to avoid him. She just had to make sure she locked the door when she used the facility, and knocked before she barged in.

She finished brushing her teeth and was about to go to her room when a cry and muffled sobs caught her attention.

Then she heard a crash.

Chapter 7

Chloe grasped the bathroom doorknob, undid the lock, and peeked into Matt's room. Moonlight poured through the antique lace curtains, bathing him in an eerie white light. Sitting on the edge of the bed with his head in his hands, he obviously had no idea she was spying.

Her first instinct was to go to him, but some inner sense told her this was not the time to intrude.

Until she heard him sob.

Not a sob exactly, but more a huge inhalation accompanied by a watery sigh that caused his body to shudder. A wave of pity flooded her heart when she heard the pathetic rasp. Coming from such a grouchy and argumentative man, the sound seemed twice as desperate and full of despair.

Matt straightened, and the light played on the

muscles of his broad shoulders and back, casting shadowed hills and valleys down to the top of his buttocks. When he shifted to a quarter view, she glimpsed his molded pecs, ripped abs, and concave stomach. Heat rushed to her cheeks as she gasped at his bare, buff, and amazing form. Who would have guessed that behind his ordinary facade hid the body of a god? If judged by his physique alone, Dr. Disgruntled was actually Dr. Studly, even by Mount Olympus standards.

At her intake of breath, he swiveled on the mattress. He waited a long second before saying, "Sorry if I woke you. I'll try to be quieter in the future."

His dark voice resonated through her from head to toe. The change in his position revealed a line of stitches running from his ribs around to his back, and she imagined they were somehow connected to his facial wounds. "You didn't wake me. I was in the bathroom getting ready for bed and I heard a . . . noise." Was he in pain, or had something else awakened him? "I thought you might need some help."

He glanced to his right and bent to retrieve whatever was on the floor. "Just a bad dream. Guess I knocked some stuff off the nightstand."

"Is there broken glass?" She took a step farther into the room. "I can get a broom and dustpan."

He repositioned the digital alarm, then righted the shade on the table lamp and set it behind the clock. When the bulb flickered to life, he ran a hand through his hair. His head jerked, and Chloe guessed he'd just realized he was naked as a newborn babe.

"Go to your room and forget about it." He tugged the covers to his waist. "I'll be fine."

She smiled at his modesty. Since her arrival on earth, every mortal she'd had sex with had a body that resembled a god, and not one of them had gone to the trouble of hiding their impressive form. In fact, most had strutted their "assets" like peacocks in mating season.

Instead of taking his suggestion, she reached around the door, grabbed his robe and walked to the bed. "Here, why don't you put this on"—*or not*—"while I get you a drink of water." She dropped the garment on the mattress, went into the bathroom, and ran the tap. Taking another deep breath, she returned and handed him the glass.

He muttered a thanks and downed the cool liquid, his throat moving seductively with every swallow. He'd put on the robe, but it was partially open, giving her a moonlit glimpse of his sculpted chest and curling dark hair. When she realized she was gaping, she closed her mouth. Though she was curious to see the rest of his manly form, it would be more than embarrassing if Matt Castleberry found out he made her weak in the knees.

He finished the water, placed the glass on the bedside table, and focused on his entwined fingers. "I'm . . . okay. You don't need to hang around."

"I don't mind," she said, and sat next to him on the bed. She couldn't help but wonder what had happened to upset a suspicious, bossy know-it-all so much it would cause nightmares. "Do you want to talk about it?"

Matt shrugged. The dream didn't rear its ugly head every night, but often enough that it no longer terrified him or came as a surprise. Still, he was always thrown for a loop by its intensity. And the last person he wanted to discuss it with was Baby Blue Eyes. She'd probably toss him a thimbleful of pity, then find a way to use the incident against him.

Chloe leaned close, grazing his thigh with hers, and a jolt of electricity slammed his gut. He pictured a scantily clothed Suzanne kneeling in the limo with her coat thrown open. While a lot of men might have taken her up on what she offered, she hadn't excited him in the least. But Chloe Degodessa had brought his dead zone to life from the moment they'd met. And even though she hadn't done it in a way that was blatant or desperate like Suzanne, she'd gotten his full attention.

"It's not late," she continued, oblivious to his thoughts. "I don't mind."

Inching away, he bunched the robe around his lap to hide his burgeoning erection. "All I need is a good night's sleep."

"How long has it been?"

Months, he almost answered, his mind still on his lack of sexual fulfillment. "Since I had an uninterrupted eight hours? On and off, maybe a year, not counting last night."

"Wow." Chloe sighed. "That's ten times a bummer."

"Tell me about it."

"Why don't you tell *me* instead?" she offered again. "I promise not to give you a hard time."

Determined to remain polite yet distant, Matt scraped up the courage to meet her stare. Pearly teeth bit at her lower lip, her beautiful eyes filled with concern. His gaze traveled her bountiful curves, took in the peaked tips of her centerfold-perfect breasts, barely covered by her shimmering blue gown, her flaring hips and the indentation centered above her shapely thighs. Long legs shifted under the gown, and ten tiny toes, painted a rosy pink, flashed from beneath the hem.

No wonder Chloe Degodessa had half the bachelors in Chicago beating down her door. The woman was every man's fantasy, a living, breathing dream girl come to life.

"It's personal," he ground out, annoyed at the direction his thoughts had taken. "If I need that kind of help, I'll make an appointment with a shrink."

She blinked. "You mean a psychiatrist?"

"Maybe," he grumbled, pissed he'd said such a stupid thing. He wasn't crazy, just exhausted. Which had to be the reason he was having such inappropriate ideas about his grandmother's assistant.

"Miss Belle will—"

"Do not even think of telling Belle about this. Or Ruby or your catering buddy." Matt stood, tightened his belt, and half lifted her from the mattress. Grabbing her elbow, he began to lead her from the room. "And since I'm a little old for a babysitter, I think it's time you returned to bed."

They reached the bathroom, and Chloe jerked from his grasp. Pressing her back to the door, she gave him a mutinous glare. "I don't enjoy being manhandled."

Matt dropped his hand. He was a big man, so he always made a point of being gentle, especially with women and children. This primitive reaction to someone who was virtually a stranger was almost as frightening as his nightmare.

"I apologize. It's just—"

"You know," said Chloe, her voice as haughty as a debutante's, "I was beginning to feel sorry for you, but I've changed my mind."

"I don't need your pity," he growled in return.

"Well, you need something. Maybe a sledgehammer to knock that chip off your shoulder where I'm concerned."

Her snotty attitude freed his conscience of all restraint. "It figures you'd be the kind of woman who'd find a way to turn this into something about you."

Chloe arched a brow. "What the heck is that supposed to mean?"

"It means I'm not like one of the goggle-eyed

guys who've paraded through your life and
thrown themselves at your feet. I don't need you
to show me pity or bolster my masculinity or—"

"Well, I don't need you either, you big jerk."

"Oh, yeah?"

"Yeah."

Matt scowled. If ever a person was begging to
be put in their place, it was Chloe Degodessa. Intent on telling her so, he took a step forward, but
she held her ground. When her nipples grazed his
chest, his dead zone rocketed to attention, and
every frustration he'd experienced over the last
few months screamed to the fore.

Angry that this woman had managed to crack
his usually calm facade, he flattened himself against
her mounded flesh. Pinning her, he captured her
hands and raised them up against the door. She
quirked her lips in a taunting grin, and he lost all
control. Bending forward, he plundered her sassy
mouth, just to show her he was in charge of this
show.

When his tongue broke through the barrier of
her lips and invaded her warm wet heat, Chloe
softened beneath him, molding herself to his
frame from shoulders to pelvis as if daring his
newly awakened dead zone to join in the dance.
Shocked by the level of his desire, Matt fell into
her gladly, achingly . . . fully.

The kiss went on forever, erasing the nightmare
and freeing his memory of every atrocity, every
inhumane moment he'd witnessed in Ituri, until

there was nothing but Chloe filling his hands and his mind.

She raised a leg and wrapped it around his thigh. He savaged her lower lip, and she returned the pained pleasure. Then he ran his hands to her breasts and cupped them in his palms, plucking her turgid nipples, moaning when she groaned in encouragement.

Gasping for air, he drew back, prepared to drown in Chloe's sweetness, but when he gazed into her eyes his heart slowed to a near stop.

She stared at him for a long moment, her face a pale mask of confusion. The last minute fast-forwarded in his brain, and he released her, silently cursing his rash actions.

"I'm sorry," he mumbled, retreating to give her room. "I don't know what . . . how . . . that happened."

Her expression was unreadable, as if she'd closed herself off to his scrutiny. "Don't think a thing of it," she said, squaring her shoulders and smoothing her gown. "Because I won't."

She slipped behind the door before he could say another word, leaving him more lonely than he'd felt in two years.

Chloe stumbled through the bathroom, into her bedroom, and sagged against the door. Sucking in a huge gulp of air, she swiped at her tears, then banged her head on the wooden panel.

"No, no, no," she whispered. "No!"

She raised her fingers to her still tingling lips. Her breasts ached at the memory of Matt's touch, her nipples begged for the feel of his hands. Her body longed to surrender to his. If only she hadn't challenged him with that so-what-are-you-gonna-do-about-it grin.

She trembled and told herself it was the chilly night air turning her to a quivering mass of goose bumps. Not Matt Castleberry. Stomping to her bed, she plopped onto the mattress, flung herself backward, and pulled a pillow over her head. The phone call she'd shared with her sisters popped into her mind, and she recalled her smart-ass comments. She'd been an idiot, lording it over them as if she alone was capable of controlling her feelings and corralling her emotions.

Over the past year, she'd become an expert where mortal men were concerned, carefully choosing only those who were as self-absorbed and unattainable as she professed to be, just to spare herself this moment, and it had all been for naught. Because somehow, the very worst thing imaginable had occurred.

She was in love with Matt Castleberry.

It was ridiculous, she knew, to be so certain of such a frivolous emotion. Mortals fell in and out of love as easily as they changed channels on their televisions. It was the reason she'd found it simple to flit from man to man, dating each one just long enough to satisfy her sexually and then move on.

She was Chloe, daughter of the mighty Zeus,

the Muse of Happiness, and a demigoddess. She'd been created to inspire eternal joy in mankind. She gave mortals the will to laugh and love for a lifetime with the partner of their dreams. It had never been destined that she or any of the muses fall in love. For them, the sexual joining was but a pleasurable nanosecond in time, meant to be over in the blink of an eye.

Never had she thought she could lose her own heart in the process. Even worse, she'd been felled by a human, a man capable of condemning her to who knew what type of cruel and unjust punishment instead of the immortality she'd been promised.

Chloe rolled to her back. How could she have been so stupid to think she was above it all? She'd teased her sisters about love, bragged about how clever she was in her dealings with mortals, yet she'd fallen for a man who . . .

A thought flickered in her brain, then blazed into being like a forest fire.

She couldn't be in love. Nothing of such importance would happen that fast—as if she'd been hit by a freight train or pierced by an arrow.

She smacked her forehead with the heel of her hand. Well, duh! Hadn't she and her sisters just discussed the mother goddess and her ability to sneak around while manipulating mortals and the situations in which they were involved?

Didn't Hera hate her, Zoë, and Kyra for their beauty, their parentage, their creativity?

And hadn't they agreed she would stop at nothing to see them fail?

It all made sense, Chloe assured herself. She wasn't in love, not really, but there was definitely something malicious afoot.

"Eros?" She said the name out loud, in case the impish god was still nearby. Then she scooted off the mattress, searched the dresser drawers, checked behind the mirror, peeked in the closet. Finally, she dropped to her hands and knees and peered under the bed. Standing, she inspected her body for any sign of a tender spot or bruise.

Finding nothing, she again threw herself onto the mattress and listed her thoughts in a logical manner. Hera had a hold over all of Olympus's citizens, so it was simple for her to employ Eros, one of the oldest and most troublesome of the gods. The irksome deity enjoyed nothing more than imparting intense feelings of devotion and care into couples who were totally unsuited for each other, causing some of them to only *think* they were in love. And he did it by striking one or both of the unsuspecting subjects with a golden arrow.

It would be just like the jealousy-ridden mother goddess to stick her nose into an innocent muse's business and concoct a plan that would lure her into unknowingly disobeying Zeus.

Hera was clever enough to realize that because Chloe was famous for her beauty, it would be the ultimate jest to have her fall in love with a positively ordinary mortal. Though Matthew Castle-berry didn't possess a great bulbous nose or a wart-covered body, he was scarred, and he was grumpy, bossy, and suspicious of her. It was simply impossible for her to lose her heart to such an unattractive and contrary man unless trickery was involved.

She fanned her face with a shaking hand as her concern abated. Now that she'd sorted it out, everything made perfect sense. She'd just have to be on the lookout for Eros whenever Matt was in her presence. If another bout of the light-headed and decidedly stirring feelings struck, she'd squelch it with humor or venom, whichever seemed appropriate at the moment.

And she would continue to deny, deny, deny, until she arrived on Mount Olympus for her final review, where she would then report her thoughts to her father. He would punish the love god for doing Hera's bidding and put his meddling wife in her place as only Zeus could.

The next time she and Matt were alone, she'd ignore his hard-muscled body, wouldn't think about his demanding lips—a solid fifteen on the kiss-o-meter—or the ecstasy she felt when she was encircled in his warm, strong arms. She'd managed to live without the love of a man for thousands of years. Surely she could avoid intimate contact with Matt Castleberry for a few more weeks.

* * *

Well hell!

Matt ran a shaky hand over his mouth and jaw, tasted Chloe on his lips, and muttered a second, fouler curse. What the heck had they—had he— just done? If her tears hadn't put a halt to their raging lust, they'd probably still be sucking face, or more likely humping the night away on his bed. Thank God, one of them had the sense to know when they were headed in the wrong direction.

He was to blame for the entire incident. Sure, Chloe had egged him on, but it was his idea to step over the line and invade her personal space. It was his hands that had held her prisoner, cupped her satiny flesh, teased her nipples to tight knots of heat.

And he'd initiated that mind-blowing kiss.

He could chalk up the impulsive deed to his long bout of abstinence, but it would be a cop-out. Something primal had stirred inside him from the moment he'd seen Chloe Degodessa in the foyer, looking regal, unattainable, and as beautiful as an angel fallen to earth. Intrigued, he'd wanted to investigate every facet of her personality, understand each of the women who resided inside, and claim them for his own.

He tugged off his robe and tossed it on the end of the bed, then lay down and drew the covers to his waist. Damn if he wasn't still tenting the blanket at the mere thought of her. He'd have to start sleeping in pajama bottoms if they continued to share a bathroom, and learn to listen for her presence in the shower.

The image of Chloe standing naked under running water brought his already engorged penis to a throbbing ache, and he hissed out a laugh. Maybe he did need a shrink, though he couldn't imagine how he'd explain his predicament. Damn Suzanne for continuing to flaunt that ring. Thanks to her inability to accept reality, all of Chicago still believed they were engaged. As soon as word of the breakup got out, they'd think it had just ended. Before he had a chance to comment, word would somehow leak that he had dropped Judge Haywood Armbruster's daughter for his grandmother's assistant.

His only hope was to stay as far away from the sexy Ms. Degodessa as possible.

The ridiculous idea brought on another round of silent laughter. He'd promised his grandmother he'd take charge of the business and act as her replacement. As such, he'd be expected to interact intimately with Belle Castleberry's second-in-command. With his need for on-the-job training, he'd also have to hold one-on-one sessions with Chloe, because it was obvious she'd been running things for the past year. That meant long hours spent together examining the books, discussing clients, consulting on pricing and contracts, and making whatever decisions were best for Castleberry Hall.

If he refused, Miss Belle would start asking questions; questions he didn't want to answer. Especially now that she knew he'd broken it off with Suzanne. In fact, Belle would be so elated she'd probably go on the hunt for his next fiancée, and logically that would lead to Chloe.

He had to harden his resolve, be the consummate professional, and dive head first into the company mechanics without seeing Chloe Degodessa as anything more than his coworker. His mentor. His link to the ins and outs of his family's business.

Matt stretched out an arm and doused the light. Punching the pillow into a ball, he tossed and turned, searching for a comfortable position. But once he found one, his mind still raced, so he decided to concentrate on something innocuous, like fishing or counting sheep. He closed his eyes, and remnants of the nightmare edged into view.

Children, thousands of bleeding children, lined up and waiting for surgery, stared at him with expressions so filled with hope it made his heart twist. Then, Migani, the little guy he'd let down that first day, smiled at him . . .

Cursing the scene, he envisioned himself in a boat on Lake Michigan with a rod and reel in his hands . . . and saw Chloe lounging on a deck chair wearing a tiny bikini the same color as her toenails.

He imagined himself sitting on a blanket in a field, watching a herd of sheep hop a fence . . . and

Chloe appeared beside him, wearing a bright red halter top, denim short-shorts, and a beguiling grin.

Frustration set in as he scoured his brain for something . . . anything that would allow him to sleep.

Finally, he dozed off, his last memory of Chloe and the way she'd melted in his arms.

Chapter 8

"How about if I tag along behind you this morning, just to see how you handle your duties as CEO?" Matt poured a cup of coffee, then turned and smiled at his grandmother. Dogging her footsteps instead of Chloe's would be the easiest and safest way to start his day. "I promise not to get in the way."

"Tag along? Then it will have to be with me and Ruby." Giving him an impish grin, Belle stirred sugar into her tea. "Though I doubt you'll learn anything of value at the Lovely Lady Salon."

From as far back as Matt could remember, his grandmother's cropped, curly, medium brown hair was kept picture-perfect thanks to monthly visits to her hairdresser. Belle's continued pride in her appearance was a positive sign that she and Ruby were feeling up to par.

"Did I hear my name?" asked the housekeeper, trundling into the dining room. Dressed in a mauve suit, with her braided gray hair coiled on top of her head, and her false teeth flashing a brilliant white smile, she looked the epitome of matronly elegance. "By the way, remind me again, Belle. Whose turn is it to drive?"

Matt took his seat, cringing at the question. Trying to decide which elderly woman was best capable of steering a tank-sized, twenty-year-old Mercedes through loop traffic was mind-numbing, but he'd put his money on the arthritic seventy-sixty-year-old over the myopic eighty-three-year-old any day. And even though the idea of spending the morning in a beauty parlor with said women was downright scary, he had to do something to avoid Chloe while he figured out how to handle his insane attraction to her.

Playing chauffeur would give him down time to find a solution. "I could drive you. It'll be good to get behind the wheel again. I can take a walk and you two can get . . . whatever it is you get done."

"A walk? In this cold? Absolutely not," said Belle, pushing her glasses up the bridge of her nose. "Besides, we're perfectly capable of navigating on our own, aren't we, Ruby?"

"That we are."

The housekeeper brought her coffee to the table just as Clark walked in from the kitchen carrying a breakfast-laden tray. "Here you go, girls. Cinnamon buns, hot from the oven. Ruby, yours are the two without icing." He set a separate plate in front of her. "Have you checked your sugar this morning?"

Matt took note of the subtle reference to diabetes, not surprising for a woman Ruby's age, and recalled his phone conversation with her physician. "I meant to tell you earlier, I spoke to Dr. Kellam yesterday and he—"

His grandmother's teacup clattered in its saucer. "You did what?"

"I phoned Dr. Kellam. I told you I planned to call him when we talked in your room."

"Well, it's nice to see you didn't let any grass grow while you were waiting." She tore into a cinnamon bun with a vengeance. "I thought you might take a few days in order to judge how well I was doing yourself, but you just had to—"

"Hold your horses, Belle." Ruby chomped on her naked roll. "This is dandy, Clark," she said as she chewed. "Now, what about Dr. Kellam?"

Matt smiled at the housekeeper and hoped his simple explanation would placate Belle. "I wanted a report on each of you. Ruby, he said he would relay your status only if you gave him permission to speak with me. As for you, Grandmother, I merely wanted to hear straight from the good doctor about the condition of your health."

"Don't I have to give my permission too?" Belle groused. "I'm still of sound mind, after all."

"No one said you weren't, but as your next of

kin, it's an automatic courtesy for him to fill me in."

"Now see here—"

"Oh, leave the boy be," ordered Ruby. "He's gonna worry and fuss until he gets answers, so why not make things easy for him? Besides, there's nothin' we've got he can't know about. Ain't that right, Clark?"

"That's right, my darling." Clark sat and snapped opened his napkin. "You're both fit as fiddles, or however they put it these days. Now eat, or you'll be late for your appointment. Oops, I almost forgot." He stood and headed for the kitchen. "I'll get in touch with the ground crew and have someone bring the Mercedes to the front door."

Before Matt could make another plea for escape, Chloe entered the dining room from the foyer and went directly to the sideboard for coffee. Dressed in a slim, powder blue skirt and matching jacket, she gave the appearance of a respectable businesswoman—until his gaze traveled to her sinfully long legs covered in sheer, seamed hose, and her three-inch, open-toed, sling-back heels the same shade as her suit.

"Are you two planning to have lunch in town?" she asked without giving Matt a good-morning. "Because if you go to the tea room, I'd love a box of baklava."

"It's a standing order, dear," said Belle. "Unless you'd like to accompany us."

"Not today." She sat and smoothed her shoulder-length fall of wavy, wheat-gold hair. "I had a trim last month, and someone has to be here to supervise the luncheon meeting."

"You're lucky to be a natural blond with no roots to worry about," said Ruby. "I had hair your color once upon a time, but I owed it all to Ms. Clairol."

"Ms. Clairol and Jean Pierre," added Belle with a laugh. "Chloe is one of the few women I've met who doesn't need to dye her hair, or curl it, for that matter. Her beauty is one hundred percent her own." She glanced at Matt. "Which is such a rarity these days."

He lowered his eyelids, determined not to take part in a discussion on Chloe's goddesslike appearance, especially if it was accomplished without the use of chemicals or cosmetics. The fact that the woman brought his dead zone to life, even while dressed for a business meeting, irked the hell out of him. And that was just the beginning of his problems with the tempting assistant.

"Car's on the way," said Clark as he sauntered through the swinging door. "Finish up, or you'll be late."

The caterer plopped into his chair, and everyone ate in silence for the next few minutes. Matt peered at Chloe over the top of the morning paper's sports section. She had nerve, studying the front page as if last night hadn't rattled her, while he'd stewed like a hormone-riddled teenager.

Was she purposely acting as if he didn't exist because of what had transpired in his bedroom, or was she pissed because Belle had told her he was now in charge? The way his luck had been going, he wouldn't be surprised to learn his grandmother was saving that tidbit for a big fat friggin' surprise.

Miss Belle dabbed at her rose-colored lips. "Chloe, I'd appreciate it if you'd fill Matthew in on how we handle things, and I believe the Optimists' lunch is a good place to start. You ready, Ruby?"

"As I'll ever be."

"Let me get the door and see you to the car," Clark said. He followed them out, almost as if he knew a disagreement was brewing in the wings.

Matt finished his coffee, waiting to speak until the trio disappeared. "So . . ."

Seconds passed while he gathered his thoughts. *Good going, jackass.* He took another stab at conversation. "What's first on your agenda?"

Chloe continued to peruse the headlines.

"I guess we'll be spending a lot of time together over the next couple of days."

She turned the front page and made a fuss of folding the newspaper in half.

All right. If that was the way she wanted it, he'd barge right in and find out what was what. "I suppose Grandmother forgot to mention that I'd be taking her place as manager for a while. Since I'm not sure which direction to go with my career, we both figured I might as well focus on the family business."

Yep, he thought, when Chloe's expressive face registered shock. A big fat friggin' surprise.

"You're the new manager of Castleberry Hall?"

"For now."

She glanced around the room, as if scanning for a listening device, then stuck out her chin. "What about medicine?"

Matt had already accepted that sooner or later a lot of people would pose the same question, so he might as well start with the lie closest to the truth. "Belle is a priority, and she's most concerned about the Castleberry, which means it's my primary concern as well."

After Chloe blew out a breath, she opened and closed her mouth. "That is the stupidest thing I've ever heard. My guess is you're going to follow me around and act as if you care, then, just when I've taught you everything I know, decide to return to practice."

If only that were true. He sat back and crossed his arms. "What's it to you? Aren't you leaving town?"

"I am. Soon." She pushed away from the table. "But I haven't told Miss Belle yet, so I'd appreciate it if you kept quiet until I do."

"I don't care for the idea of deceiving my grandmother."

"I'm not deceiving her. I'm simply putting off

something I'm sure will be painful for both of us." She carried her cup to the sideboard. "Besides, if you're taking Miss Belle's place, and you already know I'm leaving, it's just as good as giving notice, isn't it?"

Unable to fault her logic, he stood. "Okay, I'll buy that—for a while. But Belle will have to know, and you're going to be the one to tell her."

"I will, when it's right." Chloe marched ahead of him like a general going into battle. "I'm late for work, and so are you. Get your butt in gear."

"So nice you could join us," said Chloe, nodding to the thirtieth—or was it fortieth?—person to tromp through the reception foyer. Her lips felt locked in place, as if she were destined to forever smile, no matter how uncomfortable or miserable the situation. "Allow me to introduce Miss Belle's grandson, Matt Castleberry. He and I will be working together."

Matt's announcement had taken her by surprise, but she should have seen it coming. Miss Belle had made no bones about the fact that she wanted the party hosting business kept in the family. Who better than her grandson to carry out her wishes? But Chloe got the feeling it wasn't Matt's first choice, and couldn't help but wonder why he was doing it.

When they arrived at the office after breakfast, she'd carefully checked the room for signs of Eros. Finding none, she'd coerced Matt into jumping in with both feet, even though he'd argued against attending the Optimists' function. Now, at the reception hall, she'd stationed him beside her, determined to introduce him to every individual who came through the oak doors. Once he seemed at ease, she retreated to let him make small talk. If he expected to be of help to Miss Belle, he needed a crash course in diplomacy, and today was as good a time as any for his first lesson.

After shaking another club member's hand, Chloe let Matt take over the conversation. When she heard the guest mention Doctors Without Borders, she concentrated on the next round of attendees. If the concept of a dedicated doctor running Castleberry Hall brought in more business, she was one hundred percent behind his involvement.

"We're pleased you've come to the Castleberry today. Let me introduce you to Miss Belle's grandson Matthew," she said, leading what she hoped were the last arrivals to Matt. Then she sidled up to Maurice Plummer, the club's exalted president, to make sure things were running the way he wanted.

"Ever since word got out that we shifted our meetings to Castleberry Hall, attendance is up ten percent," said Mo, a diminutive yet dapper man of indeterminate years. "Looks like we'll have lots of volunteers for the next Birthday Party."

"I certainly hope so." Chloe nodded to a straggler, then turned to Mo. "What do you think of Miss Belle's grandson?"

The old gent frowned. "He's a commendable young man, but it's a pity about his face."

Chloe deemed the comment inappropriate but couldn't be rude. Matt's charming demeanor and warm hazel eyes seemed to work magic on the guests, and though they probably wondered about his disfigurement, it didn't appear to bother any of them.

"I hope he goes to a plastic surgeon," the president continued. "Because those marks are hard to ignore."

A sudden desire to protect Matt Castleberry rose in Chloe's chest. Last night, after she'd decided Hera and Eros were the reason for her and Matt's ridiculous encounter, she'd drifted into a fitful sleep. It was only this morning, when she'd awakened and pondered the situation all over again, that she realized she hadn't given Matt's scars a second thought while they were wrapped in each other's arms. The wounds had intruded afterward, when she tried to reason her way out of the dilemma.

"He has mentioned it," she said, her gaze riveted on her nemesis. Even now, the damage seemed to fade when he smiled at the customers. Did the nightmare have something to do with his face or the wound she'd seen in his side? If so, whatever occurred had probably been traumatic to have had such an impact.

The question made her ashamed of her focus on his injury. She'd never had so much as a zit; the citizens of Mount Olympus had no blemishes of any kind. But if she had even the tiniest amount of scarring, she doubted she would have the courage to leave her room, let alone meet a group of strangers, as he was doing today. Matt Castleberry might be a royal pain, but he'd been injured while sacrificing two years of his life for the world's less fortunate. And now he was willing to give up a career to help his grandmother keep her business.

"I hope he has the sense to take care of it," Mo droned. "People don't always feel comfortable being around someone with a deformity."

Deformity! Chloe again reined in her temper. It wasn't as if the scars couldn't be repaired, and besides, wasn't what was on the inside of a person more important? "I don't think it's anyone's concern but Matt's," she said, forcing a smile to remove the bite from her answer.

Mo must have caught the edge in her tone, because his cheeks turned red and his expression softened. "You're right, of course. Um . . . shall we go in?"

They entered the dining hall together. "How are the donations coming for this month's party?" Mo asked. "We've got several volunteers lined up for balloons and prizes. Think you'll need more bubbles?"

"I'll let you know after the Meyers-Whidden

wedding," said Chloe. "And Clark's willing to donate another cake."

"Wonderful, I'm—"

A female voice called to Mo, and he waved. "That's Madeline Bumpers," he said, referring to the current vice president. "Looks as if it's time to start the meeting. I'll talk to you later."

He trotted to a tall thin woman dressed in basic black and gave her an air kiss. The woman was a busybody and a fusspot, but she reeked of money and didn't mind spending it on a worthy cause. She'd taken to the idea of holding a monthly birthday party for the youngsters being treated at Children's Memorial like a Greek to ouzo and now acted as if it had been her suggestion instead of Ruby's and Miss Belle's.

And truly, it didn't matter who had the thought first. The center for kids undergoing treatment for leukemia and other forms of cancer would be the beneficiaries of a fun-filled monthly event that brought joy and laughter to hundreds of ailing children, which was the most important thing.

Chloe slipped into the kitchen and passed an army of wait staffers carrying trays laden with steaming cups of soup and baskets of rolls out the door. Judging by the scent in the air, Clark had once again outdone himself with the offerings.

"Everything smells fantastic," she said when she reached his side.

Facing a lineup of plates holding a variety of sandwich triangles, he grinned. "So far, the menu's

been simple to keep down the cost, but if they
don't up their per person charge soon, I'll be
forced to serve spaghetti and—dare I say it?—
meatballs."

"How about peanut butter and jelly? I hear
that's a real budget saver," Chloe joked.

"It is. Too bad it won't fly with this group."
Clark rested his backside against a counter. "So,
is Dr. Do-good learning the ropes, or has he run
to the big house?"

Chloe raised her eyes to the ceiling. "Uh-oh. I
left him alone with the latecomers. I'd better find
him."

She raced into the dining room and circled the
far wall, then edged to the back of the room. A
quick survey of the tables showed no sign of Matt,
so she went to the cloakroom, donned her Blackglama, and walked to the foyer, which also was
empty. Heaving a sigh, she headed into the single
digit outdoor temperature. The persnickety Eros
would never flit about in this frigid climate, even
on Hera's orders, so it was likely she'd be safe
with her new boss.

Hugging the mink close, Chloe scanned the
grounds and parking area and saw him, dressed
in his jacket and gloves, resting against the brick
wall ringing the lot. His gaze appeared focused
on the bottom of the hill upon which the Castleberry property sat. Even though the view of Lake
Shore Drive and Lake Michigan was breathtak-

ing from here, she could tell by the tilt of his shoulders that he was not a happy camper.

"You giving up on the party planning business already?" she quipped when she reached his side.

Matt's warm breath fogged the air as he continued to stare at the panoramic scene. Regretting her snippy remark, she opted for sensitivity. "I hope being dumped into society so quickly after your return wasn't too much of a strain."

Matt gave a tentative smile. "Not enough to change my mind about doing this, if that's what you're asking."

"Then why did you leave the hall?"

His ruddy cheeks grew darker. "Right in the middle of the last batch of polite talk, I remembered one of the reasons why I chose medicine. I was never able to see myself in the corporate world, yet there I was making nice with that very group."

Chloe rested her arms on the top of the chest-high wall. "Doctors have to be people persons too, don't they? Especially pediatricians."

"Not a cold and cough pediatrician, a pediatric surgeon. I wanted to do more than monitor sniffles and prescribe antibiotics." He shrugged. "I got my wish in the Congo."

"I wouldn't mind hearing about it sometime."

Straightening, his unreadable gaze traveled her face, as if trying to gauge her reason for continuing to offer assistance. "I don't want to talk about it." He glanced at the reception building. "Are we through, or do we have to stick around until the end of the meeting?"

She let out a breath. "We're through. I'll tell Clark to put a senior staff member on duty for cleanup or find one myself. Just give me a minute."

She hurried to the building and met with Leah. "Can you handle breakdown?" she asked the girl. "I have work in the office."

"Will do," Leah answered. "I'll let Clark know."

Chloe nodded and headed outside, but the parking lot was empty. Scoping the drive, she spotted Matt in the distance walking swiftly to the main house. Was she such a bother that he couldn't wait for her?

Or did the memory of last night haunt him as badly as his nightmare?

Chloe entered the office, but there was no sign of Matt. After hanging up her coat, she picked up the mail and headed toward the kitchen. She was starving and planned to have lunch whether or not he was there. She wouldn't skip breakfast again just to avoid talking with him, and Eros be darned if she would miss another meal. Besides, when Belle and Ruby, and sometimes Clark, were in attendance, the troublesome god wouldn't dare shoot another one of his arrows. And since he'd done his dirty work only last night, he probably assumed she was still under its spell.

Little did Eros realize she was smarter than the average demigoddess. She knew exactly why her heart had raced and her stomach had quivered from the moment she'd walked into the dining room that morning. Wise to his and Hera's dastardly plan, she'd be on the lookout for more trickery.

She entered the empty kitchen and opened the fridge, where she found a container of soup and a plastic-wrapped plate piled high with sandwiches identical to the kind being served at the luncheon. Whenever Clark didn't cook, Ruby prepared their food, unless she was ill or somewhere with Belle. Chloe wasn't used to assembling her own meals, so it was nice of Clark to think of her, even when the older women were out.

She set the soup in the microwave to warm and proceeded to arrange sandwiches on two plates. Then she carried the plates to the breakfast area, poured the hot soup into bowls, retrieved utensils, and set everything on the table. Perching on a chair, she began to eat as she sorted the envelopes. Like the proverbial bad penny, Matt Castleberry was bound to show up sooner or later.

Junk mail went in one pile, what looked to be personal correspondence for Belle or Ruby into a second, and anything that had to do with the Hall went into another stack, which she usually commandeered for herself. After completing a final sort of the third group, she tossed the advertisements and opened the bills. Then she tore into another letter from Party Palaces.

"Anything interesting in the mail?"

Chloe jumped, smacking the letter facedown on the place mat. "Can't you clear your throat or . . . or hum or knock before you enter a room?"

"I could," Matt said as he sat across from her. "But it would take the fun out of things. Besides, this is my house."

Chloe ignored the remark and pretended to sift through the envelopes while she carefully folded the note from Party Palaces. "After lunch, I thought we'd go over the details for tomorrow night's baby shower. Then I have to make a few calls."

Matt rose, poured two glasses of water from a container in the fridge, and brought them to the table. "Calls to whom?"

"Mo, for one. I need to hear how the meeting went, if the members were pleased with the food, that sort of thing."

"Are you going to ask him how I did?"

Chloe had wondered if Matt noticed the subtle expression of disgust on the president's face, and now she had her answer. "I'm sorry about Maurice. He's old and not very tactful."

Matt swallowed a gulp of water. "You don't have anything to apologize for. I knew it was going to be tough, coming back in this shape. But a couple of facial scars is better than the alternative."

Chloe recalled the stitches in his side. "What was the alternative?"

He picked up a sandwich. "Let's just say it could have been worse."

She shuddered at his pointed explanation. "The scars aren't that noticeable."

"Right." He downed a bite of shrimp salad. "Just what a little kid with a debilitating illness wants to see when he visits his doctor."

"If they bother you, why don't you make an appointment with a plastic surgeon?" she asked, echoing Mo's suggestion.

"I plan to. Unfortunately, my personal physician retired while I was gone, so I have to find someone to give me a referral." He finished the last of his soup. "Mind if I take a look at the mail that pertains to the Castleberry?"

Chloe pushed the stack to his side of the table, but kept the letter from Party Palaces. She'd have to wait until she had some privacy before she read whatever Jeremy Jadwin had to say this time.

"Do the bills go to our accountant?" he asked, returning the last one to the pile.

"Nope. I pay them, give them a date stamp, and put them in a file for the accounting firm. They balance the checkbook and keep things straight for taxes and the end of year report."

"You pay the bills?"

Chloe had been on the receiving end of dozens of similar comments since she'd begun work here, first with the bean counters, as Miss Belle called them, then with several fathers of brides who thought she didn't have the smarts to decipher a cost sheet or explain a contract. Leave it to mortals to let the color of a person's hair determine their IQ level.

"Yes, but only if the amount doesn't go into triple digits. I can read and write too, but the words with more than five letters give me a headache." She batted her eyelashes for emphasis. "And I hate it when I run out of fingers and toes to count on."

"Okay, okay. Sorry," Matt said with a snort.

"You should be. Give your grandmother credit for having the sense to hire someone with a brain, will you?"

"I will . . . I mean I do. It's just that a woman with your . . . ah . . . features doesn't usually spend her days behind a desk."

"Oh? And what do women with my *features* do?"

Matt shrugged. "Model? Entertain? Do commercials for shampoo or cosmetics?"

Chloe rolled her eyes. "Puh-leeze. Besides, I have several sisters in the entertainment field, and believe me, it's not all it's cracked up to be."

"Several sisters? What do they do?"

"Nothing you'd ever recognize them for," said Chloe, aware she was giving away more of her background than was necessary. "They don't live in the area, so I doubt you'll ever meet."

"Are you leaving to be with one of them?"

"I'm leaving to be with my entire family."

"And where might that be?"

"Greece . . . er . . . near Greece."

"Sounds nice. On an island?"

"In the mountains, actually." She pushed from the table and carried her dishes to the sink. "But enough about me. It's time to get back to work."

"Can I listen in on those phone calls?"

"Of course. I might even let you make one, if you promise to be a good boy." She smiled to herself. "How much do you know about hosting a baby shower?"

Chapter 9

Matt lathered and rinsed in the steaming spray, his mind centered on the first day of his new career. Once he'd been able to control the urge to jump Chloe's bones, he'd found her surprisingly easy to work with. The concept of hiding behind the facade of a party and event planner was safe and nonthreatening, even if several of the attendees at today's affair knew who he was. His luncheon duties had been simple, but he had the feeling he'd need to be more involved when his smart and savvy assistant left town.

He shook his head when the mere thought of Chloe brought his dead zone to attention. He was getting used to his body's ready, willing, and able reaction to the delectable Ms. Degodessa, and judging by the stares she'd thrown his way several times during the afternoon, he felt certain she was experiencing the same erratic rush of hormones. Too bad they couldn't just hop into bed and go at it like a pair of sex-starved rabbits. Once they were over each other, they could get down to running the business.

The afternoon had passed quickly, and before he knew it, they were enjoying a conversation-filled dinner with Clark, Ruby, and his grandmother. To Chloe's credit, she'd recounted the fine job he'd done both at the luncheon and on the two phone calls she'd allowed him to make: one to a florist and another to the linen service.

He still wasn't sure this position was the right one for him, but polite small talk with customers and suppliers was definitely less dangerous than dodging crazed, knife-wielding natives, and far less stressful than being responsible for the life of a child.

Stepping from the tub, he dried off, hung up his towel, and pulled on a pair of flannel pajama bottoms. Once he ran a comb through his hair, he twisted like a contortionist, examining what he could see of his remaining sutures in the fogged-over mirror. The stitched slash marched from the middle of his side around to his back, and ended an inch above his left kidney. Itchy as a row of mosquito bites, they were overdue for removal. Trouble was, in addition to the Castleberry family physician having retired, he'd lost touch with most of his medical school buddies.

Finding a new doctor seemed his only recourse,

but the task made him sweat. Besides having to wait for an appointment, his name might be familiar to the professional he chose. He didn't want to address a barrage of questions about Ituri or how he'd gotten the wound because, eventually, he'd be asked the inevitable: when and where was he going to practice?

The incision began to twitch, returning him to the problem at hand. Taking a cab or borrowing the Mercedes to reach a walk-in clinic wouldn't work, because when Belle or Ruby heard about it, they'd want to know why, which meant more questions. His grandmother had been upset enough over the story of his facial scarring; learning how close he'd come to dying was sure to overtax her delicate heart.

He needed to find a totally uninvolved source, someone who wasn't interested in his future or his past. Someone who had no stake in what he did with his career or his personal life . . .

"Oops, sorry."

He started when Chloe Degodessa opened the door leading to her bedroom. Dressed in a near-transparent, off-the-shoulder white gown that brushed her ankles, she resembled an angel come to earth.

"It wasn't locked, so I thought the bathroom was free."

A rush of heat filled Matt's chest and rose to his cheeks. Clutching a hand towel to the front of his pjs, he stared at the tile floor. When his gaze rested on ten pink-tipped toes, he whipped up his head and met her befuddled gaze. "Uh . . . my fault. I heard the shower earlier and figured you were through."

Chloe's face flushed the same color as her toenails. "Okay, then. I'll come back later to take care of . . . things."

He latched onto an idea, and before he could stop himself, asked, "How are you around blood?"

Her baby blue eyes widened. "Around what?"

"Blood . . . stitches."

"Blood?" She swallowed. "Real blood?"

"The amount would be minimal, a drop or two at the most."

She leaned against the doorjamb and scoured the room, as if searching for a hidden camera. Then she met his gaze. "What in the world are you talking about?"

Matt did his best to ignore the outline of her bountiful breasts and the slightly darker area at the V of her thighs. "I need help removing the sutures from my side." He turned to give her a better view. "All it takes, besides a steady hand, is tweezers, scissors, and some antiseptic. I bet everything we need is under the sink."

Eyes still open wide, she inspected his wound. "You want me to take those black threads out?"

"That's the general idea. I can reach the first two or three, then I'm stuck." He bent and retrieved a shoe box holding medicinal aids from under the cabinet. Working quickly, he dribbled liquid on a gauze pad and set it on the counter. Then he found tweezers and a small pair of scissors, and doused them in the same solution. "Watch what I do. It's pretty simple."

Raising his left arm, he snipped at the black thread and used the tweezers to pull it from his skin. "There. Nothing to it. Sit while I do the next one." He gestured toward the commode. "Then you can give it a try."

Chloe swallowed again, but her mouth was as dry as a cotton ball. No one on Mount Olympus ever fell ill; never even got a hangnail, let alone needed stitches put in or taken out. She'd seen enough medical shows on television to know of the procedure, of course, but she had never seen a suture holding repaired flesh together up close and personal.

The tingle she'd felt the moment she entered the bathroom had grown to a full-body rush. After checking for and not finding Eros, she decided it had to be because of what Matt was suggesting. If the parties Eros struck with his barbs didn't have sex within twenty-four hours, the pesky god's love arrow was supposed to lose potency and, eventually, release the couple of its spell. Without another shot from the troublemaker, she'd not be so naive as to again fall into Dr. Studly's steely arms or—

Wrong picture, she chided herself. But still . . . removing stitches? It seemed like such an intimate act. And she'd have to touch his skin to do it right.

His naked skin.

"Are you ready?"

She stared at his left side. The loose pajama bottoms rested on his hip bones, while his sculpted abs were directly in her line of sight. And below the waistband dipping under his navel was a long, thick bulge she instantly recognized.

"Okay, one more," he said with a hint of impatience. Or was it desire turning his voice into a growl? "It's the last one I can reach. Try to focus."

Chloe cleared her brain and paid full attention. Deftly, he snipped, pulled, and dropped the thread on the counter. Then he dabbed the spot with the gauze pad.

Butterflies danced in her stomach, threatening to two-step her dinner straight to her throat. She inhaled a breath. "Is this necessary? You must know someone who's experienced. What about going to a walk-in clinic or an emergency room?"

"E.R.s and clinics are for people who need immediate critical care, not basic treatment. This procedure is routine."

"Can't you see a doctor on your own?"

"Mine retired, and it would probably take a couple of weeks to get an appointment with a new one." He scowled. "If you're not capable of helping out, just say so. I'll find a way to get it done."

She bristled at the implication. He wasn't making a dumb blonde joke, but it sounded as if he was headed in that direction. She retrieved the scissors from the counter. "I'm capable. But I don't want to do a bad job . . . or hurt you."

"I'll bite on a strip of leather, if it will help," he quipped. When she didn't answer, he placed two fingers under her chin and tilted her head. "Just keep your hands steady, snip, and pull. At the most, I'll feel a little pinch, which will be nothing compared to . . . how I got the wound."

"Why didn't whoever put them in use those staple thingies, or dissolving stitches? Didn't I read about them somewhere?"

"This was done in the middle of the night, in a makeshift O.R. with basic supplies. No time for fancy doctoring, just plain old repair-the-damage-and-sew-it-up work." He smiled. "You'll do fine."

"But what if I—"

"You won't."

"But—"

"Please. Just do it."

Chloe inhaled, slowly exhaled, and inhaled again. Then, before she could dwell on what she was about to do, she spread her left thumb and forefinger around the wound, brought the scissors to the next stitch, maneuvered them into place, and cut. Still bracing her hand on his ribs, she exchanged the scissors for tweezers and pulled out the thread.

"You did great. I didn't feel a thing," Matt praised. "Ready to move on?"

Prepared to tackle the rest of the stitches, she took another deep breath, nodded, and bent her head. Intent on her work, she steadied her fingers on his warm smooth skin and snipped and pulled until finally she removed the last thread. After setting the tweezers aside, she dampened a fresh pad with antiseptic and dabbed it across the scar line.

A second passed before the enormity of what she'd accomplished sank in, and she slumped against the commode tank. First she began to shake, then tears overflowed her eyes, dampened her cheeks, and slipped to her chin. According to Matt, this was a only a small part of a doctor's duties, not even complicated enough to be considered a medical procedure, yet it had turned her stomach inside out. She couldn't imagine doing any of the more serious tasks he'd done every day.

"Hey, hey. It's over." He gathered the supplies and returned them to the shoe box. When she continued to sob, albeit from relief, he pulled her to her feet. "You're fine, I'm fine. We're finished."

Chloe nodded and took another shuddering breath. Meeting his gaze, she swiped at her tears and smiled. "I've never had to do that before."

"No kidding?" He grinned in return. "I figured you for a regular Florence Nightingale." Cupping her jaw, his thumbs grazed her cheeks. "And you didn't even need a lollipop to stop your crying."

She stood, and he placed his palms on her shoulders and stared into her eyes. Chloe blinked, again aware of the tremors overtaking her body. When had the touch of Matt's hands changed from comforting to arousing? At what moment had her breathing, her very heartbeat, aligned with his?

He bent toward her, and she inched closer, as if drawn by an invisible string. "I should go," she gasped, trying to remain in control.

"Common sense would say that's a good idea." He rubbed his nose against hers. "Trouble is, I seem to lose all sense, common and otherwise, whenever I'm within ten feet of you." His palms slid down her arms to her waist, then around to her bottom. "You have an amazing body."

"I know," Chloe said, her tone matter-of-fact. Each of the goddesses had been formed to drive a man wild. Though hers was one of the more voluptuous figures, Zeus always bragged she was one of his finest creations. "It's a curse as well as a boon."

"I do love an honest woman," he responded. "Maybe it's the reason I can't stop touching you . . . I'm cursed."

"I doubt it," she whispered. Her hands rested on the finely sculpted wall of his chest. "You have a nice body too. What do you do to stay so . . ."

"Fit? I run, though it was tough keeping with the regimen in the jungle. Instead, I did a lot of lifting. I must have carried fifty ten-gallon barrels of water a day, when I wasn't seeing patients. I carted a lot of kids too." He pressed his forehead to hers. "So, what are we going to do?"

"Do?"

"About this . . . this attraction that surfaces whenever we're together." His palms slid from her bottom to her lower back. "I assume you feel it too?"

"There is no attraction. It's simply—" Her gaze scanned the bathroom, then linked with his. "—hormones."

Matt drew away, still grinning. "Probably, considering you started driving me crazy the moment I saw you. And before you take offense, I don't think it's just because of your dynamite figure."

"It isn't?"

"Nope. For some reason I find impossible to fathom, you've worked your way under my skin."

"But—But you accused me of taking advantage of Belle," she stammered. "You as much as said you didn't trust me."

"I didn't, until I spent a day in your presence. You're easy to work with, and your people skills surpass anything I could ever manage. I'm still a little concerned that you didn't give Belle any references, but . . ." His fingers caressed her nape, encircling the curve of her throat. "Are you really going to leave soon?"

"Absolutely," she answered, though the thought filled her with regret. Matt had presented a new side of his personality today. Even without his

Eros-induced sexual allure, she was beginning to enjoy his company. If only . . .

Leaning forward, he halted her thoughts with a gentle kiss that built in intensity until he nibbled, tasted, feasted, as if he was becoming accustomed to the feel of a woman's mouth for the first time. Caught up in his passion, Chloe met his thrusting tongue with her own, filling herself with his essence and erasing all thoughts of the amorous god.

His skin scorched hers, burning through the gossamer of her chiton, melting her flesh until it puddled like heated candle wax. No mortal man, and certainly no citizen of Mount Olympus, had ever made her feel this lost yet found, this weak yet powerful . . .

This needy for love.

Remember Eros! Her brain shouted the words like a battle cry. Pulling away, she took a third survey of the room.

"What are you looking for?"

"Um . . . nothing." Then she remembered something Clark had said. "I thought you were engaged?"

"I was. Suzanne and I called it off six months ago."

"Does your grandmother know?"

"She does now. I should have written and told her, but I didn't want to upset her. Imagine my surprise to learn she was thrilled with the news."

He tipped his head. "Would it matter if I had a fiancée?"

Chloe pushed at his chest, ready to bolt at the insult. "Of course it would matter. Ruining relationships is tacky, definitely not my style."

"Sorry." He grabbed her elbows. "I didn't mean to make it sound as if you did. I was just hoping . . ."

"What?"

"That maybe we could find out where these sudden bursts of sexual attraction are headed."

"It isn't attraction," she lied. "At least, not on my part."

"Really. Then why else do you suppose we can't be near each other without sparks flying?"

She met his eyes and sighed. "We were in the office a big part of the afternoon, and—"

"The electricity arcing around the room was blinding."

"Who says?"

"No one had to say. My body is so attuned to yours that, whenever we're together it's as if someone is holding a nine volt battery to my feet." He frowned. "Which is pretty much the way it feels right now, only the voltage has quadrupled."

"You've been living in primitive conditions; returning to the real world has you confused, that's all. We have nothing in common, and no reason to . . . to . . ."

Chloe closed her eyes, unable to look at him. Instead of finding the proper words to express her thoughts, she was making a mess of things.

"Chloe?"

She raised her head. His honey gold eyes traveled her face, then he let go of her elbows and his lips stretched into a grim line. "Is it the scars?"

Shocked at the question, she opened her mouth. "Of course—" She stopped and shrugged. If her answer would get him to keep his distance, did it matter what he thought? "I mean yes, it's the scars," she continued. "I'm not . . . turned on by men with physical flaws."

Matt's sharp, condemning gaze filled her with sadness. He raised his hands and stepped back to give her room. "Sorry, my error. It—this—won't happen again."

She sidled from the room without a word.

Damn! Damn! Damn!

Chloe dropped onto the bed and pressed a fist to her lips so Matt wouldn't hear her sobs. His expression, so disappointed yet so angry, had cut to the bone. But it was better this way, she told herself, for both of them.

Let him think she was shallow, uncaring, and more concerned with physical appearances than emotions. He never would have believed her if she'd told him about Eros, so when he brought up the scars, it seemed the perfect answer to her problem. After her pronouncement, she deserved his disgust, and any other negative feeling he might have about her.

Taking a calming breath, she closed her eyes and began to think with her head instead of her libido. She hadn't spotted Eros, but that didn't mean he wouldn't be in the bathroom, hiding behind the light fixture or crouching atop a bar of soap, gleefully watching the damage he'd caused. It was completely plausible that he'd struck both her and Matt with another of his golden arrows, just to bedevil them.

And, of course, Matt wouldn't have a clue to what was really going on. His body would do what came naturally and, thanks to Eros, his heart would follow. If she tried to explain away their passion, or confess she was a goddess who would soon return to Mount Olympus, he'd think her crazy or worse.

There was no true attraction between them, she again told herself. Just an uncontrollable lust that, thanks to the troublesome god, pushed them into each other's arms. And if they succumbed to that lust, it would consume them both. She would be on the receiving end of Zeus's wrath, and Matt would be left alone, without an explanation as to why she couldn't return his love.

Drying her eyes on her bedsheet, Chloe pulled up the covers, hunching beneath her pillows as if they formed a secret cave where no one could reach her. Though she wasn't the self-absorbed snob Matt thought her, it was best if he believed her prejudice to be true. Not only could they never be together—they weren't even right for each other.

He was intelligent, brilliant even, while she was an uneducated muse who'd charged through centuries living by her wits as well as her beauty.

Matt was a humanitarian, someone who gave of himself without a thought as to what he might receive in return, while she always put herself first, no matter the situation.

He needed a woman who, like him, was noble and caring, not a demigoddess sent to earth as punishment, with no hope of remaining by his side.

If she gave in to her desire to sleep with him, there would be no way to protect him from the disaster that was sure to follow. It was better if he hated her, because the hatred would keep him at a distance, where Eros's nasty arrows could cause no harm.

Chloe snuggled a pillow to her chest. Tomorrow she and Matt would continue as coworkers, nothing more. She had a reputation to uphold, after all. As the most beautiful of the muses, gods and mortals fell at her feet with the quirk of her finger. When finished with them, she dropped them to the wayside without a second thought, as she'd done to all her sexual partners throughout the centuries.

Now that she'd done the same for Dr. Stud—

Matthew Castleberry—he wouldn't enter her mind again.

Matt choked back a curse as he strode to his bedroom and turned out the light. He'd been an idiot, practically a raving lunatic. Thank God the truth had dawned, and he realized he'd taken Chloe's reaction to his presence completely wrong. While he'd been mooning over her like an adolescent in the throes of his first crush, the oh-so-perfect Ms. Degodessa had been experiencing a totally different type of sensation.

He should have figured Chloe was as thoughtless, self-absorbed, and status-seeking as Suzanne the second he'd laid eyes on her expensive shoes, designer clothes, and that damned mink coat. Even his mention of a plastic surgeon wasn't good enough. The woman didn't want a relationship with a flawed man, no matter what sizzled between them. Period. End of sentence.

He had a good mind to let the scars remain as they were, almost as a test. His grandmother was right. If people couldn't accept him for his talent as a surgeon and—dare he say it—being a nice guy, he'd have no use for them either.

Dropping onto the bed, he scrubbed his face with his hands, wincing when he pulled at his scars. He'd treated children with slashes ten times worse than what he'd received, and they'd never have the luxury of a plastic surgeon to erase the

.blemishes, or make their wounds acceptable for public viewing. Hell, most of those kids were so happy to be alive, they wore their scars as a badge of honor.

He leaned back on the pillow and heaved a sigh. At least he'd found out about Chloe and her intolerance for imperfection before things got out of hand. She'd said she was leaving, so a relationship with her couldn't have gone anywhere. He just had to get through the next couple of days, or weeks, without making a fool of himself again.

Lusting for a woman he disgusted would definitely put a damper on his dead zone. And though he had to work with her, he was damned sure he didn't have to go one step beyond courtesy to get the job done.

He tossed and turned, trying to find a comfortable position that allowed him to sleep, but events of the past two days kept nudging their way into his head.

Was he so desperate for a woman that he'd only imagined the electricity arcing between them whenever they were together?

Was the desire he felt when she trembled in his arms all in his mind?

Had he completely misconstrued the way she'd responded to his kisses?

Though he'd never burned up the sheets with any of the women he'd taken to bed, none of his past lovers had complained that he was inconsiderate. He enjoyed the opposite sex, liked listening to their laughter, and was sometimes inspired by their logic. They could be intelligent, as were all the female nurses and doctors who'd served with him in the Congo, but they could also be mercurial, argumentative, and downright silly.

Either way, he reveled in the quirks and inconsistencies that made up a woman. Their soft, generous touch, their compassion for those in pain, their ability to comfort a terrified child, amazed him.

Too bad he'd missed the boat where Chloe Degodessa was concerned and allowed his dead zone to guide him.

Happily, tomorrow was another day.

Chapter 10

The next morning, Chloe woke in a mood so foul she barely noticed the sunshine streaming through her bedroom window. She'd never had to handle unrequited desire before, and last night's dreams hadn't helped with the challenge. Instead of a peaceful sleep, the taste of Matt's lips and touch of his hands had seduced, taunted, and thrown her into a sexual frenzy so intense, every nerve ending screamed for release.

She heard the shower run and closed her eyes, but the sight of Dr. Studly standing in the steamy downpour appeared on her eyelids. Water cascaded over his hardened pectoral muscles, drizzled down his washboard abs, and pooled in the dark hair surrounding his engorged shaft.

Her breath came in a rasp, and she realized she was—to use a vulgar human word—horny.

Sitting up straight, she threw her legs over the side of the mattress and squeezed her thighs together. Mortal men had flocked to her from the moment she'd set foot on earth, and the last year had been no different, but the thought of phoning Bryce or any of her past lovers and arranging a meeting sent a shiver of distaste down her spine. There had to be a single man somewhere who fit her criteria and was capable of fulfilling her body's demand for satisfaction.

The shower stopped and she heaved a breath, erasing the tempting picture of Matt Castleberry from her mind. Though he'd let it be known he was ready and willing to take her to bed, he was the last mortal she wanted, while at the same time the only one her body craved.

Gritting her teeth at the contradiction, she peeked into the bathroom, saw that it was empty, and locked the door leading to Matt's room. After finishing her morning ritual, she scraped her hair into a demure bun and returned to her room, where she searched for the frumpiest clothes in her closet. She slipped into a long, black wool skirt, white silk blouse, and black cashmere cardigan, then added heeled, ankle-high black leather boots, and checked herself in the mirror. The outfit was exactly what a spinster schoolteacher might wear if she were employed by a stodgy institution of higher learning.

Dowdy and puritanical, the clothing was sure to deflect any prurient thoughts the doctor had about her, especially after she'd voiced her feelings on the importance of a person's physical appearance. Between her bland look and arrogant attitude, she was sure even a jolt from one of Eros's love arrows wouldn't take hold in his veins.

Encased in fabric body armor, she headed downstairs, prepared to act noncommittal and completely disinterested in Matt, while still remaining polite and friendly to Miss Belle, Clark, and Ruby. Entering the dining area, she smiled at the room in general, noting Dr. Studly had yet to come downstairs. "Good morning."

Clark took one glance at her and choked on his coffee. After Ruby patted him soundly on the back, the older woman said, "Holy Hannah, girl. Who died?"

"D-Died?" sputtered Clark. "That getup isn't fit for a funeral." He leaned over his plate. "Where *did* you find the skirt and sweater, in the donate-to-the-dismal-and-boring bag?"

"The sweater is DKNY—"

"From her designs for a nunnery, no doubt," jibed Clark.

"And the skirt is Dior," Chloe added. "Not to mention the one-hundred-percent silk blouse and Ferragamo shoes."

"Yeah, but I bet none of those designers ever intended for the pieces to be worn together. The half boots need form-fitting leather pants, and that skirt would look fa-boo with a red bustierre, or maybe a gold lamé off-the-shoulder slip-on. As for that sweater—"

"It's perfectly acceptable. In case it's escaped your notice, it's ten degrees outside, and I have several sales appointments today, plus the supervision of a baby shower this evening." She chose a blueberry scone from the sideboard and brought it to the table, along with a steaming cup of coffee. "I'll be doing a lot of running around in the cold."

Miss Belle took that moment to arrive. "What's all the chatter about?" she asked. After hooking her cane on the back of her chair, she headed for the teapot.

"Chloe's dirge-wear of the day," Clark quipped. "It's ghastly, and I'm being kind."

"Clark's right, but I don't think he's being kind at all," said Ruby. "What do you think, Belle?"

Chloe stood and made a production of pirouetting in place so Miss Belle could run an inspection, then sat down with an annoyed plop.

Her employer furrowed her brow. "Black and white are classic, so the blouse and sweater need something classic to set them off. Say . . . a string of pearls." She shifted her gaze to Ruby. "Real pearls."

"Now why didn't I think of that? I'll be right back." Ruby pushed from the table and charged through the swinging door as if her tail were on fire.

"No, no!" Chloe called after her disappearing form. She caught Miss Belle's grin and frowned. "You know how much those pearls mean to her. What if I lose them or—"

"You won't. Besides, Ruby has to leave them to someone. You're the prefect choice."

Chloe inhaled a breath. "I'm the . . . ? But I'm not. Surely Ruby has relatives who would appreciate the one quality piece of jewelry she owns."

"Nope. We're her only family, and it's unlikely I'll survive her. Unless Matthew gets married and gives me a granddaughter-in-law very soon, I don't have anyone to leave my baubles to either. You might as well come to my room someday soon and help me sort through my jewelry box. That way you can tag whatever catches your fancy."

Clenching her fists in her lap, Chloe shook her head. "I'll do no such thing. And stop talking about who'll get what when you're . . . gone. Everything is Matt's. He'll be married *someday*, and his wife and children should be the ones to inherit family heirlooms."

"Did someone say my name?" Matt sauntered in. Dressed in tan slacks and a red crew neck sweater over a white shirt, he looked comfortable yet businesslike.

"No," said Chloe.

"Yes," said Belle at the same time.

He continued to the sideboard. "Well, which is it?"

"I was just telling Chloe that she could come to my bedroom and take a gander at my jewelry." Belle sniffed. "Since it doesn't appear you're going to give me a great-granddaughter any time soon."

Matt walked to his chair, set down his coffee and plate of food, and rested his arms on his chair back. Narrowing his eyes, he stared at Chloe. "Oh, really?"

"And I told her I wouldn't do it," Chloe said in a challenging voice. "I don't want anything from Miss Belle, or Ruby, for that matter."

"You'll wear these today, young lady, or I'll—I'll—toss 'em in the trash," Ruby threatened as she made an entrance and circled the table. Draping the pearls across Chloe's throat, she did up the clasp.

Chloe swiveled to face her as she fingered the necklace.

"Hell's bells, but they're perfect on you," said Ruby. Taking a step back, tears pooled in her dark eyes. "If I didn't love them so much, I'd insist you take 'em now, instead of waiting for me to pass on."

"Good idea," Matt said, still giving Chloe a smug stare. "I'm sure Ms. Degodessa will be happy to *take them now*."

Chloe jutted her chin and waited until Ruby sat down, then said to her, "I'll wear them today, and thank you, but you're getting them back tomorrow. Now, if you don't mind, I have work to do." Standing, she picked up her breakfast and the society page and stomped from the room.

Matt scanned the comic section of the morning paper a third time. Hagar and Helga were arguing, the Family Circus was living up to its name. Snoopy was still penning the great American novel, while Woodstock fluttered behind him chirping nonsensical advice. He sighed. Maybe he should have been a jet pilot, or a cartoonist, or an accountant. Each career would have been rewarding and infinitely less stressful than the training he'd endured to be a surgeon.

Then again, he didn't much care for heights, couldn't draw worth a darn, and he had a hard time balancing his checkbook. For as long as he could remember, the only thing he'd ever wanted was a profession in medicine.

Now, here he sat, his life in flux while he fantasized about a woman who thought he was disfigured and, probably, pathetic. What's worse, he suspected said woman was a snob and a user, just like his ex-fiancée. So why in the hell did he continue to fall for women who had such unappealing character traits? Not that he'd *fallen* for Chloe, exactly, but he was attracted to her. And why did her opinion of him matter?

When the answer didn't automatically come to mind, he decided it wasn't worth dwelling on. He simply had to exercise self-control in her presence and not let his insecurity keep him from succeeding with his latest endeavor. He pushed from the table and stood as Clark entered from the kitchen.

"How are you doing?" the caterer asked, loading a tray with used dishes and silverware.

"Fine. Great. Why?"

Clark grinned. "Just asking. I thought I felt a little tension between you and Chloe during breakfast."

Tension? The air had been so charged with electricity, Matt was surprised the lights hadn't flickered. "Nothing two adults can't handle," he answered. "I know you're a fan of hers—"

"But . . . ?"

Matt shrugged. "I can't figure her out. One second she's warm and caring, the next she's cold as an ice cube and twice as hard. Is there something I should know about her?"

Clark folded his arms, his expression blank. "I don't gossip about friends."

"I'm not trawling for gossip. I just want to understand where she's coming from, especially where Belle is concerned," he said, playing a trump card. If the caterer truly had his grandmother's best interest at heart, he would agree she should be protected. "I have to focus on her welfare, and the Castleberry, of course."

"Chloe wouldn't do a thing to undermine Miss Belle or put Castleberry Hall at risk. She's been nothing but considerate since she began working here." Clark fisted his hands on his hips. "Maybe she thinks you're the danger."

"Me?"

"Let's face it, you haven't gone out of your way to hide your suspicion of her, and you seem to enjoy insulting her in front of us." He cocked his head. "You do realize the remarks are upsetting Belle and Ruby?"

Okay, so his grandmother had told him the exact same thing about a dozen times already. "Really?"

"That crack about Ruby's pearls was crude, and there've been other comments . . ."

Matt sighed. "I get your point."

"Chloe isn't used to being questioned or challenged. Belle and Ruby adored her on sight, and so did I. As do most of the people who meet her."

"Don't you mean most of the men?" *Damn, where had that comment come from?*

"Men and women. Though I can't deny all the men she meets are taken with her, but why not? She's personable, pretty, and honest." Clark's bland expression turned sly. "But I guess you've already noticed."

"Am I that transparent?"

"To another man, yes."

Matt raised a brow.

"I'm gay, not dead. I can admire a beautiful woman as much as the next guy, even if I don't plan on hooking up with her." As if putting a period on the discussion, he picked up the overladen tray. "Give Chloe a chance, is all I'm saying. You might be surprised by the woman hiding behind the bluster and beauty."

Clark slipped through the kitchen door, and Matt turned to leave. The caterer's logic was too close to comfort where he was concerned, which irked him no end. He didn't enjoy knowing that his attraction to Chloe was so obvious even a gay guy noticed. And why did the fact that he had questions about the woman make him look like the problem instead of her?

The front bell rang, and he hustled to the foyer to greet whoever was calling. It was time to put his misgivings about his assistant on the back burner and get on with his job. As he entered the lobby, the door opened and a man strolled in sporting a used-car-salesman grin. Dressed in a top-of-the-line navy suit, hundred dollar tie, and classy Italian loafers, the Colin Farrell clone stretched out his hand.

"Good morning. I'm Jeremy Jadwin. Is Isabelle Castleberry available?"

"Mrs. Castleberry is indisposed," said Matt, accepting the gesture.

"What about Ms. Degodessa? Is she free?"

"I believe she's expecting a client, but I'm Mrs. Castleberry's grandson. Maybe I can help you."

"Perhaps. I'm here about—"

Chloe strode into the foyer and clasped Mr. Jadwin's hand before he finished his sentence.

"Mr. Jadwin, how nice to finally meet you. I was afraid we'd never coordinate our schedules for an appointment."

"You were?" Jadwin's narrow-eyed gaze traveled over Chloe as fast as a hungry fox sizing up a rabbit. Clearly taken by what he saw, he showed enough teeth to rival a piano keyboard. "You're right. It's about time we got together."

She tucked her arm in his elbow and led him to the door. "Allow me to take you on a tour of the property." Then, almost as an afterthought, she turned to Matt. "Answer the phone, would you, Mr. Castleberry? And if the Kings show up for their ten-thirty appointment, please handle it."

"But—"

"They'll need a quote on a bar mitzvah. You know where the contracts and rate tables are."

Matt stifled the urge to drag Chloe to his side and give her a good shake for treating him like a hireling, though punching the movie star wannabe square in the nose for looking so smug would have been a pleasant alternative.

Instead, he said, "I'll be happy to take care of it," and watched them trot out the door.

He shook his head. Jadwin asked for Isabelle Castleberry first, yet Chloe had taken over without a care to Belle, or to him, for that matter. What the hell was she up to?

Chloe led the surprisingly handsome Jeremy Jadwin through the last of the reception halls.

Because of the businesslike tone of his letters, she thought they'd been dealing with a more mature man, instead of this thirty-something go-getter with a killer smile and an equally appealing face. As they'd taken the tour, Mr. Jadwin had made it clear that he'd arrived without an appointment on purpose. He was tired of Miss Belle's refusal to meet with him, and he'd had enough of Chloe's terse telephone rejections and negative letters to know the only way to make his point was to appear at Castleberry Hall in person.

She'd managed to rein in her temper when he'd confessed to the unprofessional action. Though relieved she could deflect his speaking with Matt or bothering Miss Belle in one swift stroke, it still rankled that he thought he could make an unannounced visit in hopes of wearing down her fragile employer.

"I've saved the kitchen area for last," said Chloe, hoping they wouldn't find Clark hard at work on food for the baby shower. "It's the heart of our operation." After striding into the empty room, she swung open a few cupboard doors, then showed him the massive stainless steel refrigerator. "As you can see, our equipment is large enough to accommodate the most lavish of affairs. There's even a walk-in freezer through the hall to the left, though our caterer uses fresh ingredients whenever possible."

Arms crossed over his broad chest, Jadwin scanned the kitchen, then hoisted himself onto one of the island stools. "It's quite an operation, but I knew it would be."

"And it still isn't for sale," said Chloe.

"I thought you might say that, so I've brought another offer." He reached into his inside suit jacket pocket and drew out a white envelope. "Don't take offense, but I have orders from the top brass to present this one to Isabelle Castleberry, and only Mrs. Castleberry, in person."

Chloe kept her smile in place. Jeremy Jadwin had been polite yet flirtatious during the entire tour. He'd asked questions, made the proper comments, and been so charming she'd actually considered, for one brief moment, that he might be a good candidate for her final fling. But his too-smooth demeanor made her wary, and she didn't think it had a thing to do with his being a Party Palaces representative.

"I'm afraid that will be impossible. Miss Belle doesn't see clients anymore."

"I'm not a client, Ms. Degodessa, I'm a buyer. And I've been authorized to make her—and only her—another very lucrative offer." He tapped the envelope on the counter. "Unless, of course, you can do something to help persuade her for me."

In lieu of snarling at him, Chloe shut the cabinet doors. Was he offering her a bribe—to sell out dear, sweet Miss Belle? Gathering her composure, she turned and rested her backside against a far counter. "Persuade her? Could you be a little more specific?"

"How about I get 'more specific' over dinner tonight? That way, we'll be guaranteed privacy." He grinned boyishly. "I'm staying at the Drake."

A Chicago landmark, the Drake was one of the swankiest establishments in the city. Since she'd taken over the day-to-day running of the Castleberry, they'd beaten the high-class venue out of several corporate meetings and wooed away more than a dozen weddings.

"The Drake is an impressive hotel."

"Our company does things first-class. That's why we've been courting the Castleberry."

"Even if it isn't for sale?"

"Everything's for sale. For the right price."

"Mr. Jadwin—"

"Jeremy, please."

"Jeremy, I'm not quite sure what you're asking, but I'm unavailable tonight. I'm scheduled to supervise an event."

"Then maybe I should speak with Matt Castleberry."

"No! I mean, I don't think so. Matt's just returned from a visit . . . to . . . to Europe. He's only helping out until he decides how to proceed with his own career." *And he'd probably encourage his grandmother to accept your offer in a nanosecond, which would, eventually, break her heart.* "Besides, he has no say in Castleberry business."

"But as a part of the family, I assume the company will one day belong to him. Surely he'd want to be involved in a decision that would mean millions to his family."

Clark took that moment to push through the kitchen doors. "I heard we had a visitor," he said, "and I was hoping I'd find the two of you here. Mr. Jadwin, have you seen the wedding chapel?" he asked, grasping both Jeremy's and Chloe's elbows.

"Clark," said Chloe, slipping from his grip. "Let me formally introduce you to Jeremy Jadwin of Party Palaces Corporation. Mr. Jadwin, this is Clark Parrott, our very talented but sometimes crazed caterer."

"Nice to meet you," said Clark. He gave the rep's hand a quick shake and again latched onto Chloe's and Jadwin's elbows. "Now about the chapel . . ."

"It's the first thing I was shown," said Jeremy.

Clark talked as he walked. "Uh . . . what about the gardens? They're particularly lovely this time of year."

"Clark, it's ten degrees outside." Chloe stopped in her tracks and focused on his pale face. The caterer's wide eyes darted to the kitchen's reception room doors.

"But—"

Jadwin grinned. "I can take a hint. It's obvious you're trying to get rid of me, so let me tell you what I'll do."

"What?" asked Clark in a clipped tone as he continued escorting them to the side door.

"If Ms. Degodessa agrees to have dinner with me tonight, I'll leave."

The trio reached the delivery entrance doors. "Of course she'll have dinner with you," said Clark. "Chloe's always up for a free meal."

Chloe gritted her teeth. "I can answer for myself, Clark, and I'm not free tonight. There's a baby shower."

"Either Leah or I will handle it. And don't forget Matt. He can get his feet wet, and we'll rescue him if there's a problem. Now, might I suggest you return to the house via the gardens." Practically shoving them out the door, he slammed it shut behind them.

Chloe shivered as the icy wind gusted. She had half a mind to march back inside and confront the contrary caterer, but she'd heard the lock click in place a second after the slam. It was too cold to do more than hurry to the house before both she and her guest froze.

Heading up the path, she spotted Matt, a man, and a woman entering the reception hall, and finally got the message. Clark had somehow guessed what was going on with Jeremy Jadwin and taken it upon himself to prevent Matt and the Party Palaces rep from meeting.

Another gale force breeze blew in, and Jeremy clasped her hand in his larger one and pulled her to his side, blocking her from the frigid wind. Trotting in double time, they raced to the porch and into the foyer, where Chloe tugged from his grip and rubbed her upper arms to ease the chill.

"So, are we on for dinner?" Jeremy asked, as if nothing unusual had occurred.

Chloe gave the invitation further consideration. An evening in the company of a handsome man might be just what she needed to erase the lingering effects of Eros's nasty arrow.

"I can take a cab to the Drake. You don't have to make the trip."

"Fine. I'll be waiting in the main dining room at seven. If that's all right with you?"

"Seven is good." Chloe opened the door.

Without warning, Jeremy grabbed her free hand and brought it to his mouth. After a quick brush with his lips, he said, "I look forward to dinner. And whatever the night will bring." Giving her a practiced smile, he sauntered out the door.

Chloe peered through the intricately etched panel of leaded glass and watched the salesman drive away in a late model Corvette. The man was smooth, a real charmer, and the only type of guy she felt safe fraternizing with in her short time left on earth.

Though she didn't warm to the idea of being wined and dined by Jeremy, it might be the only way she could find out what Party Palaces wanted and take her mind off Matt Castleberry at the same time.

Feeling justified in her plan, she went to her office to wait for her new boss's return.

Chapter 11

Only thirty more minutes and he would be free.

Matt propped himself against the entry foyer door frame and closed his eyes, but it didn't shut out the vision of a dozen children, from toddlers to kindergarteners, laughing, running, and shouting at the top of their lungs while their mothers oohed and aahed over cuddly stuffed animals, frilly dresses, and a cornucopia of baby gifts.

If he'd known the twenty scheduled guests were bringing kids, he would have complained of an old jogging injury or whatever it took to get him off the hook. Unfortunately, feigning a trick knee would have been totally impractical. First, Chloe had informed him she had a business meeting with Jeremy Jadwin—*informed* being the operative word—and gave him the responsibility of handling the event. Then Leah called in sick.

When he realized this baby shower shindig was all his, he'd actually thought about taking the coward's way out and turning it over to his grandmother.

Thank God he'd come to his senses before complaining to her. The affair had worn him out. Belle would have exhausted herself waiting on this herd of boisterous children and gushing women, and given him a huge case of the guilts in the process.

Just for spite, he decided to blame the entire evening of misery on Chloe. If she hadn't agreed to a night on the town with that pretty boy, he wouldn't be in this position. For all her claims of wanting nothing but the best for Castleberry Hall, she had some nerve taking time off to be wined and dined when she should have been here fulfilling her duties even if her absence was, according to her, for the good of the Hall.

It figured Chloe would be interested in a guy who was his exact opposite. She'd already confessed she was only attracted to men who were good looking—not physically flawed. He could tell she'd been taken with Jadwin the second she latched onto the guy's arm and led him from the house.

"Mr. Matt?"

A youngster's voice came from somewhere around his knees. Matt stared down at a dark-haired boy of five or six, balancing a plate in his chubby hands. Though the boy bore no resemblance to any of the children haunting his dreams, his expression was still painfully innocent and full of hope.

"That's me," he answered, trying his best not to scowl.

"My mom said to give you this." He raised the plate high. "It's cake to celebrate my new sister. She's gonna be here in three weeks."

"You're going to have a little sister?" Matt noted the child's eager grin, squatted to kid level and accepted the plate. "Are they sure?"

"Uh-huh. Mom said the doctor did a sun-e-gram that showed her picture." He rubbed his nose. "I saw the picture too, but it didn't look much like a sister to me."

"Have your parents picked out a name or are they still thinking about it?"

"They're naming her Jessica," the boy answered. "But they said I could call her Jesse, just like Jesse James, the outlaw." He raised a hand fixed in the shape of a gun. "That way, she'll be ready to play cowboy with me when she grows up."

Just then another kid came by and gave the boy a shove. "You're it," he shouted, and took off running.

" 'Bye," his little buddy yelled as he broke into a trot.

"Thanks for the cake," Matt shouted in return. Standing, he breathed a sigh as he cut into the snow-white layers separated by a chocolate and raspberry filling, relieved he'd been able to speak to the child without experiencing a panic attack. Then again, all these kids appeared healthy and well-adjusted. Chances were they'd grow up with every advantage and would live to a ripe old age instead of ending their life by getting raped or chopped with a machete.

The cake melted in his mouth, and he made a mental note to tell Clark he'd done a superior job. It was a comfort knowing that someone besides Miss Belle took pride in the work they did for Castleberry Hall. Maybe someday he would feel the same sense of kinship with his family's venerable institution.

He checked his watch and read the time. The bash was scheduled to end at nine, and he wasn't about to let it last a moment longer. The sooner he got rid of the crowd, the sooner he could go to bed. Though he wasn't expecting a good night's sleep, he had his hopes. He'd worked hard today, maybe hard enough to send him into a coma for at least a couple of hours before the nightmare reared its ugly head.

At exactly nine o'clock Clark walked through the kitchen door with the three waitresses who'd served at the party. The mother-to-be took the hint and said good-bye to the guests. Matt offered to help cart out presents, the leftover cake, and a box of table decorations. The caterer led the cleanup crew in the removal of silverware, plates, and the remaining food, and disappeared into the kitchen, while the guests corralled their kids, got into their coats, and headed for the door.

It took about thirty minutes to empty the hall. Since making sure everything was in its place and closing the building went with the territory of event supervisor, he said good-night to the waitresses and sat in a folding chair to wait for Clark.

"You did okay for a newbie," said the caterer when he returned a few minutes later.

"You did a great job. That cake was terrific. I only had a taste, but—"

Clark shrugged into his coat. "You couldn't finish it because there was a lot to do, right?"

"I had no idea overseeing a small event could be that much of a chore." He scooped up the dirty table linens and continued collecting napkins. "Where does this stuff go?"

"There's a pantry next to the walk-in freezer where we store canned food, clean linen, and keep the hamper. Dump everything into the basket, and the laundry service will collect it first thing in the morning." Clark glanced at his watch. "I can stay if you need help."

"I've got it. Are you sleeping here tonight or going to your place?"

"My place. But I'll be back Friday to start the wedding reception preparations. There's no need to lock up, by the way. The security team will check the building in a couple of hours and make sure things are tight."

Matt entered the kitchen with his arms full and

set the linen on the island. After checking to make sure the cabinets were shut and one of the two industrial-sized dishwashers was running, he gathered the laundry, found the room Clark had told him about, and tried to open the door. When it didn't budge, he dropped his bundle, fumbled with the knob, and pushed until the door slammed open. Just as he picked the linen off the floor, he heard footsteps.

"Clark, are you still here?"

The sound of Chloe's voice sent a chill of awareness tripping up his spine. Even though she'd assured him the date was strictly professional, she was home earlier than he'd expected. According to Chloe, Jeremy Jadwin worked for a remodeling company and they were going over a plan to renovate the reception areas. But he'd seen the once-over Jadwin had given her in the foyer, and he had no doubt the guy was on the hunt for more than a successful meeting.

"I'm in the pantry," he called, determined to remain polite yet distant. It was no skin off his nose if Chloe wanted to get up close and personal with the guy.

"Oh, I thought you were Clark."

Matt tossed the dirty linen into a large wheeled hamper, then turned to face her. "He went to his place for the night. Said he'd be back on Friday to start cooking for Saturday's wedding."

"How did the baby shower go?" she asked, tucking a curling strand of flyaway hair behind her ear.

"Fine. How about your date?"

"It was a professional meeting," she reminded him. "And we got a lot accomplished."

Matt crossed his arms and leaned against a wall of shelves, intent on presenting a casual facade. "Really?"

"Yes, really." After scanning the closet, she stepped inside and let the door close behind her. "Jeremy has some great ideas for remodeling the reception halls."

"Like what?" Matt asked, stifling the urge to voice his real question: since when did women wear figure-hugging dresses, sheer black nylons, and three-inch heels to business meetings? Not to mention a softly tousled hairdo that begged for the touch of a man's hands.

"We discussed a change of table and chair styles, for one thing. Maybe some new flooring and . . . other decorative enhancements."

"I thought he was in the remodeling business, additions and renovations, that sort of thing. Or did I misunderstand?"

"Jeremy works for a remodeling company, but he's the . . . the interior designer. He's more of an idea man than an architect."

"Maybe he and I should schedule a meeting of our own," Matt offered. Pushing from the wall, he stood behind the small table in the center of the room. "Since I'm the one who'll be picking up the tab for these *ideas* you claim he has."

Chloe set her handbag and coat on the table. "I

didn't realize you'd put any of your personal money into Castleberry Hall."

She had him there. "The Hall is a family business and I'm the only one who'll inherit. I'd say that makes it mine, so be careful how you spend it."

She jutted her chin. "Miss Belle gave me full control over the project."

"But Belle isn't in charge any longer. I am," he pointed out, his gaze drawn to her mink. It looked as expensive as his ex's, but she acted as if it were made of plastic. Still, the expensive garment was a glaring reminder of how much she valued things that were perfect. "And I don't give full control over anything I'm in charge of to just anybody."

She placed her fists on her hips. "I'm not an *anybody*."

"You are if I say so."

"And besides, I'd bet my last quarter you're going to sell this place to the first bidder when I leave."

Though annoyed that she could read him so adeptly, he found himself enjoying the sparring. Aside from his unease with the children, she'd been on his mind fifty-nine out of the sixty minutes of each preceding hour. It was about time he gave her something to gnaw on too. "Why should you care?"

Chloe gritted her teeth. "I care because I respect Miss Belle and her wishes," she countered. "I'm not happy about leaving either."

"Then you're rescinding your notice?"

"I can't. It's time to move on with my life and—"

"Castleberry Hall isn't a part of that plan? What's the matter? Aren't we upscale enough for you? Or are you taking a job with that Jadwin character?"

She'd had a feeling Matt would want a detailed report of her dinner with Jeremy, but the last thing she'd expected from Dr. Studly was a jealous attitude. Or that his jealousy would grate on her nerves and bring goose bumps to her skin.

Or make her weak in the knees.

She did another quick survey of the room. She was going to slap Eros silly if he was lying in wait behind a jumbo jar of mayonnaise, poised to hit her with another of his love arrows. "Mr. Jadwin has nothing to do with it."

Matt took a step nearer. "Can't stand working here with me as your boss?"

"Don't be ridiculous."

"You sure Mr. Tall, Dark, and Obnoxious didn't offer you a better position—something with *fringe benefits* the Castleberry can't match?"

"What in the world are you talking about?" He moved toward her, and she inched backward. "You're not making any sense."

"It makes perfect sense. Lots of people use one business as a stepping-stone to the next. Negotiation over salary requirements, a personal discussion on benefits, a little push and pull on an expense account—" He took a step forward with every sentence, until the door was at her back. "—and the next thing you know you're being offered a new job with better pay, less hours, and a lot of extras."

"You're crazy. I'm going to bed. Good night." Turning in place, she grabbed the doorknob and gave it a tug.

Matt smacked his palms on either side of her, caging her between his arms. "Take it easy. I didn't mean to insult you."

Chloe refused to face him. "Hah! That's not what it sounded like to me." She gave another jerk, but the knob wouldn't budge. Frustrated, she kicked the door for being so uncooperative. Pain radiated up her ankle and into her calf, and she knocked Matt out of the way as she hobbled into a corner.

Matt took over and used both hands, jiggling and twisting the knob until his fingers turned white. When that didn't work, he leaned sideways and dug in his feet, pulling with his entire body. The panel shuddered but held its ground.

"Great." He speared his fingers through his hair. "Leave it to Belle to turn an old bomb shelter from the fifties into a pantry. If I remember right, this thing was made of reinforced steel." He shot the door a dirty look. "How long has it been giving you trouble?"

Chloe's shoulders slumped. It was her responsibility to report this sort of problem to maintenance, and thanks to Dr. Studly's surprise arrival, she'd failed to do so.

"A while," she muttered. Limping over, she pushed him aside with a swing of her hips, grabbed the knob in both hands, and gave another jerk, but all that did was loosen the hardware from its mooring.

Matt snorted. "Nice going."

"Okay, smarty pants, do you have a better idea?"

He heaved a sigh. "Yeah. We keep trying."

Chloe decided the entire stuck-in-a-closet-with-a-grump incident was Matt's fault. If he hadn't come home a month early, she wouldn't have met him. If she hadn't met him, she wouldn't have been distracted by his bossy attitude and hunky body. If she weren't distracted, she would have paid more attention to her job. If she'd paid more attention to her job, she would have called maintenance or a locksmith when Leah first informed her of the problem with the door.

Now, at a little before midnight, they were no closer to escaping from the pantry than they'd been at ten. She'd shoved Matt aside a few times and tried her best to break the door's hold, but for the most part Matt had taken charge. Trouble was, he'd been no more successful at freeing them than she had.

She pulled her coat tighter around her and

gave him her best diva glare. "The heat shuts off automatically at twelve. We'll freeze if we spend the night here."

Matt slammed a palm against the door, something he'd done about a hundred times in the past two hours. Walking to the wall of canned goods, he rifled through the foodstuff, something else he'd done before. Then he turned in a circle, as if scoping out the room.

"Now what are you doing?"

"Searching for a hammer or screwdriver, anything to break the lock." Huffing out a breath, he headed to the wall holding the clean linen, pulled down a stack of tablecloths, and spread them on the floor.

"If you ask me, that's a strange way to look for a hammer."

"I'm done for the night," he answered, ignoring her indignant glare. "As far as I can tell, we're stuck here until morning, and I don't plan to stretch out on a hard-as-rock floor without something to cushion my ass—or give me a little warmth, for that matter."

Chloe opened her mouth, realized he was probably right, and snapped it closed. Too bad her short list of powers didn't include controlling inanimate objects, as did Kyra's and Zoë's, or she'd simply zap the door free.

Matt slipped out of his jacket, rolled it up like a pillow, and stuck it under his head. Then he lay down on the makeshift bed and attempted to cover himself. But every time he pulled the cloth to his shoulders, his feet stuck out. Hah! It was exactly what he deserved for being so big and muscular and . . . and . . .

The memory of his hard-molded chest and wiry strength warmed Chloe all over, which ratcheted up her own grumpiness quotient. If her mind continued on this perilous path, she'd need an air conditioner instead of a heater to regulate her temperature. But Matt shouldn't have to suffer because she hadn't done her job. Stomping to the wall, she snatched one of the larger and heavier brocade tablecloths from a top shelf, unfolded the fabric, and tossed it over him.

"Thanks," he muttered, scooching around on the linen. "How about turning out the light?"

"Fine." She crossed the floor, flipped the light switch, and shivered when the room was thrown into a black void as dark and as cold as the Underworld. Stumbling forward, she found a chair and sat, pulled over her handbag, and rested her cheek on the cool leather. Thirty seconds later her neck felt as if it were caught in a vise.

"You're going to regret sleeping in that position come morning," Matt said in a matter-of-fact singsong.

How does he know what position I'm in? It's so dark in here I can't even see my own hand.

Chloe moved her purse, readjusted her head, and leaned down. Then she heaved a sigh and sat up straight, ticked because her back, as well as her neck, was complaining. "How else am I supposed to sleep?" she demanded. "You've claimed all the tablecloths and most of the usable floor space."

"Don't be such a grouch," he answered, his voice tinged with amusement. "I do have an idea."

"Okay. I'm open to suggestions."

A heartbeat passed before he said, "Body heat."

"Excuse me?"

"We share body heat. If I move a few of these tablecloths and you join me, we can use the mink as a throw and snuggle up underneath. That way, we should be warm enough to get a couple of hours rest."

Chloe drummed her fingers on the table, awash in another rush of heat. As far as she knew, Eros hadn't invaded the closet, and even if he had, it was too dark for the mischievous god to hit either of them with an arrow. Which meant they'd be safe from their emotions until there was light in the room. Still, getting cozy with Dr. Studly . . .

"Chloe?"

"What?"

"Are you pouting, or are you thinking about it?"

"Thinking about it."

"We'll have to get close. Is that going to be a problem?"

"Why should it be a problem?"

"My face, remember," he said flatly.

Chloe swallowed the lump in her throat. She knew her remarks had been callous, but they were for his own good. She just didn't want to be reminded of what she'd said, especially when she hadn't meant it.

"I'm sorry if I hurt your feelings. I—It's—"

"No problem. You gave me your honest opinion. I should be grateful you told me before I made a complete fool of myself."

"It's not—you didn't—" She hissed out a breath. "Maybe we can talk about it in the morning, when things are less tense." She rubbed her nose, now the temperature of an ice cube, and gave him a chance to take back his invitation. "Are you sure you want me down there?"

"I'm sure." *But not really.* In fact, he absolutely did *not* want Chloe Degodessa in his arms, especially in a horizontal position. But what else was he supposed to do? If she slept draped over the table, she'd need traction to straighten out her back. If that happened, he'd be in charge of the Castleberry all by his lonesome, an idea he didn't want to ponder. Besides, he was an understanding guy. He knew where she was coming from with her comment on his scars. She wasn't into men with physical flaws. Why should she be? A woman as beautiful as Chloe had every right to pick and choose, and it stood to reason she'd choose a man like Jadwin over him. Still, he could hope . . .

"Okay. But I have to go slow. I can't see a thing."

"Take off your shoes and slide over. It won't do either of us any good if you stab me with one of those spikes you're wearing."

"My feet will freeze if I remove my shoes." The sound of her voice told him she was getting closer.

"I got rid of mine. You can wear my socks, if you want."

"Um . . . no, thanks. I'll manage."

He heard a clumping noise and guessed she'd toed off her heels. Then the tablecloths rustled. Chloe's summertime scent wafted gently through the air as she settled down and arranged the flowing mink coat over them. Her body skimmed his thigh, then his chest, as she stretched out at his side. When she inhaled but didn't move near, he closed the gap.

"What are you doing?" she asked in a small voice.

"I told you we'd have to get personal in order to share body heat. Let me put an arm under your shoulder . . ." She raised up, and he slid his limb under, clasping her to his chest. "Now, curl against me so I can tuck my knees behind yours."

She wiggled her behind, then let out a frustrated sigh. "I can't possibly sleep here. This floor feels like a bed of nails." Tossing and turning, she humphed, "Can't you think of something else?"

"Sorry, but no. I'm all out of ideas. If you relax, it might get a little better."

Bit by bit Chloe softened in Matt's arms. And as she softened, he edged closer, until her curvy bottom gloved his penis like a hand on a gearshift. Unfortunately, the intimate position brought his dead zone from second to full throttle in the blink of an eye.

"Comfortable?" he asked, almost choking on the word.

"Sort of." She squirmed, and his dead zone all but broke the speed barrier. "There, that's better."

When she clutched his bicep and adjusted her head, his arm turned downward, his palm grazed her breast, and he felt her budded nipple. "Sorry." He jerked away and his hand tangled in her hair. "Sorry."

"Stop apologizing," she mumbled. "I'm willing to accept part of the blame for us being stuck here. I should have taken care of the door as soon as I knew it was a problem."

Matt smiled at her semiadmission of guilt. It had probably taken a lot for her, a woman who was used to being in charge and always seemed to know what was right, to own up to her error. She'd even sounded a bit ashamed of the way she'd talked about his scars the other night.

As if they had a mind of their own, his fingers sifted through a cluster of curling tendrils. Before he could stop himself, he said, "You have hair like spun silk. I don't think I've ever felt anything so—so—"

"Thank you."

Chloe's gratitude, along with the press of her hips and improved manners, spurred him on. He continued the gentle exploration, massaging her scalp and stroking her nape, enjoying the way she warmed to his touch.

"That feels nice," she hummed in satisfaction.

"So do you," he confessed.

His other hand grasped her waist, and she rolled to face him. Nuzzling her nose in his neck, her fingers traveled down his chest to his belt, then his zipper . . .

"Are you sure you want to do that?" His breath caught as she gauged the size and shape of him. Swallowing, he said as evenly as possible, "Maybe this wasn't such a good idea. I'm only human, and you're . . . well, you're . . ."

"A woman?" she offered.

He grabbed at her wrists with his free hand. "Don't touch me like that unless you mean it."

"And if I do mean it?" She stroked him more boldly, learning the length and strength of him.

He closed his eyes as desire took over, pushing him to the edge of reason. "Then we'll probably end up doing something we'll both regret."

Her hands stilled and she drew back, but he held her tight. She moved her head and her nose brushed his chin, his lips, his cheek . . .

"It's so dark in here, I can't see a thing, can you?"

"No," she answered, her voice a mere breath of sound.

"And out of sight is out of mind, right?"

"Matt, I truly am sorry for what I said. It's just that this—this thing we have for each other—"

"You think we have a *thing* for each other?"

"What else would you call it?"

He thought a second, then came up with something light and breezy. If she turned him down, he could pretend he was joking, call himself an idiot, and move on. Since she insisted she was leaving, what could it hurt?

"Pumpkin pie."

"Pumpkin pie?"

"Like at Thanksgiving. Ruby makes a chocolate cream pie, an apple pie, and two pumpkin pies every holiday. I think about them for weeks, imagine their smooth texture, the mellow tang of the spices, the way the whipped cream topping is going to blend with the filling and taste rich and sinful in my mouth. When the big day arrives, I admire the beauties from afar and claim one entire pie for my own. I eat a double piece after the main meal, and have another slice before bed. The next day I have a piece for breakfast, then again after lunch, and another after we finish the leftovers Friday night. I eat so much pumpkin pie, I can't look at another serving . . . until the following year."

"And then what?"

"The yen starts all over again, but it's a different pie."

"So you want to sleep with me until you're sated, the way you gorge on pumpkin pie?"

"I know it sounds crazy, but you seem to be a modern woman with no ties, and I'm not ready for a committed relationship just yet. If you can overlook my scars—" Matt stopped mid-sentence. He'd never had to beg for sex before, yet that's exactly what he was doing. Talk about a blow to his ego. "Never mind. It's a dumb idea. Just close your eyes and keep your hands to yourself."

"Shh. I'm thinking."

"Thinking?"

"About pie. I really love pie."

Chapter 12

Matt's desire pulsed through his dismissal and grabbed Chloe deep in her core. Now that she'd apologized for her cutting remarks, it was obvious he still wanted her, just as she wanted him. She'd complained to her sisters about not having a man to dally with during her final weeks on earth, and here was Dr. Studly, offering himself for the task a second time, with no strings attached.

Could anything be easier?

As far as she could tell, Eros's shenanigans had nothing to do with Matt's longing. He was a man, and all males, be they mortal or not, were drawn to her. Now that she was forewarned where Hera and the pesky love god were concerned, it seemed logical the two of them could share a night of passion freely, without any of the silly sentiment usually associated with intimacy.

Because with or without Eros's influence, she was attracted to Matt in the most basic of ways. If he could keep his emotions in check and think of her as pumpkin pie, it stood to reason she could imagine him as baklava. The sticky sweet, honey and phyllo concoction was her favorite, and she feasted on it with relish, but after eating an entire box, she didn't want to see another slice for at least a month.

Engaging in a single night of impersonal sex with Matthew Castleberry was sure to satisfy them both and allow them to move on. And if the worst happened, and she craved more of him before she returned home, she would control her libido and wait until her arrival on Olympus, where she could have any of the hundreds of men living there who were willing and able to take his place.

"Are you sure you can treat our interaction as nothing more than a fling?" she asked, just to be doubly sure. "Because I wouldn't want any emotional interference or sappy sentiment gumming up the works."

His hand tightened around her waist and his thumb traced delicate circles on her rib cage. "I'm willing to give it a shot if you are," he said in a rasp.

"Well, then—"

Matt wasted no time. Brushing his lips against her temple and down her cheek, he searched for her mouth. When he found it, he groaned, and Chloe's stomach clenched. He deepened the kiss, and she let her body lead her into new yet familiar territory. She'd always believed men were the same the world over, though some had more clever mouths, and hands that knew better where to touch and tease and stroke.

And if they didn't, she was an expert at guiding them until they did exactly what she wanted.

He plied her lips with his tongue, and she opened to the erotic invasion. The kiss permeated her senses and sent a cluster of shock waves from her head to her toes. He threaded his fingers through her hair, sifted the curling tendrils, and spread them over her shoulders. Then his palms cupped her chin, grazed her neck, and caressed her back, where he found the zipper of her dress and inched it down.

Chloe unbuttoned his shirt and inhaled his spicy scent, lingered over the rough texture of his chest hair, his pebbled nipples, his ripped abs. He pulled at the top of her dress, and she shrugged it from her arms. She tugged at his shirt, and he drew it from his pants. Moving quickly, they undressed each other under the cover of her coat, tossing aside the cumbersome clothing until they were skin-to-skin.

Entombed in a black hole, her hands became her eyes. She smoothed the raised line left by his stitches, slid her palms over his firm cheeks, squeezed his slim hips, grasped his engorged shaft and gauged its steely length. After weighing the heavy sack at the underside of his member, she ran a thumb to the tip where a bead of moisture had formed, and his penis grew larger in her hands.

At her touch, he hissed out a breath. "Jeez, Chloe, you're killing me."

A smile curved her lips as power engulfed her. When he captured her breast and plucked at a hardened peak, electricity sizzled through her veins. She moaned her pleasure, and he drew the nipple into his mouth and suckled, flicking with his tongue. The sensory torture seemed to go on forever, until she arched into him, demanding to be taken to the next level.

As if reading her mind, Matt delved into her navel, smoothed his fingers over her belly, and feathered her feminine curls. He lifted her knee, anchored her leg over his hip, and returned to her swollen core, where he explored her intimately. Inserting one, then two fingers, he found the bundle of nerve endings that longed for his caress and plied them with an age old rhythm, circling, stroking, then circling again.

For a single fleeting moment Chloe was impressed by his expertise, the thrill of his lips, the certainty of his touch. Then her heart stuttered. She'd done all of this and more with other men, so where did these tingles of first-time infatuation come from, why did his tender fondling make her feel as if she'd flown to the top of Mount Olympus and jumped off without a bungee cord?

Taking a deep breath, she reminded herself to live for the moment. No entanglements, no distractions.

No falling in love.

Then he raised her hips and shifted to kneel between her thighs. With his mouth still at her breast, he teased her with his penis, entering and withdrawing at will. He traced her collarbone with his tongue, moved to her ear and whispered, "I was wrong. You're so much better than pumpkin pie, I don't know if I'll ever get enough."

Matt's heart rate increased, his breath came fast, and his stomach clenched the way it had when he'd run his first five minute mile. From the second he realized he would be alone with Chloe, his primary focus had been self-gratification. Now that he'd feasted on her, laved her satiny skin, explored her intimately, he felt compelled to drive her to a frenzy so tumultuous she'd scream when she came apart in his hands.

Entering her inch by inch, he prolonged the moment, guiding himself as he stroked slowly, then thrust forward to the hilt. Increasing the tempo, he pumped onward as he bent low to again pull a turgid nipple deep into his mouth and taste the swollen bud. Chloe twined her fingers in his hair and held him close, but he sensed something was wrong.

"Am I hurting you?"

"No. But this floor is a pain in the—"

"I'll fix it," he promised. Still locked inside of her, he rolled to his back so she could straddle him. Determined to heighten her enjoyment, he raised his hips and surged upward, taking them both on an erotic ride of sensual completion.

Chloe groaned encouragement as she rose and fell against his pelvis. Her mewls of passion became crazed moans of pleasure as she tightened around him, spurring him on until he thought he wouldn't last another second. She called out his name in time with her thrusts, and the friction they created blazed in his core, burned in his brain, and exploded in a flash of heat and sensation.

Moments passed as his body floated back to earth. Chloe melted across his chest, her pliable body molding to his every muscle. She quivered in his arms, and he crushed her to his torso. When she continued to breathe in short little gasps, he used his fingers to take her on a second—or was it a third?—trip to completion. She arched up and whimpered, then slowly returned to spread herself over him like a blanket.

Unable to say a word, Matt turned on his side, pulled her close and pillowed her head on his shoulder. Positive he would sleep free from his haunting nightmare, calm washed over him, and he tugged the mink coat around them, cocooning them in a nest of safety and peace.

Chloe woke with her entire body shivering. She wasn't under familiar covers; the fabric draping her was too slippery, the surface she laid upon too hard and cold to be a bed. Raising a corner of the throw, her fingers touched something soft and thick, and she recognized the luxurious texture of her mink coat.

Peering out from the fur-covered shroud, she jerked when bright light stabbed her eyes. After blinking at the overhead fixture, she saw a man's stockinged feet slide into worn yet well-cared-for shoes. Then a hand reached down and pulled a jacket from under her coat.

"Chloe, are you awake?"

Matt Castleberry's voice, soft and thoughtful with just a hint of amusement, cleared the fog from her brain . . . and reminded her of exactly where she was. And what she'd done.

"What time is it?" she muttered, running her tongue across her teeth.

"Close to six. I heard a truck a minute ago, probably the linen service. Unless you want to hide under there, I think you'd better get dressed and put on your coat."

Chloe rose to her hands and knees, moaning when pain wracked her aching muscles. Glancing down, she realized she was naked and scrambled to her feet. After shrugging into the mink and drawing it tight around her, she sorted through the tablecloths, found her clothing, and stood. Matt grinned, and she turned her back, wriggling to get into her dress as quickly as she could. His knowing gaze had already sent a quiver down her spine;

the last thing she needed was more temptation.

The knob rattled, and she jumped. Then the door shook.

"Hey," Matt shouted. "We're locked in here."

"It's McGuffy's Linen Service, come to pick up your hamper," announced a muffled voice. The knob rattled again. "You say you're stuck?"

Well, *duh*, thought Chloe. We spent the night in a cold, dark pantry because we didn't have anything better to do.

"Yeah," replied Matt. "And we'd appreciate it if you could find a screwdriver and take off the knob. If not, search the grounds for one of the maintenance men and see if they can help."

"Will do," their rescuer said. "Hang tight."

Tugging the mink to her chest, Chloe spun around and sized up Matt, who was fully dressed and none the worse for their forced togetherness. Darn men, anyway. Why was it they always seemed to look presentable, even after spending half the night rolling around on a cement floor the temperature of a funeral slab? With some attractive chin stubble and an unruly curl gracing his forehead, Dr. Studly appeared as appealing as ever.

Determined to salvage a bit of her pride, Chloe raised her hands to smooth her hair, but pain locked her arms in place. Wincing, she lowered them slowly, biting her lip against the nagging ache.

"Stiff?" asked Matt, sounding more than a little cheerful. "Me too." He rotated a shoulder in commiseration. "As soon as we get to the house, I'll find us a couple of pain relievers. If we're lucky, Gram might even have a muscle relaxant in the medicine box, or maybe Ruby will have something."

Chloe stuffed her bra, panties, and stockings into her coat pocket, and dropped into a chair. She'd never had the need for any type of medication and wondered if whatever he dug up would work on a demigoddess. Then the rest of the sentence hit her, and she frowned. "I forgot about Belle and Ruby. What are we going to tell them?"

"Nothing, if we don't want to." Matt sat in the opposite chair, still sporting a goofy grin. "In fact, if we make it to our rooms before they go to breakfast, they'll never know we spent the night here."

"Hah!" Ruby and Belle might be old, but they were still sharp as needles and shrewd as Zeus. No way would the fact that Belle's assistant and her grandson shared the pantry for a night escape either one's notice. And she didn't even want to think about Clark. "Nothing slips past those two. If they were younger, they could work as interrogators for the FBI."

"Trust me, it's not a big deal. If we act like nothing happened, they won't catch on."

"That's what you think." She spied her shoes and stood to retrieve them. Back in her chair, she slipped on the pumps as she said, "What's taking that guy so long?"

"It's only been a couple of minutes. I imagine

he didn't find a screwdriver so he's on the hunt for a maintenance man."

Now that she'd worked out a few of the kinks, Chloe was able to raise her arms and finger-comb her hair. Then, so she didn't have to meet Matt's gaze, she began gathering the linen, folding it, and stacking it back on the shelves.

"Uh, just an idea, but you might want to toss those in the hamper," he suggested. "If anyone found out what we—ah—used the tablecloths for, I doubt they'd be happy to see them on their dinner table."

She stopped fussing and sighed. He was correct, of course. And since the linens for all their upcoming events were probably on the service truck, none of this would be needed for a few days. Removing the tablecloths from the shelf, she dumped them into the hamper and wheeled it to the door, shoving the cart into the back of Matt's knees in the process.

"Excuse me."

"Not a problem," he said, moving out of the way.

Hands on her hips, she glared at their exit. "This is taking way too long."

"What's the matter?" His breath tickled her ear, telling her he'd somehow inched behind her for a sneak attack. "Ashamed to be seen with me?"

"I already told you I didn't mean those things I said," she answered, refusing to face him.

His arms encircled her waist and pulled her

back to his front, enveloping her in his firm and somewhat possessive grip. "Then who cares what the McGuffy man thinks if he sees us together, or anyone else for that matter?"

"It's not—I don't—"

His lips brushed her nape, then her ear, and she sagged against him, determined not to turn and melt into his arms.

"Last night was more than I expected, Chloe. A lot more."

His words, so soft and sweet, called to mind all they'd done to each other in the dark and what she'd like to do with him in the light of day. She longed to see the nicely muscled body parts she'd touched and tasted, just as she wished he could see her. There'd been something naughty about having sex in a black hole, but watching his reaction to her caresses would have increased her pleasure ten times over.

Not that she was complaining. Matt had been intense but, unlike the lovers she'd had the past year, was still considerate enough to meet her every demand. His seeking fingers, clever hands, and tender lips had driven her wild with passion and satisfied her completely, yet left her longing for more.

The erotic thoughts caused her to firm her resolve. She hadn't spotted Eros lurking about, but she wouldn't put it past the troublesome god to slip in and do his dirty work the moment the door opened.

Matt continued to ply her neck with butterfly kisses, forcing her to muster every ounce of willpower to stay focused and uninvolved. She didn't want to admit that her night of baklava overload had exceeded every other sexual experience she'd had with a mortal—and all the gods, if she was honest—and then some.

"You promised you wouldn't get sappy on me, and I'm holding you to your word," she huffed out.

"I intend to stay unsappy." He bit gently on her earlobe. "But it's also important you know the truth."

"No. It isn't." She struggled from his grasp. "What's important is we act as if last night never happened."

"Chloe—"

There was a knock on the door. "Who's in there?"

"It's me, Stan," Chloe replied, grateful to hear the familiar voice of their senior maintenance engineer. "Dr. Castleberry and I spent the last six hours locked inside. Do whatever it takes to get us out."

"Yes, ma'am. Just give me a minute."

Matt folded his arms, propped himself against a wall and narrowed his eyes. "You're acting totally immature about this. It's not as if you were taken prisoner by Jack the Ripper."

"In case you've forgotten, we have a business to run. I won't get a shred of work done in here, and neither will you. And we have to make it to the house before Belle and Ruby find out where we spent the night."

"I still say they won't give it a second thought," he insisted. "If we feign innocence, they won't have a reason to believe otherwise."

"Then stop looking at me like that," Chloe snapped out.

"Like what?"

"As if I were a—a—piece of pumpkin pie."

"Now you're being ridiculous." He jammed his hands into his jacket pockets. "And a tad too stuck on yourself."

"Stuck on myself!" She rolled her eyes. "Puhleeze. Sleeping together was your idea, not mine. I have dozens of men falling at my feet every day of the week. I should have known better than to think you were baklava."

He blinked, then smiled the same goofy grin. "Bak-la-what?"

Heat inched up from Chloe's chest, scalding her cheeks. "Never mind. Just keep your pants zipped and forget last night ever happened, and we'll be fine."

"Now wait just a darned—"

Voices echoed from the hallway. The doorknob rattled again, then came the sound of metal on metal and the squeak of screws. Chloe held her breath. The knob sagged at a drunken angle, then dropped to the floor with a clatter.

The door swung open, and she fell into Stan's arms. "Oh, thank goodness."

"There, there, Ms. Degodessa." His smile large, the elderly gentleman wrapped Chloe in a fatherly embrace and scowled at Matt. "It's okay now. You're safe."

Chloe drew back and threw Matt a look that confirmed he was Jack the Ripper reincarnated. "It's been *such* an ordeal."

Stan took her by the arm and led her from the pantry, clucking like a mother hen on steroids. "It's all right. Let me walk you to the house, where you can get warm. Then I'll come back here and start working on that doorknob so you won't get caught again."

Matt shook his head. Chloe Degodessa was something else. The word diva fit, though he had a suspicion it was a bit too harsh. He didn't buy her story of relegating last night to the history books for a single minute. Not when she'd screamed in ecstasy, milked him for more than one orgasm, and slept like a baby in his arms. No way were they finished with each other.

Not by a long shot.

By the time he'd taken care of the linen guy and spoken with Stan, Matt was running about thirty minutes behind Chloe. When he arrived at his room and heard the shower, he'd let her have some privacy, though he didn't doubt she'd remembered to lock the door.

Intent on heading off any speculation his grandmother or Ruby might have about his and Chloe's whereabouts last night, he figured he could clean up later. Now, he sat at the table buttering a large slice of one of his grandmother's famous breakfast specials, cinnamon crumb coffee cake. Belle and Ruby had made the treat together, stating that ever since Clark had commandeered the kitchen, they enjoyed taking advantage of the room whenever they could. Fixing the culinary delight had them both so proud of their handiwork, they didn't even notice his bleary eyes and stiff-legged walk.

"It's clear you have yet to shower or shave this morning," said Belle. Her eyebrows arched gracefully over the top of her glasses, as if she'd just seen his day old beard. "Did you have a problem sleeping?"

"Not at all," said Matt. "But Chloe was in the bathroom when I got up, so I thought I'd take care of things after I ate breakfast. How was your night?"

"Miserable," she answered with a *humph*. "Ruby and I met in the kitchen at two A.M. There was some kind of celebration going on at the lakefront, fireworks, music, and enough noise to wake the dead. Kept us up half the night." She sniffed her displeasure. "I can't believe you slept through all the racket."

Chloe walked in from the foyer at the same moment Ruby entered from the kitchen carrying a coffee refill. Wearing a pair of dark green wool slacks and a buttery yellow sweater set, her upswept golden curls made her look fresh as a daisy.

"Noise is right," the housekeeper snapped, setting the carafe on the warmer. "We should have called the police."

"Noise?" Chloe ignored him, brought a cup of coffee from the sideboard to the table and sat down. "What are you talking about?"

"A big shindig at the lake. The racket about shook the house," said Ruby. "Isn't that right, Belle?"

"Quite. Didn't you hear it either?" Belle asked Chloe.

"I was out with Mr. Jadwin until midnight. I came home exhausted by all his remodeling ideas and went straight to bed. He has some very interesting things we need to discuss . . . when you have the time, of course."

"Did he take you dancing?" Ruby laid a hand on her heart and did a little shuffle. "The mister and I used to go regular like, every month, until they closed down the dance hall. Then Wendall died, and my arthritis set in. But I still love to watch, especially those not-so-famous folks who star on that television show every week. They set my feet to tappin' like nothing has since the mister."

"Um . . . no, no dancing. We talked business."

"For five hours?" Ruby set her hands on her hips. "How much remodeling is the man planning to do?"

"Speaking of renovations," Matt said to Belle, "I've been meaning to talk to you about the plans."

Belle kept her gaze on Ruby. "Didn't I tell you? I'm considering a total overhaul of the dining rooms. I want bright and cheery with a modern twist—new window treatments, new flooring, the works. And it has to translate well to the brochure Chloe designed. That's why I'm letting her handle it."

Matt frowned. "I'd like to talk with this Mr. Jadwin, maybe offer some input in the designs." *And stake my claim in case he gets any ideas about Chloe.*

"No!" Belle half rose from her chair, then sat and adjusted her glasses. "I mean, why should you when I've already left it all in Chloe's capable hands? Besides, you need to learn about the business, host a few more events, negotiate a contract or two, and all that. Don't you think so, Chloe dear?"

"I certainly do," Chloe said emphatically. "He needs to work on the basics."

"In that case, I guess I should stay beside you in the office today. All day," said Matt, tossing out the dare. "I can stick like a shadow, so I won't miss any of your . . . expert technique."

"Come to think of it, your *technique* could use a bit of work," Chloe rebutted, her smile so sweet Matt couldn't miss her sly innuendo.

"I believe the best way to improve technique is

with practice . . . hours and hours of it," he said with a smile.

Chloe sipped her coffee, then wrinkled her nose as she said, "Far be it from me to keep you from practicing. But you can always work on your technique alone and get the same result, you know. I hear men do it all the time."

She was such a kidder. And she didn't fool him with that high and mighty attitude about his lack of technique. If his moves had been any better, both of them would be in bed right now, too tired to face the day. He sent her a cocky smile, planning to make her sorry for every jibe. So sorry she'd beg him to ply her with his inadequate *technique* morning, noon, and—

"Whatever you two are jabbering about, it's over my head," Belle interjected. "Chloe, you look a little . . . disturbed. Are you feeling all right?"

"I'm fine," she said, sending Matt a glare. "But I have another date with Jeremy tonight, and there are some things you and I need to talk over before I meet with him."

"I'll be happy to take Belle's place—"

"No, no, Matt, it's fine. I'll speak with Chloe while you, um . . . do something . . ."

"You can keep my ten o'clock appointment with the Hadleys," said Chloe. "They want to hold a christening party for their new baby, and they want a weekend date. You'll have to get their requirements, go over the calendar, and see if we can work them in. If they're planning for less than fifty guests, they can use the smallest dining room, but that's the maximum for a sit-down affair."

"Ten o'clock?" Matt glanced at his watch. "That's less than an hour away."

"More than enough time for you to take that shower and refresh yourself after your sleepless night," said Belle. "Go on now, while Chloe and I have our chat."

Chapter 13

"So, tell me about the meeting you had with that Jadwin person, and don't leave out a thing," Miss Belle said the moment they reached her suite and Chloe shut the door. "I hope you kicked his butt."

Chloe helped the older woman settle into a chaise in a corner of the sitting room before she replied. Though last night's interaction with Dr. Studly continued to take center stage in her thoughts, that problem could be handled by giving Eros a piece of her mind. Getting Isabelle Castleberry to accept reality was a totally different dilemma.

Now, as she faced her employer in a slipper chair upholstered in a rose-and-peony-covered fabric identical to that of the chaise, her stomach lurched. There was no way she could talk about her meeting with Jeremy without confessing her plans to leave. After straightening her shoulders, she crossed her legs, assumed a businesslike pose, and gave Miss Belle a smile of encouragement.

"Mr. Jadwin came here with another offer for Castleberry Hall, and he's been instructed to deliver it to you in person. I did my best to pry the information out of him, but he refused to say another word."

Belle frowned. "I assume you told him I wasn't interested, and advised him to go away."

"I did, but he isn't about to go home," Chloe admitted. "He's planning to remain in town for however long it takes to get you to speak with him. Unfortunately, I don't think he was joking."

"That's ridiculous," the older woman muttered. "Why won't Party Palaces accept my decision?"

"I imagine they see Castleberry Hall as the easiest way to break into the Chicago market, for a number of reasons. We're an established institution, they know we've improved our bottom line, and it's common knowledge you've been running the business without a successor. Whatever their logic, Mr. Jadwin claims his superiors want to make their final best offer and hear the refusal from your lips alone. No more stalling from me or anyone else." She recalled the man's veiled attempt of a bribe. "He's very persuasive."

Belle's brow rose with interest. "Is he good-looking?"

"Movie star quality, not that it matters." *With a smooth delivery, a killer smile, and an oily air of presumption I abhor.*

"Then he's your usual kind of man."

She knew Miss Belle was correct, but that only made her feel worse. "Not really. Lately, I seem to be more interested in—" *Your grandson.* "Never mind. This isn't about the type of mort—ah—guy I date. This is about your future."

"I'm sure you can sway him into disappearing."

"I doubt it."

"Oh, come now. You and I both know that if men were thousand dollar bills, you'd be a millionaire. I've yet to meet one who can resist you, when you set your mind to it." Miss Belle grinned. "Don't tell me he isn't attracted to you."

"Whether or not Mr. Jadwin is attracted to me is irrelevant." She heaved a sigh. "I think you should hear what he has to say."

Placing a hand on her heart, Belle gave a wounded sniff. "You too? Chloe, how could you?"

"How could I what? Care about you and Ruby so much that I want both of you to be comfortable in your final years? Or that I'd like to see Castleberry Hall continue the twenty-first century as one of the city's premier event houses?" She sat back in the chair. "I don't want to sound cruel, but it's time you retired, Miss Belle, and sold the business to someone who can keep it going."

"Nonsense. Matthew is proving he can fill my shoes—"

She leaned forward and took her employer's hand. "I don't enjoy giving you the news, but I'm fairly certain Matt is not planning to take over the company."

"But he knows how much it means to me—"

"Your grandson is a doctor. He has a career, a very important career, that he should be allowed to pursue. I hate to say it, but it's selfish of you to expect him to devote his life to something in which he has no real interest, especially when he could be saving lives."

Belle opened and closed her mouth, as if searching for the words. Then she pulled her hand from Chloe's grip and folded her arms. "The boy is interested." Tears filled her eyes. "And he's doing a fine job—"

"He's been making an effort, for your sake, but his heart isn't in the work. Surely, you can see that. If you love him, you'll encourage him to return to medicine, where he belongs."

Wiping the drops that trickled down her papery cheeks, Belle gave a sad sounding chuckle. "You're right. And I'm nothing but a foolish old woman for not seeing it before this. I just kept hoping he'd grow to love Castleberry Hall and what it stood for, the way his grandfather and parents did. But it's true. He's too fine a doctor to be involved in something as mundane as a catering service."

"There's nothing ordinary about the service you provide. People have come to Castleberry

Hall for generations to celebrate weddings, births, religious events . . . even funerals. It gives them a sense of unity, of hope . . . of love."

"I'm so happy to hear that you say so, dear, because, well, I've been thinking—"

"I'm almost afraid to ask," Chloe interrupted, "but what have you been thinking about?"

"Why you, of course."

"Me?"

"Yes, you. What if I sold you the business, with the contingency that Ruby and I remain here as advisors of sorts? That way, nothing would change. Matt could practice medicine, but he couldn't fuss about my continued involvement or harass me about retiring . . ."

Chloe's heart ached for Belle. Thanks to Hera, she and the other muses had never known their own mother, but if she had been able to choose, Isabelle Castleberry would have been at the top of her list for a mother and a mentor.

Now that she'd heard Belle's impossible idea, she had no choice but to confess that she was leaving. It wasn't fair to let her friend hold onto a dream, when it could never become a reality.

"I'm honored that you would trust me to protect and guide your life's work." She swallowed and forged ahead. "But there's something I should have told you a few weeks ago. First, Matt threw me a curve by coming home early. Then, I thought he might be able to convince you to sell to Party Palaces. When you asked me to keep quiet about the offers, I respected your decision and gave him a chance to take over, but I just don't see that happening now, so I have to be truthful." She took a deep breath. "I'll be gone from Castleberry Hall by the end of the month."

"Wh-What are you saying?"

"I tried to tell you once or twice, but something always seemed to get me off track. I'm so sorry."

Belle placed a hand over her heart. "You're leaving me?"

"Not you—never you, Miss Belle. I'll write, and we can talk by e-mail or on the phone." *If Zeus lets me. And if he doesn't, I'll find a way to stay in touch, even if I'm tending the chicken coops.* "But it's time I went home."

"Home? I got the impression you had no home. Just your sisters, who are spread throughout the states. Are you going to live with one of them?"

"Not exactly. I have a father . . . in Greece . . . in the mountains. And he's expecting me soon."

"How soon?"

"In a matter of days. I know it's sudden, and I didn't mean to spring it on you like this, but there isn't anything else I can do."

"Does Matthew know?" Her expression stern, color flushed Belle's cheeks. "Clark? Ruby?"

"Please don't get upset," Chloe said. "I told Matt, but no one else. And I wouldn't have confided in him if he hadn't been hinting that he wanted me gone."

"I'm going to take that boy over my knee and—"

"No, you're not. I think he's finally seen the light where I'm concerned, and he won't actively push me out of the Hall. But he cares about you and wants to see you comfortably settled before— in your final—in your retirement."

"I'm not planning on dying just yet, so both of you can stop your worrying. I'm aware he cares; I thought you did too, but it's obvious I was in error."

Chloe let the insensitive comment, spoken in sorrow, not anger, pass. "I've given it a lot of thought. It's time you sold to Party Palaces. Accept their money and take yourself and Ruby to one of those swanky assisted living communities where you can share an apartment and spend your days playing canasta or reading, or simply relaxing. Do all the things you never could when caring for this place."

A childish pout graced Belle's lips, as if she were about to have a tantrum. "Don't want to."

Chloe suppressed a smile. "I know you don't, but think about it. No more going to bed late and rising with the sun. No more fussing over menus or contracts. And no more listening to complaints from the staff or whining customers."

"That's what I hired you for," Belle muttered.

"And since I won't be here to do it, it makes sense for you to give it up. I'm sure Party Palaces will agree to keep the name, so Castleberry Hall will live on."

Belle gazed about the room, her eyes still bright with tears. "Do you think they'd let me live here for a while, until Ruby and I found the perfect place for us?"

"I'm sure they would, and if they won't, then you can explore other options." Again she took Belle's hand and squeezed her frail fingers. "Just think about it."

"And you won't tell Matthew about them until I say so?"

"I'll try. But Mr. Jadwin could be a problem, unless we can keep him on hold. How about if I set up a lunch date for the two of you? Then you can ask questions, hear what he has to say, and tell him you need some time."

"Only if you promise to be there."

"I promise. Now, I'm going to get some work done and check on Matt." Chloe stood and headed for the door, then turned. "Why don't you read a book or take a nap? I'll bring up a tray for lunch."

Matt heaved a sigh as he slid the fully executed contract for the Hadley christening into a folder and wrote their name on the tab in bold black letters. The family had attended several functions at Castleberry Hall, so the negotiations had been a snap. He was fairly certain he'd done everything right, but he still wanted Chloe to check the paperwork, just to be certain.

He glanced around the office and was overwhelmed with a feeling of loss. He didn't belong here; he belonged in an operating room or a clinic where he could help children. Too bad he wasn't sure how to accomplish that, satisfy his grandmother, and still keep his sanity.

On the plus side, he could stick like glue to the delectable Ms. Degodessa and let her teach him all she knew, both professionally and personally, while he weighed his options. Together, they could go over his "technique," and maybe discuss a few improvements. If nothing else, his presence would remind her of everything they'd shared last night and, if he was lucky, make her long for more.

Though their evening had been stellar, and he'd touched, teased, and tasted just about every inch of Chloe's incredible body, two things nagged at him. He hadn't been able to lay eyes on the voluptuous territory he'd been exploring, and he hadn't used protection.

Not that he thought his bed partner was foolish enough to have contracted an STD or risk a pregnancy, but these days it was better to be safe than sorry. As to seeing her up close and personal, well, he intended to right that error tonight. Which meant he had to borrow the Mercedes after lunch and make a trip to the nearest drugstore for a jumbo-sized box of condoms.

The ringing telephone brought him back to business, and he lifted the receiver. "Castleberry Hall."

"This is Jeremy Jadwin. Is Chloe Degodessa available?"

Not for you, hotshot, he almost said. "She's out of the office at the moment. Can I help you?"

"I'd rather speak to Ms. Degodessa . . . unless Isabelle Castleberry is free?"

"Sorry, she's not available either. Can I"—*toss you a live hand grenade, throw you into Lake Michigan?*—"take a message?"

Jadwin rattled off a number and said a polite good-bye.

"Who was that?" asked Chloe, stepping into the office as he disconnected.

"Your remodeling buddy. He left his cell number." He pushed the small square of paper across the desk with one finger. "He's waiting for your call."

She picked up the paper, glanced at it and frowned. "You really did choose the correct profession. Are those threes or eights, and is that a one or a seven?"

"All threes and a one," he answered, recalling the number. "And I didn't choose this profession—"

"Not the event-hosting profession—the doctor profession. Aren't physicians noted for their bad handwriting?"

"Ha-ha," he replied, relieved to see her lips turn up in a half smile. "You going to get back to him?"

"Of course. He's a business connection." She took a seat on the opposite side of the desk. "When are you returning to medicine?"

"I'm still not sure, and why is that topic so important when we have other things to discuss?"

"If you're talking about what happened in the pantry—"

"Is there something else you and I have to go over? Like what this Jadwin guy really wants?"

Her blue eyes narrowed. "Never mind Jeremy. And forget about last night too. I already have."

"You are such a terrible liar." He grinned, then stood and circled the desk. When Chloe reached for the Hadley file and flipped it open with a slight tremor of her hands, his grin grew to a full-blown smile. Sidling behind her, he set his palms on her shoulders, and was immediately surrounded in her intoxicating scent.

"You smell like honey and flowers," he whispered.

Chloe straightened in the chair. "Tell it to my shampoo."

His fingers itched to remove the pins holding her hair in a tousled upsweep of curls. Instead, he breathed on the tiny blond hairs trailing down her nape. "Have lunch with me in the kitchen?" She couldn't deny she had to eat. "I'll even put it together."

She gave an annoyed sounding *hmmph* and rose from the chair, as if breathing his air was enough to raise her body temperature. His courage bolstered, Matt let her pass and followed her through the foyer and dining room. On the way, he admired the sway of her hips and the curve of her shapely legs. Legs that ended in a pair of sling-back pumps the exact color of her hot pink skirt.

In the kitchen, she placed the folder on the table, walked to the refrigerator and perused the contents, then took out a container. "I think there's still some of each sandwich filling on the second shelf. Why don't you make sandwiches while I heat the soup? And don't forget to include Belle."

"What about Ruby?"

"It's her day to attend a monthly garden club luncheon. She won't be back until three."

"Ruby gardens?" he asked, pulling out the fixings and carrying them to the island.

"She dabbles. Putters in the roses, trims some of the bushes, directs the landscapers like a battalion sergeant when they're here. It's hard to do more with her arthritis, but she refuses to let it hold her back. Says it keeps her nimble."

"That makes sense."

They worked in silence until they sat across the table from each other. "So," Matt began, "what do you suppose Jadwin really wants?"

Chloe studied the Hadley paperwork while she spoke. "Input on the ideas he has for the renovation, of course."

"And you're going to get the contract for the job signed before you go home?"

"Yes. I also plan to arrange a lunch date, so Belle can meet him." Her expression turned dour as she heaved a sigh. "I told her I was leaving, by the way."

Matt had been on the receiving end of his grand-mother's disapproval plenty of times and knew she was a master at heaping on the guilt. "How bad was it?"

"I ended up feeling like a traitor." Raising her head, she met his gaze. "She cried, and it was all I could do not to join her."

"It doesn't surprise me. She thinks very highly of you." He shrugged, wishing for a moment that he and Chloe could start over, man to woman, without the underlying mistrust that had tainted their initial meeting. Now that sex had entered the mix, he wasn't sure they'd ever get on track. Maybe it was best she leave, before things got complicated and he did something stupid . . . like fall in love with her.

"Guess I'd better put an ad in the newspaper for someone with experience to help me hold down the fort. I don't know how much longer I'll be able to do this on my own." *Or how long I want to.* "Can you hang around until I find someone?"

"Leah's been trained to take care of the day-to-day tasks. As long as she can fit them into her college schedule, she'd probably be glad for the extra hours."

"Are you certain you have to quit? Because I've decided to take back all the negative things I said about you." He made the apology in hopes of a smile; instead he received a hesitant grin. "If I went back to medicine, I'd get my own place. You could work and live here without interference from me."

She scanned the kitchen before answering. "Why?"

"*Why do I want you to stay?*" *And why do you always check out the territory whenever we're alone, as if looking for a spy?*

"Yes, why?"

"Because my grandmother's come to depend on you, and now that I've given it a try, I don't think I'm the right person to run Castleberry Hall . . . and you are."

Her expression unreadable, Chloe raised a finely arched eyebrow. "You're not just saying that because we hit it off in bed, are you?"

"We weren't in a bed, if you'll recall, though I was hoping we could rectify that situation tonight." Then he realized what she'd just said. "So you thought we hit it off? Despite my poor 'technique'?"

Her cheeks flushed pink. "I didn't say it was poor, just that it needed work."

His smile grew. "But you did enjoy the night?"

"I'll bring a tray to Belle as soon as I finish taking a look at this contract," she said, ignoring the question. A second later her eyes opened wide. "You scheduled the christening for the last Sunday of May?"

"I guess so. It's far enough away I didn't think there'd be a problem. There wasn't anything else on the calendar but a birthday party."

"I believe it said 'The Birthday Party,' in caps."

"Yeah, so?"

"Don't you remember my telling you about 'The Birthday Party'?"

"Vaguely. Something about kids from the hospital—"

"Not *from* the hospital, *at* the hospital. It's the one day we set aside each month to hold a party for all the children being treated there who celebrate a birthday in that month. Their parents and the other kids attend as guests, share in the gifts, and in general have a great time."

"Whose idea was that?" he asked, working to keep his voice even. He still loved kids, just couldn't stand to see them so joyous, so trusting, when the world seemed to have it in for them six ways to Sunday.

"Belle and Ruby. They were at loose ends once I arrived and started to handle things, so they talked with Maurice Plummer and a few people on the Optimist board, and came up with the idea. Clark donates a cake, and the people who hold receptions here usually let us keep the leftover party favors. We've only done it for the past five or six months, but it will continue until the hospital says we can't do it any longer, or no one wants to assume the responsibility."

"That means the next one is—"

"A week from Sunday, so clear your schedule."

His stomach clenched in concern. "Me? Why me?"

"Because Belle and Ruby can't do it alone, and we don't think it's right to force Clark to come along, especially if he can make money catering a private affair. I'll be there, but I'm not sure for how long, so you should probably take charge."

"So you'll stay through the weekend, at least until your plans are firm?"

She frowned. "It doesn't matter. You'll have to call the Hadleys and ask them to change the date of their event. And you'll need to be at the next Birthday Party to see how it's done, whether I'm here or not."

He sighed. Yet another reason not to like this job. He hated disappointing people. "How about if you call them and I listen in? I should have an example before I do any of the dirty work, don't you think?"

Chloe sat alone in the office, thinking about the past few minutes. When Matt expressed concern over phoning the Hadleys, they returned to the office together and she'd gotten hold of the family herself. After she finished the conversation, he complimented her on her people skills, kissed her in an arousing and totally proprietary manner that left her reeling, and said he had errands to run.

Now that she was alone and able to think rationally, she remembered the message from Jeremy Jadwin and returned his call. He reminded her of their tentative dinner date, but she begged off and changed the meeting to a business lunch on Monday with both she and Belle in attendance.

With Ruby and Belle in the kitchen fixing

supper, and no appointments scheduled for the rest of the day, Chloe closed and locked the French doors leading to the foyer and gave herself some much needed privacy. Instead of keeping her distance when alone in Matt's presence, she seemed to gravitate toward him in a completely ridiculous manner. Spending even a few hours with him set her nerves to thrumming and her heart to hammering with every suggestive glance and meaningful word he tossed her way.

For whatever reason, the effects of Eros's love arrow were taking far too long to subside. It was time she took matters into her own hands where the prissy love god was concerned, and get the issue with Dr. Studly resolved once and for all.

Leaning back in her chair, she tried to recall the chant the gods used when they needed backup. She hadn't summoned any of the Olympians in over a century, and wasn't sure the SOS would work unless the verse was letter perfect, so she was prepared to stumble over several versions before she got it right.

"God of the mountains, god of the seas, god of all hearts, thee I beseech. Though Mount Olympus is a gas, come to me now before I kick your . . ."

Clever, very clever, she thought, fighting a giggle. And oh so very wrong. Sighing, she started again.

"God of all hearts, god of the sea, god of the mountains, I do beseech thee. Olympus is old,

Zeus is tired, come to me now or I'll have you . . ."

Grinning like a fool, she decided to give it one more try. If the next chant was incorrect, she'd wait until tonight, when she was in her room.

"God of the mountains, god of the seas, god of all hearts, I do beseech. Though on Olympus you reside, I need you now by my side. Eros, if you hear my plea, obey me now and come to me."

Positive it was as correct as she could make it, she crossed her fingers and closed her eyes.

Chapter 14

Chloe held her breath and waited, but her office remained the same. Fading sunlight still dappled the walls, warm air continued to rise from the floor vents, and she was alone.

Serves me right for not trying to reach him sooner. I should have sent an SOS the second I knew there was something fishy afoot.

She sighed and leaned back in her chair. Now what?

As if on cue, a parade of goose bumps marched up her arms. She focused on the air shimmering around her as heart-shaped rose petals whirled like snow flakes. Swirling colors joined in the dance, immersing her in a cloud of fluttering pink, yellow, aqua, and white.

The atmosphere ripened with the exotic aromas

of musk, rose, and patchouli, mixed with a hint of sandalwood. The storm of petals gently ebbed, and Eros appeared, first as a tiny diaper-swaddled cherub holding a bow, then as a young lad in a loincloth, sporting an arrow-filled quiver across his back. A moment later he morphed into a fully formed deity of manly proportions. Dressed in a flowing white chiton, his blond ringlets waving in an imaginary breeze, he posed in his usual pompous, magazine-model fashion.

"Chloe, darling," he greeted her, his sensual mouth set in a teasing smile. "What a wonderful surprise. I'm honored you have need of me."

She crossed her arms and rolled her eyes. "I have 'need of you' all right. But only because I want to know one thing: how low can you go—and why?"

The god of love quirked a brow, then strode to the opposite side of the desk and loomed over her, anger etched in his handsome face. "I do not take lightly to false accusations, *ma petite,* so think twice before you besmirch my good name."

"Don't trifle with me," she said in return. "What did Hera promise you in exchange for hitting me with that arrow?"

"*Moi?* Hit you with one of my barbs?" His lips firmed to a thin line. "Nuh-uh. Not me."

Chloe stood and met him toe-to-toe. "A couple of nights ago? In a bathroom in this very house? Me, Dr. Studly, and a breath-stealing, knock-your-socks-off kiss?"

The arrogant deity grinned. "Are you referring to a few nights ago, here in this very house?"

"Yes."

"Then . . . no. I don't remember."

"And you haven't spoken to Hera or joined her in a plot to ruin my chance at eternal glory?"

"Of course not."

Chloe threw back her shoulders and glared. "I—I don't believe you."

"Well you should." Eros gave a wounded sniff. "I haven't spoken to the old bag in months. She's been off the mountain for weeks now. Rumor has it she's up to no good, and since the only gods down here are you, Kyra, and Zoë, the rest of us figured you three were the reason." He threaded his fingers through his hair. "But it has nothing to do with me. I've been too busy overseeing the veritable cornucopia of lonely hearts sites on the Internet to even begin doing her bidding."

"Lonely hearts sites?"

"You know, those Internet websites mortals visit to find their soul mates. After they fill out a lengthy questionnaire, they're matched with another mortal who might be Mr. or Ms. Right. It's my job to intercept the e-mails before the website owners bungle things and link up the wrong people. Alas, I can't always get to them on time."

"Why in the world would you want to do that?"

"I don't want to. Unfortunately, it's my new assignment. Zeus decided using the Internet was the modern way to fall in love and gave me the job. But as much as the old goat says he's into technology, he still can't resist dabbling in the lives of mortals in a very hands-on manner, especially where matters of the heart are concerned."

She'd heard of the sites, but she'd never met anyone who used them. "Do all people of today fall in love that way?"

"Have you listened to the hip-hop-rhyming-slam-bam-whining excuses for love songs making the rounds these days? It's enough to send Cole Porter spinning in his grave. In the modern world of *amour* there are few enchanted evenings, less glances across a crowded room, and only the tiniest amounts of love at first sight. And definitely no arrows." He shuddered. "If you ask me, it's positively barbaric."

Chloe thought so too, but it wasn't her place to comment. Her only goal was getting to the bottom of her near-obsession with Matt. "I don't understand," she muttered. "If I haven't been hit by one of your barbs, what's happened to me?"

"I won't know until you tell me exactly what you've been experiencing."

"I'm—I—I think I might be sick."

"Impossible. Deities don't get ill."

"But my stomach is churning. I'm dizzy, I'm—"

"Hmm. Your complexion is a bit green." Eros gave her a sympathetic smile. "There there, let the love doctor help. Give me all your symptoms, and I'll try to come up with the ailment *toute de suite*."

"Symptoms? As if I had a disease?"

He shrugged. "What is love but an ailment of the heart?"

Chloe brushed past him to pace the room, working to make sense of it all. Throughout the centuries, Eros and his quiver had sometimes been more of an epidemic than an ailment. But it wouldn't help her cause to argue. Better she listed her so-called symptoms, and let him think she agreed.

"Besides my queasy stomach and intermittent rushes of dizziness, I get hot and cold all over whenever I see him," she began. "It's almost as if I'm standing at the North Pole while surrounded by a ring of fire."

"Hm-mmm."

"First, I start to shake, then my head feels as if it's filled with helium, and I find it difficult to form a coherent thought or utter a sensible word."

"Ah-hah."

"My knees grow weak when I'm near him, and I want to fall into him and pretend there isn't anyone else in the world but the two of us. His strong arms surround me, and I know I'm safe and cared for. And when he kisses me—"

"Then you've already done the lip-lock thing?"

"Boy, have we ever."

He frowned. "Anything else? And I mean *anything*."

Chloe's face heated to blast furnace level. "We did *it*."

"It! You did it?" Eros raised his hands to the ceiling. "Oh, sweet goddess, say it isn't so."

She flinched at his over-the-top plea.

"Tell me it was terrible, a disaster, the worst experience you've ever had between the sheets."

"To say so would be a lie." She swiped the tears she just realized were trickling down her cheeks. "The one night we spent together was wonderful. I felt it as a communion of bodies, minds, and hearts, even if we did the deed on a cement floor."

He waggled his eyebrows, and she stomped over to stand before him. "Don't ask." Her throat clogged and she heaved a breath at the memory of Matt's clever hands, his tempting mouth . . . his warm concern at fulfilling her totally before seeing to his own desire. "He's all I think about, all I want . . ."

Eros embraced her and held her to his chest. "There there, *ma petite*. It happens to the best of gods, if they let their guard down—which you obviously did. You're due back on Mount Olympus in a matter of days, correct?"

"Y-Yes."

"Simple. Leave him, and those unnerving feelings will disappear—" He snapped his fingers. "—like that."

"Leave him? But I can't go anywhere until Zeus sends for me." Chloe grabbed the hair at her temples, prepared to yank in frustration. "You have to give me something to ward him off until then. A potion—an antidote—a spell!"

Grasping her upper arms, Eros gazed into her eyes. "Alas, but there is no such thing. The only cure is returning home and losing yourself in your old life."

"But—But—what should I do in the meantime?"

He gave a sassy grin. "Enjoy yourself, *ma petite chou*. Spend every second you can together, because once you're back on Olympus he'll be nothing more than a warm, fuzzy memory."

She leaned forward and dried her tears on his chiton. "You're sure that will work?"

"Of course I'm sure."

"You wouldn't lie to me, would you?" she asked, sniffling. "Because, right now, your prediction is the only thing I have to look forward to."

"He's a mortal, correct?"

She nodded.

"Then trust me on this. All deities who have canoodled with mortals have taken their fill and never given them a second thought once they regained the sanctuary of our mountain paradise. It just isn't done. Besides, why would they want to live a human life of toil, misery, and eventual death here when they already have eternal glory?"

The silly question needed no answer, but it did leave her feeling marginally better. Eros was spouting an idea very close to Matt's pumpkin pie theory: gorge until sated, then wait for the next pie. Maybe she should take his advice, especially since it was all she had.

"I'll try," she told him. "Really, I will. But I have a favor to ask."

"Anything. If I can grant it, I will."

"Don't repeat our conversation to a single being. Especially Hera."

He put his fingers to his lips and locked them with an imaginary key. "Mum's the word, *ma petite*. You can count on me."

Matt arrived home, pleased with everything he'd accomplished in the past several hours. He'd just about cleaned out his trust fund buying a new car, but he had to have his own wheels, and what could be better than a brand new Mercedes? Though he hadn't gone overboard and bought the most expensive model, he had purchased a peppy, four-door sedan in a deep racing green with all the bells and whistles.

Then he'd stopped at Children's Memorial, where he had a long talk with Dr. David Jones, the chief of staff. If he was going to be at the birthday party thing, it would be foolish of him to pretend he wasn't a doctor in front of people who probably knew everything about his past. During his and Dr. Jones's discussion, he hadn't come right out and stated his misgivings about resuming his practice, but he had asked for more time, using his grandmother's health as an excuse. Then he'd filled out the paperwork needed to start the process for allowing him hospital privileges, and added his name to a list of doctors available for consultation.

He hadn't experienced a complete change of heart where medicine was concerned, but he figured he might as well start the ball rolling in order to be ready, when and if he did. Even Chloe had somehow known he wouldn't make it as an event host, so it was time he stopped hedging and admitted he simply wasn't cut out to be a party planner.

Then he'd put his plan in action to keep the adorable Ms. Degodessa in his sights. First, before leaving the hospital he'd gone to the pharmacy and purchased two of the biggest boxes of condoms in their display. Then he'd dropped into a jeweler's showroom for something special, a token to prove to her that he cared. With little more than a week left to convince her to stay on, he needed to get busy, and this was his only idea.

There had been little sexual chemistry in his relationship with Suzanne, merely a sense of doing what everyone expected. His meetings with Chloe sparked like a match to kindling, though it was difficult to tell who was the more combustible. He had no doubt they were sexually attuned to one another, but was mere physical compatibility enough to build a relationship on?

And what would happen if the attraction died?

He had to get busy and see where an affair with Chloe would lead. Even if the electricity arcing between them fizzled, she'd have something to remember him by. Then he'd say farewell to the woman and funnel all his energy into deciding what was best for Belle and Castleberry Hall. After that he'd tackle his professional situation.

When Matt arrived at the house, everyone was seated at the dining room table. Clark walked in from the kitchen at the same moment he entered through the foyer.

"You're on the button," the caterer said, setting down a large soup tureen. "It's the first course for tomorrow's wedding reception. I thought everyone would enjoy a preview."

"It smells delicious," said Ruby, smacking her toothless gums. "What kind is it?"

"Shrimp bisque with a twist. Take a taste, and tell me what you think."

Matt sat next to his grandmother and across from Chloe, hoping to read her expression. Had she returned Jeremy Jadwin's call? Had she agreed to meet with him? Buoyed by the fact that she was here for dinner, instead of out with the pushy renovation expert, he opened his napkin and grinned.

"Were you busy this afternoon?" he asked.

Chloe met his gaze with a hesitant smile. "A little."

"I didn't see an appointment on the calendar. Did customers drop in?"

"No."

"Then what did you do?"

She fiddled with her silverware. "Paid a few bills."

"Is that all?"

"I went over contracts for next week's activities," she said, smiling a bit too sweetly. "I even managed to call our flower supplier all by myself and coordinate the order for tomorrow's reception."

"No need to get defensive. I wasn't checking up—"

"Then why the third degree?"

"Why are you interpreting a few simple questions as an interrogation?"

"Oh, for Pete's sake," chimed Belle. "Stop sniping, Matthew, and say what's on your mind."

"Yes, Matthew," Chloe muttered through clenched teeth. "Say what's on your mind."

Can we have sex tonight, and every morning and evening until you leave? He swallowed the thought. That would certainly be an interesting topic of conversation. Or not.

"Both of you are acting like children," his grandmother continued.

"I wasn't the one who started it."

"I don't know what you're talking about," Chloe snapped at the same time.

Belle slapped her soup spoon on the table and

gazed at Chloe from across the table. "I think we all know what he's talking about, even while he beats around the bush. Your impending departure is sitting in the room like the proverbial eight-hundred-pound gorilla. And I think it should be discussed out in the open."

"I can't tell you how sad I was to hear you were leaving," said Ruby. "Was it something we did?"

"Of course not," Chloe answered, her expression grim.

"If it's more money, I'm sure Belle will agree to a raise," offered Ruby. "Won't you, Belle?"

Before the matriarch answered, Clark added his two cents. "If all you need is a trip home, why not take a leave of absence? I could help with the client load if I knew you'd be back in a couple of weeks."

"Oh, Clark, no. I'm afraid it's nothing—there's nothing anyone can do. I made a promise to my father that I'd return, and the date is approaching fast."

"I wish you'd told me earlier," said Belle. "What with Mr. Jadwin's visit, your decision isn't coming at a good time."

"What does Jadwin have to do with it?" Matt demanded when he saw his grandmother's lower lip quiver.

"Why, nothing," Ruby interjected. "It's just that making the plans Belle needs to make to complete such a big remodeling job will be stressful without Chloe to supervise, is all. Right, Belle?"

"Yes, that's it," Belle agreed.

Matt wanted to say more, but everyone at the table grew quiet—too quiet. Either they were keeping something from him or Chloe's resignation was more devastating than he'd realized. They finished the main course, a casserole he would have sworn tasted like sawdust, in near silence. He stole as many looks at Chloe as he could without being obvious. She focused on her food, barely raising her eyes from her plate.

Finally he could stand it no longer. "I bought a car today," he announced, hoping to perk everyone up.

"Really?" Clark asked. "What kind?"

"A mid-level Mercedes. Nothing flashy, but it should be dependable. If I'm lucky, it will last as long as the one Gram owns."

Ruby leaned into the table. "When are you picking it up? 'Cause your grandmother and I would be happy to drive you to the dealer. Then you could give us a ride in the new wheels."

"It would be a nice change from sitting in the house," Belle added.

She sighed, and Matt grew concerned. Her voice sounded more like a weak warble, and her hands were shaking. When Clark removed his grandmother's untouched plate of food, he had to ask, "Are you feeling all right? Maybe you should make it an early night?"

"No, no. That talent show is on television tonight, and it's another session of bloopers. I love the part where they show the worst of the worst and the judges start their usually hilarious harangue." She stood and took a step away from the table, then laid a hand on her chest and plopped back in the chair. "Oh, dear."

Matt grabbed Belle's wrist, found her pulse, and noted the erratic rhythm. "Clark, run upstairs and bring down whatever medication is in her bathroom. Chloe, call 911, then phone Dr. Kellam, and tell him we're heading to the E.R."

Chloe paced the emergency waiting room, too restless to continue holding Ruby's hand, which had been wrapped around her fingers in an iron grip. Belle and Matt had been taken to an examining room over two hours ago, yet there'd been no information on her condition. Why couldn't someone come out and tell them what was going on? How difficult would it be to extend a bit of common courtesy to those waiting for word?

The EMTs hadn't said much when they'd arrived at the house either. They'd just loaded Belle onto a gurney while Matt watched, his face pale and set in a frown. He'd followed the ambulance to the hospital in the family car, while Clark had driven her and Ruby in his catering van, explaining that Matt would probably be allowed to stay with his grandmother, while they would eventually have to leave.

The waiting room was almost empty now, but it had been clogged with mortals when they first arrived. Over the course of time, a half-dozen people of all ages and genders had shuttled through the wide double doors, while family and friends remained here in the lounge. She smiled at a lone man propped against the wall in a far corner, and he nodded in return. A siren sounded, its pulsing wail drawing closer and closer, until it stopped and hospital personnel raced to the entry. A minute later another gurney was wheeled inside.

Despondent, Chloe swiped at a wayward tear. She'd never been in a hospital before tonight, and she now understood why so many mortals considered it a depressing and frightening place. Sitting and stewing over the health of a loved one was downright terrifying. When Clark arrived with a cardboard carrier holding insulated cups filled with hot tea, she breathed a sigh.

"Here you go," he said to Ruby as he sat down and passed her a cup. "Yours is milk only." He held the next container out to Chloe. "Honey and lemon for you. And straight up for me."

"If it's good news, it shouldn't take this long." Ruby dunked her tea bag a few times, then set it in the carrier. "What do you suppose they're doing to her?"

"Giving her drugs and monitoring her progress, I'd imagine," said Clark. "I'm sure Matt will be out soon to tell us what's going on."

Just then the double door swung open and Matt walked into the room. Drawing a chair from the wall, he placed it in front of them and took a seat. "How are you guys doing?"

"We're managing, but barely. How is Belle?" asked Chloe, setting her tea aside.

"She's stable now, but they're keeping her overnight for observation. If all goes well, I can bring her home tomorrow."

"What's wrong with her?" questioned Ruby. "Was it her heart?"

"You're aware of the details of her condition? That she's on medication?" said Matt.

"Of course, but Dr. Kellam didn't seem worried at our last visit. Should he have been?"

"Not really. Gram's got a few things wrong with her, as do most senior citizens, but none of it's been serious until tonight. The stress she's been under of late intensified the problem. She had atrial fibrillation and—"

"Atrial what?" asked Chloe. Could the news of her leaving truly have contributed to Miss Belle's collapse?

"Too put it in layman's terms, her heartbeat became irregular and a little too fast. She lost her breath, got dizzy, and the stress sent her further into arrhythmia. Dr. Kellam's upped her dosage of digoxin and added another drug."

Clark frowned. "Can we see her?"

"Not tonight. In fact, it's probably best if the three of you return to the Hall. I'll spend the night in Gram's room and, provided she's improved, bring her home tomorrow." He gave Ruby a lop-sided grin. "You can fuss over her all you want once we get her settled."

Ruby gnawed on her lower lip. "Maybe I'll move into the bedroom next door, so I can hear if she needs something or—"

"The second floor isn't a choice for someone with your arthritis," Matt responded. "If need be, I'll hire a nurse. But for now, Gram can use the phone system's intercom to call for assistance."

"You don't really think you'll be able to convince the woman to stay in bed, do you?" said Clark. "Miss Belle is used to keeping busy, even if she's no longer directly involved in the running of Castleberry Hall."

"We can set her up in the front parlor," Chloe suggested. "It's big enough for her chaise, I can keep an eye on her from the desk, and Ruby wouldn't have to climb the stairs to visit."

Matt sent her a pointed look. "You're not going to be here after next week, remember? Besides, I like the idea of a private nurse better."

"I meant until I have to go," said Chloe, miffed at his expression of disapproval.

"I know what you meant and—"

"I'm leaving to get the car," announced Clark. "The two of you can argue at home tomorrow. Come on, Ruby. I'll walk you to the exit door. You can sit there while this gruesome twosome say their good-byes."

Chloe waited until they shuffled off before

meeting Matt's glare. "Clark's right. This isn't the place to fight."

"I agree."

He walked to a window and stared into the darkness. She followed him and stood by his side while she held her breath, fearful that anything she might say would start another argument. On Mount Olympus she had eleven sisters and dozens of gods she considered family. Though she, Ruby, and Clark were worried about Belle, Matt was her grandson, and she was all he had left in the world.

Matt's shoulders sagged and he ran shaking fingers through his hair. "Jeez, she scared the crap out of me."

"I know," said Chloe.

"If anything happens to her—"

"I feel the same."

He turned to face her and captured both of her hands with his. "Then stay at the Hall."

"I—I can't."

"Belle needs you."

"It's impossible."

"What if I confessed that I need you too?"

"That is so unfair," she muttered. "You don't know what you're saying."

"Haven't you heard? All's fair in love and war." He cupped his fingers around her jaw. "And we're not at war."

Chloe gasped as she gazed into Matt's eyes. Did he realize what he'd just said? Positive his grief was forcing him to utter crazy things, she shook her head. Too confused to speak, she opened and closed her mouth.

Then she raced from the waiting room.

Chapter 15

TO: Cdegodessa@CastleberryHall.com
FROM: Topgod@mounto.org
SUBJECT: Immediate response required

Permission to receive aid from another muse never given. Eros has all he can handle managing dating sites on the Internet without sticking his quiver into matters of a personal nature, which you need to take care of yourself. There is little more than one week before recall. Don't screw it up.

   For clarification, see corporate document No. 4907, subsection 4A, paragraph 12.

Sincerely,
Zeus (still Top God)

Chloe glared at the computer screen in a state of total frustration. She'd had a long night at the hospital, and thanks to Matt's parting comment, got only a few hours of sleep before returning to the Hall. As many times as she tried to convince herself that she'd heard him incorrectly, she couldn't deny he'd used the L word. After a year of avoiding a single entanglement of the heart, she refused to believe that, with so few days left on earth, she'd finally been laid low by four tiny letters.

Miss Belle's health and Dr. Studly's passionate plea weighed heavy on her mind. Spending the morning stewing over Zeus's nasty e-mail definitely was not on her to-do list. Still, she'd be in big trouble if she didn't send the immediate response he demanded.

But what blasted corporate document was he referring to? As far as she knew, she'd never been given any list of official rules, so how was she supposed to have read them? Too bad her weekly chat with Kyra and Zoë wouldn't take place until tomorrow night, because she'd bet her last chiton they'd received plenty of chastising missives themselves and would know best how to reply. Worrying her lower lip, she began to type.

TO: *Topgod@mounto.org*

FROM: *Cdegodessa@CastleberryHall.com*

SUBJECT: Your last communication

Father: Please consider my invitation to Eros a grave error in judgment. It will not happen again. I'm in the process of studying the documents you cited in order to avoid such failures in the future.

Sincerely, your daughter,
Chloe
Muse of Happiness

She grimaced at the note's groveling tone. Completely on her own this past year, she'd grown to treasure her freedom and independence. Not having to comply with Zeus's silly demands and Hera's imperious whining had been invigorating. She hadn't felt second best to anyone, be they god or mortal, and it had been emotionally satisfying doing something useful instead of the same old *blah blah blah* she'd put up with for the past several thousand years.

She sometimes wondered why her father insisted the muses continue in the job for which they'd been created, especially because of his unfavorable opinion of the human race. Though he'd once enjoyed dabbling in the mortal world, it was apparent to all that he'd turned Mount Olympus into a poor imitation of a corporation simply to get back at the humans who had denied his existence these many years.

Mortals weren't such a bad lot. Though some were self-absorbed and unfriendly, so were many of the gods, and she'd interacted with hundreds of humans who were the opposite. Ruby, Clark, Miss Belle, the staff members working at the Hall, and most of the people who held their events at the Castleberry were all pleasant and insightful.

She'd added kind and caring to their attributes when Belle, Ruby, and the Optimists started the monthly ritual of the Birthday Party. Since then she'd met a plethora of mortals willing to go out of their way for children destined to struggle throughout their journey to adulthood. And although Matt loved to irritate her and put her in her place—hah! as if he could—she had to admit he was an admirable human being. Especially when it came to children.

The front door opened with a bang and a gust of wind returned her to the moment at hand. Sensing it was Miss Belle and her entourage, she rushed to the foyer, hoping to assure her dear friend of her support. Then she would meet Leah in the chapel and check on the pew and altar decorations for today's four o'clock wedding ceremony. After that she would visit the reception hall and make sure Clark and the wait staff had everything under control for the evening's festivities.

Ruby trundled in, her face wreathed in a smile.

Clark had dropped her at the hospital first thing that morning to give Belle a hand while Matt saw to his grandmother's discharge. It was important Ruby feel useful, and what better way to attain that goal than by helping her oldest and dearest friend?

" 'Morning, Chloe. You ready to welcome home the lady of the manor?" Ruby called as she entered the foyer.

Chloe grinned at the woman's positive attitude, noting that Ruby had deigned to install her teeth for the occasion. "Is everything all right? Where's Belle?"

"Matthew's escorting her from the car. He's making her walk real slow, which she hates, so she doesn't slip on the ice or wear herself to a frazzle." Ruby shrugged. "She looks so good, if I didn't know better, I'd think last night was just a bad dream."

Before Chloe could answer, she heard voices coming from the porch.

"Stop your fussing. I'm fine."

"Watch out for that patch of ice."

"I still have my eyesight, young man. Let go of my arm."

"Please, Gram, just take it easy for a while."

"Since I don't plan on going dancing tonight, I don't see why you're worrying. And I refuse to be treated like a baby." Still grumbling, Miss Belle tottered into the foyer and glanced around as if checking to make sure she'd been delivered to the right house. Her eyes rested on Chloe and she immediately perked up. "Hello, dear. How are you?"

"I'm fine, now that you're here," Chloe answered, ignoring Matt's scowl. One look at his day-old growth of beard, bleary eyes, and disheveled hair, and she knew his night had been as disjointed as hers. "It's good to see you so fit."

"As a fiddle," Belle added, jerking from Matt's grasp. "Or at least I will be as soon as my grandson finds something better to do with his time."

"I'll leave you alone once I see you settled upstairs," Matt said, placing his fingers on her back.

Belle spun around with surprising agility for an eighty-three-year-old-woman. "There's a wedding today that Ruby and I were personally invited to attend, and I refuse to miss it."

"Now, Belle . . ." said Ruby. "Maybe we should stay in and watch a movie or—"

"Not on your life," Belle snapped. "Unless you're feeling too ill to go."

"Now that you mention it, I have been tired of late—"

"You have not. But if you want to stay home, that's fine with me. I, for one, plan to celebrate Michael and Glenda Barnsworth's daughter's marriage as scheduled." She folded her arms and glared at her grandson. "Since it's probably the only wedding I'll be a part of this year."

Matt stuck his hands in his jacket pockets and rolled his eyes. "For the love of— Make up your mind, Gram. First you're thrilled I broke it off with Suzanne, then you're on my case because I'm not getting hitched. What the heck do you want from me?"

Belle puffed out her chest and gazed, in turn, at each person in the foyer. Then, like a child caught in a temper tantrum, her shoulders slumped. "I don't want anything from you but your love, my dear boy. I'm sorry if I'm being difficult, but last evening's episode took the wind out of my sails too." Removing her coat, she handed it to him as she smiled at Ruby. "Come upstairs, sit with me while I decide what to wear to the festivities—unless your knees are bothering you."

"Don't imagine one trip up and down will hurt if I rest in between," Ruby replied.

Matt stepped toward the staircase, and Chloe arched a brow, stopping him mid-stride. "I'll make tea and bring it to you before I leave for the chapel. How does that sound?"

"Dandy," said Ruby, following Miss Belle to the second floor. "And take your time."

Chloe left for the kitchen, and Matt hung his, Ruby's, and Belle's coats in the closet. He needed a nap, then a shower and shave, in that order. Though his grandmother had slept like a baby and awakened refreshed, his night had been miserable. It was tough convincing Belle she had to rest when she ran rings around him at every turn.

After Chloe had shot him a lay-off-you-idiot warning, he realized he'd been harsh with Belle, but damn it, his concern for his grandmother was driving him nuts. Though his professional patience had been put to the test in Africa, it paled in comparison to the personal trial facing him now.

And aside from thinking about Belle, Chloe had been on his mind all night too. Had he really been so stupid as to intimate he was in love with her? After he'd said the words, her expression had gone from shock to anger to disbelief in a split second, so he doubted she'd taken him seriously. Which was for the best, considering her plans.

Once in the kitchen, he walked to the stove and confronted Chloe, who was preparing tea, as promised. "Give me your honest opinion. How did Belle look to you?"

She removed the teakettle from the range and poured boiling water into a white china pot. "A lot better than she did last night. I can hardly believe she was ill."

"Amazing, I know."

"What did Dr. Kellam say?"

"He told her to take it slow and ease back into her regular routine, but he didn't remand her to bed or make her swear to stay quiet." Sighing, he ran his fingers through his hair. "Then he escorted me into the hall and asked that I curtail her activities for a week or so."

Chloe propped her backside against the counter. "That doesn't make any sense."

"It does to Dr. Kellam. According to him, after a minor incident, seniors used to their independence usually fight his orders for bed rest, so he merely advises them to take it easy. Then he tells their caretakers it's up to them to see that their parent or grandparent lightens their schedule. He says it helps in the patient-doctor relationship. Instead of thinking he's against them, the old folks believe he's on their side. I see where he's coming from, because I've figured out that dealing with the elderly is a lot like dealing with kids."

She arranged teacups and saucers on a tray, then set the teapot beside them and covered it with a brightly colored cozy. "How so?"

"Children and seniors are famous for testing boundaries. They hate it when they're talked down to or babied, exactly as Gram said. Even if they're not of sound mind, they don't want to admit they need extra care."

She added a plate of sugar-free cookies to the tray. "And it's better if they get angry with their families instead of their physicians?"

"So Dr. Kellam says." He hunched over, rested his arms on the sink and stared out the window. "If you want my opinion, it sucks."

A moment passed, then Chloe placed her hand on his shoulder and began to rub. "She's going to be okay."

He inhaled a breath. "No, she's not. She's going to die, if not today or next month, then next year or the year after that. And I'm going to miss her more than I can say."

She continued to soothe him, moving her hand in calming circles. "If it's any consolation, I'm going to miss her too. I've come to care for Belle . . . more than you know."

Then why are you leaving? He almost blurted the words. Talk about a whining baby. "Thank you."

"For what?"

He turned and faced her. "For being here when I couldn't. For looking after the business, helping it to grow and prosper, and letting Gram still feel she's a part of it." He grasped her elbows. "I know you've run this place almost single-handedly for a while, and I appreciate it."

Tears glittered in her baby blue eyes. "I still can't stay."

"I figured as much." He leaned forward and pressed his chin to her forehead. "It's okay."

Sniffing, she chuckled. "Then why do I feel like such a traitor?"

"Because you have a conscience?" He nuzzled her cheek with his nose, then drew back and took a long narrow box from his inside jacket pocket. "This is for you. Please accept it as thank-you for everything you've done."

She put her hand on her throat. "I can't—"

"Think of it as a bonus for all your hard work." He opened the box, revealing a string of perfectly matched pearls. When her eyes opened wide, he reached out and clasped them around her neck. "There. Now you don't have to borrow Ruby's."

She fingered the shimmering globes. "They're beautiful."

"Just like you." He tugged her to his chest and placed his lips on her cheek, meaning to kiss her in gratitude, but when their mouths met, his good intentions disappeared.

Chloe snuggled into him, and he welcomed her in his arms. She molded to his body, and he nestled a leg between her thighs. When she opened her mouth, he took full advantage, tasting her, teasing her tongue, telling her he wanted all she had to give.

Grinding her hip against his erection, she threaded her fingers through his hair. Her heartbeat thumped against his chest, syncing perfectly with his. As if one in body and soul, they rode wave after wave of desire.

She drew away first, her breath heaving. "I don't think—"

"That this is right," he said, finishing her sentence.

"I'm—"

"Leaving. I know."

"There can't be any more—"

"Between us. I got it."

She exhaled as she shook her head. "You aren't being sensible about this."

"What *this*?"

"This thing we have for each other. You know as well as I do that we can't—"

"I know nothing of the kind," he insisted. "I'm a man, you're a woman. I have needs, so do you."

"Is this something along the lines of your pumpkin pie theory?" she asked, amusement lacing her words.

"Sort of." He raised her chin with his index finger and gazed into her eyes. "If I promise not to bring it up again, can we pretend you'll be staying? Until you have to leave, that is."

"I don't know—I mean no. It isn't practical or sensible, or even logical. It's—It's—"

"Crazy?"

"Yes." She sighed and stepped from his arms. "I have to go to the chapel and check on the decorations, then I'm needed at the reception hall."

Matt hoisted the tray. "I'll take this upstairs and see if I can help those two make a decision about tonight, but I'm not betting on it. If Belle and Ruby decide to go to that ceremony, I plan to stick to them like glue. Think you can back me up and say you need me there?"

"Of course." She fingered the pearls as she smiled. "Because I do."

"I wish you every happiness." Chloe gave the just wed Ashley Barnsworth Demming's hand a hearty shake, and repeated the gesture and statement to the young woman's new husband.

She then helped the attendants find their proper

place in the receiving line, and let Leah take care of the next step. After shrugging into her coat, she hurried to the hall. Matt had convinced his grandmother and Ruby to skip the line and, with him at the wheel, drive the quarter mile to the reception. Though both women had fussed, they'd finally seen the logic in his suggestion, for which Chloe was grateful.

On her walk, she recited a mental checklist of the things she was expected to oversee in order to be certain Castleberry Hall lived up to its contractual obligations. She had to speak to the emcee/bandleader and make certain he had the program in hand, then look over the gift table, inspect the cake, and finalize the seating arrangements for both the head table and those of the guests. Once everything met with her approval, she'd visit the kitchen and have a quick talk with Clark, who always remained in control of the food. Knowing all was exactly as it should be gave her the peace of mind she needed to enjoy herself at the event.

She entered the staff coat room, hung up her mink, and took stock in the mirror. Tonight's gown, a full-length, pale green sheath trimmed with sparkling faux diamonds, hugged her curvaceous figure as if the designer had personally sewn her within its folds. She'd left her hair loose so it cascaded past her shoulders and fell in curling waves. Matt's gift complemented the hint of blush she'd applied to her cheeks, the brush of gloss she'd swiped across her lips, and the sweep of mascara she'd given her eyelashes to complete the overall effect.

In short, she appeared every inch the woman Zeus had created. A goddess.

Then why did she feel so vulnerable and unsure of herself, as if she was no longer in control of her destiny? Why did tears continue to leak from her eyes at the oddest moments? And why did her heart clutch whenever she thought of leaving Belle, Ruby, and the Hall?

And not just the Hall, she reminded herself. Because more than anything, she would miss Matt.

Closing her eyes, she recalled Eros's advice and vowed to be strong. He'd promised that once she returned to Olympus, Matt would become a distant memory, a pleasant reminder of her time on earth. Oh, how she wished he spoke the truth.

After dabbing at one of those pesky wayward tears, she set her head at a regal angle and set out for the reception. Inside the grand ballroom, she traded words with the bandleader, who was also the vocalist of a popular quartet that played at Castleberry Hall on a regular basis.

The guest book sat on the gift table, open and ready for signatures. She approved of the cake, a beautiful three-tiered confection of white icing covered with yellow roses, pale pink lilies, and curling green leaves. Dark green tablecloths and creamy yellow napkins—new colors she'd added to the list of linen choices—complemented perfectly the two dozen tables decorated with flower-filled baskets, each holding a single lighted candle. The stemware, cutlery, and china, also new and chosen by her, gleamed under the light shining from the Hall's immense brass and cut-crystal chandeliers.

A wave of pride tickled her belly. Since its inception, Castleberry Hall had always been a wonderful place to hold a wedding or any other type of celebration. Thanks to her vision, it was now superb.

Searching the room, she found Miss Belle and Ruby sitting at a table in a distant corner. Matt stood behind them, dressed in a tuxedo that emphasized his broad shoulders and trim build, a look of concern etching his noble-but-scarred face. Belle waved, which alerted him to her presence. He raised his head, their gazes locked, and he broke out in a smile.

In that instant Chloe knew for certain she was in love with Matthew Castleberry and, Eros be damned, would always love him.

Matt stared at Chloe across a sea of flowers and flickering candlelight. A dream come true in a figure-hugging gown of pale green, she appeared unflappable, imperial, and untouchable. But he knew the truth, because he'd been able to ruffle her feathers and dig below the surface of all that perfection. He'd seen the real Chloe Degodessa, brought a smile to her face, touched her delectable body, and felt her writhe beneath him in ecstasy.

If the woman didn't realize he was head-over-heels in love with her, she was an idiot. And he was positive he could never fall in love with an idiot.

"Isn't Chloe striking?" Belle said to Ruby, her stage whisper loud enough to be heard in the next county.

"I'll say. It's so nice to see that she's got a string of pearls of her own to wear." Ruby sniffed, then reached up and took Matt's hand. "You did good, boy. Real good."

The pearls, Matt thought, didn't have a thing to do with Chloe's appearance. Whether the woman wore a potato sack, a necklace made of coal, or a costly mink coat, she would always be spectacular. And she would always be . . . his.

She disappeared into the kitchen, and he exhaled a lungful of air. Glancing down at Belle, he noted and ignored her sly smile. He didn't have a formal place setting at the event, but the guests were only beginning to trickle in, so he took the vacant seat between his grandmother and Ruby. "The two of you look very fetching tonight."

"Fetching?" Belle tittered at the old-fashioned word. "Aren't you sweet?" She peered around him and stared pointedly at Ruby. "It's just sad that he's too much a coward to voice the same sentiment to Chloe."

"I am not," he muttered. "I simply haven't been able to talk to her since we left for the chapel. She's been too busy, and I've had my hands full with the two of you."

"The girl works like a demon," Ruby stated. "I'm sure gonna miss her when she leaves."

"It's so unsettling, knowing she'll be gone soon," Belle added. "I only wish there was something here that might compel her to stay. Something . . . more meaningful than a strand of pearls."

"More meaningful?" asked Ruby.

Belle dipped her head in Matt's direction, as if he were blind to her meddling.

"Oh." Ruby grinned. "I get it."

Matt glanced at the place card at his seat and saw Judge Armbruster's name. The seat on the other side of Belle belonged to Suzanne, and next to hers was a sign that read GUEST. That told him his ex-fiancée had moved on with her life, and good for her, he thought. Though they hadn't been right for each other, he hoped she had a good life with the right guy.

He smiled inwardly, knowing how thrilled his grandmother would be when she learned she'd have to listen to Suzanne's chatter for most of the evening. Perhaps it would be enough to convince Belle to make it an early night.

"I'd better see if I can be of help in the kitchen," he announced, standing. "I should be earning my keep."

"Go ahead," Belle encouraged. "We have a good view of the entryway, the dance floor, and everything else of interest. Don't worry about us."

"Easier said than done," Matt said with a shake of his head. Bending down, he kissed Ruby's cheek, then his grandmother's. "Do not leave for home without me. Understand?"

"Yes, dear," they agreed in unison.

He set off for the kitchen, nodding at a few old friends he knew from his past along the way. He'd gone to high school with Ashley Barnsworth's oldest brother, Ron, and had even attended a party or two at their mansionlike home only a couple of blocks from here. Mr. and Mrs. Barnsworth, as well as their four children, belonged to the right clubs, contributed to the proper charities, and socialized with the most influential of people. He'd never been clear about what the elder Mr. Barnsworth did for a living, but it didn't matter. Like Suzanne, the family was more concerned with appearance than substance.

As if on cue, Ron Barnsworth and his two younger brothers, all dressed as groomsmen, appeared and headed toward the waiting rooms tucked behind the bandstand. When Chloe came in from the kitchen, the three men stared with appreciation. She glided past them as if oblivious to their admiring grins, and the trio continued on while she stopped in front of the musicians. After a short conference with the bandleader, the quartet began the introductory song that officially opened the festivities.

Matt leaned against a wall while the attendants were announced, and then the bride and groom entered. Fifteen minutes passed while several standard numbers were danced. He waited until guests joined the bridal couple on the floor, then walked to Chloe, who was watching the process with a dreamlike expression in her eyes.

"Would you care to dance?" he asked when he arrived at her side.

"Me?"

He grinned. "I don't see anyone else standing here."

"I'm on duty."

"Which means it's against the rules to have a little fun?"

"I'm having fun," she stated, a smile gracing her lovely face. "And working too."

"You'd have more fun if you danced with me."

"Oh, really?"

"Yes, really." Matt clasped her hand and led her onto the floor. Twirling her out and drawing her back to his chest, he said, "See what I mean?"

The band segued from a fairly upbeat tempo to their version of "When a Man Loves a Woman," and he pulled her close. Chloe relaxed in his arms, leaned into him and followed his slowly swaying body until they danced as one.

"This is nice," she whispered. "I don't usually get to join in the dancing."

"I know the family, and they won't care. Besides, you work too hard."

Before she responded, Matt felt a tap on his shoulder. Turning in place, he came eye-to-eye with Ron Barnsworth.

"Hey, Matt. Long time no see."

"Ron. Your sister looks very . . . bridelike." That nonsensical statement alone proved he had no business as an event coordinator. "Congratulations."

"Yeah, the old man and Mom are thrilled to get her off their hands. I'm the only one still not married. What happened to you and Suzanne?"

"Things didn't work out between us."

"So I heard." His gaze roamed Matt's face. "Sorry it was so difficult."

"Now that I'm home, I'm helping in the family business," Matt continued.

"Then you'll be practicing here in Chicago?"

"I'm thinking about it. Maybe we can catch up later."

"Yeah, later. Right now, I'm cutting in." Ron smiled at Chloe. "My sister said you might be kind enough to dance, if I asked nice."

"I am dancing," Chloe answered, her eyes fixed on Matt.

"I meant with me."

"Perhaps some other time, but thanks for asking," she said sweetly.

Leaving a perplexed-looking Ron to stare, Matt's chest swelled with pride as he steered Chloe into the rhythm. "You could have finished this with Ron. I wouldn't have minded."

"Why would I do that, when I'm already dancing with the man I want to be with?"

He drew back and stared into her eyes, unable to believe the sparkle he found there was because of tears. Instead, he pulled her close, melded against her body, and set his mind to work on a way to keep her in his arms tonight.

And all the rest of his nights for as long as he lived.

Chapter 16

Chloe gave the reception hall's spacious kitchen a final inspection. The cleansing jet sprays of the dishwashers rattled the silverware and china. The service items, beverages, and leftover food were accounted for, and the heavy cleaning team was scheduled to arrive first thing in the morning.

Matt had left hours ago with his grandmother and Ruby. Chloe had read the exhaustion in his eyes and realized his overnight stay in the hospital, constant devotion to Miss Belle, and his feelings of guilt over her diminishing health had added another burden to his shoulders. Though there were days she wished for a mother, she was grateful she wouldn't have to care for aging parents, as did so many mortals. Sometimes it was all she could do to care for herself.

She grabbed the half bottle of champagne Clark

had left on the center island, then buttoned her mink coat. After sticking the bottle in one pocket and a crystal flute in the other, she headed for the rear exit. Until a moment ago she'd forgotten that her weekly talk with Kyra and Zoë was scheduled for tonight. She looked forward to something mortals called "drowning their sorrows," and couldn't do it until she made that phone call.

Chloe entered the house, locked the front door, and tiptoed up the stairs. Clark had retired to rest for tomorrow's party, and she assumed Matt was sleeping in the room adjacent to Miss Belle's suite, so there was no need to check on her.

Now, in her sitting room, she set the bottle and glass on the coffee table, dropped her coat on the nearest chair, and plopped on the sofa. Toeing off her pumps, she admired the blaze burning brightly in her fireplace. Someone—she had no idea who—had taken the time to light a fire, and by the appearance of the logs, had done it only a short while ago.

After filling the flute and swallowing the contents, she propped her feet on the table, picked up her cell phone and dialed. "Sorry I'm late," she said when Kyra and Zoë were on the line. "I had to supervise an over-the-top wedding reception and it ran late."

"I'm up," said Kyra.

"Me too," said Zoë.

"So . . . how is everyone?"

"I'm fine," Zoë muttered.

"Me too," Kyra added hesitantly.

"Well, neither of you sound fine. What have the two of you been doing?"

"Same old, same old." Kyra's yawn rang with boredom. "Sorry, I'm really beat."

"As am I," said Zoë. "And I don't have a thing of interest to discuss."

Chloe sensed the uneasiness in both women. It wasn't like them to be so blasé. It was rare when they didn't have something to complain about or comment on.

"How's Miss Belle? Is her grandson still working there with you?" Kyra asked in a sudden rush of words.

"Oh, he's here, all right," Chloe answered, marginally relieved. That sounded more like the sister they knew and loved. "Except he's always underfoot."

"And?"

"And who cares? He's a selfish, boorish bully who's continually in my way." Too bad if she sounded harsh. The description had fit Matt to a T when they'd first met, which hadn't been that long ago. "I can't wait to leave this cursed planet."

"Me too," said Kyra a second time. "Zoë, what about you?"

"Hmm?"

"You're quiet. Don't you have anything to say about Chloe and her job?"

Zoë's sigh echoed over the line. "I'm sure she's handling things, just like you and I are."

"You should know that I had a surprise visitor. Hermes, in all his winged glory," Kyra continued.

Chloe sat up straight. "No kidding? I thought he never left the computer room. What did he want?"

"Zeus sent him. It seems I was too slow responding to his e-mails and it cheesed him off."

Zoë snorted. "You've never been on time, so why start now? Can't the old poop wait another week?"

"That's what I said, but I think Hermes used it as an excuse to warn me personally. Apparently Hera's returned to earth. Our fellow gods are worried . . . about us."

"Great," said Zoë.

"Well, crap," muttered Chloe, fingering the pearls. There was no point in telling them about Eros, since Kyra had already been warned.

"The hint was subtle, but I could tell he thought it was important we knew. Since none of the others are fans of Hera, they want us to watch our backs."

Just as Eros said, thought Chloe.

"Lucky for us we're playing by the rules, huh?" said Kyra after a long silence.

"Of course. What else would we be doing?" Chloe asked in innocence.

"Absolutely by the rules," agreed Zoë on a yawn. "Sorry, I have to make this short. I'm sort of involved in planning my big exit."

"Me too." Chloe wanted nothing more than to

get off the line and have another glass of champagne. "Remember I love you both, more than I could ever say. You're wonderful sisters and—well—good night."

"Same here," muttered Zoë.

"I love you too. See you in a week," Kyra added.

Chloe disconnected the call and set her cell phone on the table. Her sisters had sounded distracted almost to the point of despair, but it had to be the jitters. They were probably nervous about their return, especially with the added news that Hera was on the warpath. And so what? To her knowledge, not one of them had done anything to give the mother goddess a reason to make trouble. As the Muse of Happiness, she herself had wished hundreds of mortals eternal joy, and she hadn't fallen in love.

Not really.

Sighing, she stared at the champagne, refilled her glass, and swallowed it down. Then she poured a third flute, which emptied the bottle, and vowed to savor it slowly. The next event on the calendar was for the coming afternoon, when the Hall hosted another baby shower. She could sleep late and still be ready to take charge of the affair.

In moments the first burst of heady sensation assailed her nerve endings. She giggled as, bit by bit, serenity, calm, and a so-what attitude she hadn't experienced in quite a while overtook her.

Who cared if she disappointed Belle by leaving? What did it matter if she never again saw Clark, Ruby, or the other friends she'd made here? Big deal if she never got a second chance to dance with Matt. She'd swayed to a heart-stirring rhythm in a dozen men's arms; why should she miss being sheltered in his?

Matt Castleberry was attractive, even with his scars. Considering his future prospects as a doctor, he was sure to find another woman, the *right* woman, to dip and twirl on the dance floor . . . to share his future.

To love.

Heaving a breath, Chloe gazed at the tiny bubbles rising and popping in the pale amber liquid while the fizzy brew painted swirling colors in her brain. Colors that melded with the flames caressed her skin and warmed her inside and out. Brilliant blues, bright greens, invigorating oranges, reds, and yellows reached from the fireplace to raise her above all her worries, until she thought she might fly to Olympus and laugh in the faces of her bossy father and his mean-spirited wife.

Perhaps if she drank nothing but champagne until her return to Olympus, leaving here would be a no-brainer. The mind-numbing buzz of the fizzy wine would bolster her *who cares?* attitude and offer a much needed cocoon of emotional protection. She raised the flute in mock salute. When she arrived home, she would share the glory with her sisters, accept the accolades due her as a true goddess, and be free to live as she chose.

Matt stood in the doorway, his gaze focused on Chloe as she sat before the fire inspecting what appeared to be a glass of champagne. After bringing Ruby and his grandmother home, he'd chatted with them for a time before seeing them safely to bed. Then he'd showered, found a few candles and set them to burning in Chloe's bedroom, and laid a fire.

When Chloe didn't make an immediate appearance, he'd returned to straighten his room, hang up his tux, and locate a book. He planned to read while waiting for her in front of a roaring fire. In the few minutes it had taken him to attend to the tasks, Chloe had sneaked in, made a phone call, and gotten comfortable with her own supply of bubbly.

"Glad you finally decided to come home," he said, sauntering to the sofa.

She jumped and whipped up her head. Eyes wide, her gaze skimmed his face, his bare chest, and his low riding pajama bottoms. Then she giggled.

"Well, well, well. If is isn't Dr. Stud-dud-ly."

"Dr. who?"

"You scared me half to death," she went on as if she hadn't heard the question. Still giggling, she nodded toward the fire. "Thank you for the blaze, by the way, but it's not going to change anything. I still don't intend to sleep with you again."

Matt ignored the pronouncement, positive he would change her mind. "I meant to be here waiting for you, but you beat me to it." He sat and focused on her glass. Though champagne wasn't his beverage of choice, he'd drink any amount necessary to bring him closer to her. "Is there enough of that stuff to share?"

Instead of answering, she straightened, finished the glass, and raised the bottle high. After swigging down the dregs, she placed the flute and bottle on the table and gave him a silly grin. "Nope. Good night."

He shrugged. "Not a problem. I don't need a drink. How did the reception go after I left?"

"Things went well." She settled against the cushions and hiccuped. "Is Belle all right?"

"Fine and dandy, according to her. She didn't even complain about having to share a table with Suzanne. Since both Belle and Ruby warned me not to wake them in the morning, I expect they're sound asleep." He leaned back, mimicking her relaxed pose. "What about you?"

"Ron Farns—barns—" She hiccuped again. "Ron what's-his-name asked me to dance a second time, and I said yes."

"Did you enjoy it?"

"I did. He wanted to know if I'd go dancing with him at some club in town."

Over my dead body! "And you said . . ."

She gave an unladylike snort. "No, of course. I'm leaving."

"Oh, yeah, that's right. You're jumping ship."

Stiffening visibly, she threw him a glare. "I am not shumping jip . . . skipping pip." Another round of hiccups led to another burst of giggles. "I have to leave."

Matt couldn't help but smile. Clark had told him that Chloe and champagne were a lethal combination. If it wasn't so late, he'd go to the Hall's wine cellar and dig up another bottle, just to see what she'd do.

"Okay."

"Okay?"

"Yes, okay. I got the message. You made a commitment to your father, and you're too honorable to break it. I'd feel the same if I gave that kind of promise to Gram."

"I'm glad you understand." She returned her gaze to the fire. When he didn't continue, she said, "Isn't it past your bedtime?"

"I'd hoped we could spend a little 'bed time' together," he replied, mentally crossing his fingers.

"I just told you—*hic*—that wasn't a good idea."

Smothering a grin, he inched sideways, until his thigh touched hers. When she trembled, he moved closer. "Pumpkin pie, remember?"

"You've already had your slice, *remember*?" she retorted, still seemingly entranced by the fire.

"A slice, yes," he whispered, nibbling on her ear. "But I was shooting for the whole pie."

Encouraged by a flurry of giggles, he moved in for what he hoped would be the final strike. "There's still a week left before you're scheduled to leave. It sounds selfish, I know, but the thought of sex with you is the only thing keeping me sane right now."

"Trolling for an entire pity pie? You are a glutton."

"Hey, I'm thinking of myself, as most guys would in this situation. I accept that you're leaving, which means there can't be anything serious between us, but . . ." He cupped her jaw and turned her head so they were face-to-face. "I want you, Chloe. For tonight, and as many nights as you're willing to give."

Drawing back, she rested her head on the sofa. "Hmm. Don't you just love it when the fire reaches out and touches your skin? It's so warm and sensible and—"

"Sensible?"

She huffed out a breath. "Sen—sue—al. I said sensual."

"I'd rather have you touching me than the warmth of the fire."

When she glanced up, Matt leaned forward. Capturing her mouth, he traced her lips. She opened, and he accepted the invitation, tasting the sweet-tart tang of champagne on her tongue.

Entering her warm wet heat, he stroked in a time-less rhythm of desire until he was completely lost in the kiss.

Then he pulled away and focused on what he had to do. Standing, he drew Chloe to her feet and hoisted her into his arms. "Don't take this the wrong way, but you're a handful," he said, smiling.

Lacing her fingers around the back of his neck, she raised a finely arched eyebrow. "For a man who's heard the word no as often as you have, that's a pretty risky comment."

"How about if I tell you I want to work on my 'technique'?"

"And what if I tell you I'm too much woman for you and your 'technique' to handle?"

"Trust me, sweetheart, that isn't possible."

"Then I guess you're *up* to the task?"

"And then some. Whatever you have to give."

They arrived beside the bed and Matt set her on her feet. Chloe noted the candles scattered about the room and recalled his earlier statement. They both wanted the same thing: a night of shared passion and mindless surrender. If he could treat their coupling as a balm to his sanity, who was she to resist?

Resting her head on his shoulder, she ran her fingers over his firm pectoral muscles, through the crisp hair on his chest, and lower to his navel. Entranced by the warmth of his finely sculpted body, she dropped her palms to his pjs, slipped them under the waistband and caressed him intimately, gauging his steely length.

He groaned and she nuzzled his chin, meeting his lips in another stirring kiss. He moved his hands to her back and inched the zipper down, down, down, until she wriggled out of her dress and the one-piece body suit she needed to safely wear the figure-hugging gown. Standing in nothing but his gift of pearls and ivory-colored, thigh-high hose, she basked in the admiration shining from his eyes.

"You are a goddess," he whispered. "But you've probably heard that from every man you've dated."

"Some have said words along that line, but it's never sounded so romantic." Unable to tell him the truth about herself, she glanced at the candles a second time. "Of course, I had no idea there was such a sappy streak hiding behind your all-work-no-play attitude."

"I'm not—it's not—" He wrapped his fingers around her nape and slowly massaged her neck. "Is being romantic such a terrible thing?"

"No, but I don't want you to think what we're about to do means more than it does."

"You already said so, along with the fact that you're—"

"I can't stay."

"I know, and I'm not asking you to." He caressed her jaw with his palms. "Right now, I just want you to make love with me. Everything else can wait until later."

Chloe sighed, losing all hold on her resolve. It was difficult arguing with Matt when he was so sweet and so . . . so . . . He palmed a breast, circled the nipple with his thumb, then bent and licked the hardened tip.

"You don't play fair," she muttered, melting against him.

"I'm fighting fire with fire, sweetheart. You make me burn, I do the same to you."

As one, they sank to the mattress. He covered her with his body, kissed her collarbone, moved to her breast and suckled, drawing the bud deep into his mouth.

Shuddering, she rode a wave of pleasure, let it ripple through her veins and turn her liquid inside. He nuzzled her ribs, feathered her navel with his hot breath, and brought his lips to her woman's mound. Then he parted her thighs and delved into the center of her desire.

She ran her fingers through his hair, holding him tight while she writhed in rhythm with his tongue. The colors of the fire reappeared, flashing, pulsing in her brain, and sizzling along her nerves until she screamed her release. He nipped the inside of her thigh, laved her belly, and inched up to again take a breast in his mouth. His fingers opened her still quivering center, and he slipped his penis inside, filling her with need and a sense of empowerment at the same time.

He kissed her then, his tongue filling her with the taste of their shared passion. When he began to move, she moaned.

"Tell me what you want," he whispered.

"You," she said on a rasp.

He quickened his thrusts, and she raised her knees to take him more fully.

"Like this?"

"Faster . . . harder . . ."

"Is that any way to ask?"

"Please," she pleaded. "Please."

He groaned his approval and drove into her to the hilt. Then he rose to his knees and brought her with him so she sat with her legs wrapped around his back. Clutching his shoulders, she rode high on his thighs, moving in time with his pulsing rhythm. Words of encouragement mingled with throaty gasps and pleasure-filled sounds, until she fell onto the mattress and he spasmed over her, cradling her while she found her release.

Moments passed before Chloe opened her eyes. Matt was stretched across her body like a living blanket, his head resting on her shoulder, his breathing slow and deep. She blew into his ear, and he chuckled.

"That tickles."

"I'm not too excited about the thought of you falling asleep on top of me."

"I wouldn't do that to you." Turning his head, he grinned. "Though I'm so relaxed right now I probably could."

"Not funny." She wriggled. On Olympus, the gods did whatever pleased them after having sex, but no mortal had ever spent the night in her bed. She'd always gone to their apartments and left shortly after they'd finished the act. She had a sneaking suspicion that mortals who slept together were on the road to something more. "Do you plan on staying here until morning?"

"Beside you in bed?"

"You do have a room of your own."

"Yeah, but you're not in it." He eased off her and onto his side, and propped his head in his hands. "I don't snore. At least, no one's ever told me so."

"It isn't the snoring that bothers me—"

"I don't hog the covers either."

"It's not the covers—"

Reaching out, he tucked a curl behind her ear. "Your hair is amazing. Even in the candlelight it's obvious you're a natural blonde."

Heat rose to her cheeks when she realized what he meant. "We're not allowed to alter what our father gave us."

"Your father? As in, he didn't allow you to wear cosmetics or dye your hair when you were growing up?"

"Um . . . yes, that's exactly what I'm saying."

"But you're not a teenager any longer. You're living on your own, paying your way, supporting yourself."

"Of course, I am. It's just—"

"Then why should he still be able to dictate the color of your hair or where you're supposed to be at any given time? You're of age." He brushed the damp tendrils from her forehead. "How old are you, anyway?"

"Never mind how old I am." She pulled the covers to her breasts with a *humph* of annoyance. "Men who ask that question are considered rude."

"Actually, it was the start of a compliment." He brushed her temple with his index finger. "You don't have a single line or freckle on your face—or on your body that I could see." He studied her. "If I didn't know better, I'd bet you could pass for sixteen."

"I'm way past my teen years," she answered. "Now, let's drop the subject."

"Whatever you say."

She frowned when he joined her under the sheet. "I don't think this is a good idea."

"You keep saying that, but it always works out."

"Your grandmother might walk in on us, or Ruby—"

"Have they ever surprised you before?"

"No, but—"

"Then they won't do it tomorrow." Snuggling her close, he ran his fingers through her hair and down her back. "What are you afraid of, Chloe?

Why can't you just enjoy what we're doing for the moment? I've already told you I understand your reasons for going to your father."

"Maybe, but your actions speak differently."

"All right, I'm pretending." He tucked her head under his chin. "So sue me."

"That's not funny."

"How about if I admit I'm also hoping something will happen to change your mind? I believe it so much, I'm thinking about joining the Optimists Club."

"That's not a—"

"Good idea. I know." He heaved a sigh. "Is your father ill? Is that why you have to go home?"

As far as she knew, Zeus hadn't had so much as a splinter in his several thousand years of existence, and neither had any of the other gods. "Not exactly."

"Family reunion?"

"Sort of."

"You're not being very clear about it."

"And you're not being understanding, like you promised. Please, can't we simply forget this— this—"

"Forget that we've slept together?" He snorted. "Fat chance."

"Maybe you should sleep in your own bed."

"Fat chance on that too. I'm here for the night . . . and every night until you're gone. If I can't have the whole pie, I plan to get as many pieces as possible."

She gazed at him, then traced the pink line crossing his cheek with her thumb. "When are you going to see a plastic surgeon?"

"Soon. Right after I decide about Belle."

"Decide what?"

Furrowing his brow, he rolled off the bed and paced the room, blowing out the candles. Then he returned and settled by her side. "I have to make some decisions about Gram and Castleberry Hall, and none of them are simple. I'm not looking forward to doing what I have to do."

"Then don't. Wait, and give Miss Belle the chance to make her own decision. She'll be desolate if you take things out of her hands. Give her a little time, and I know she'll do what's best."

He wrapped his arms around her and snuggled her bottom against his thighs. "We can talk about it later. There's another baby shower scheduled for tomorrow, and I need to get a good night's rest if I'm going to be of any use to you."

Moments later Matt's breathing turned deep and even. Chloe clenched her fists to keep from jabbing an elbow in his stomach. Just like a man to fall asleep when there was more to be said. She and Belle had a lunch date with Jeremy Jadwin on Monday. If his terms were good, and he met all of Belle's stringent requirements, perhaps they'd strike a deal that would satisfy Matt and enable Miss Belle to keep her dignity.

If not, Castleberry Hall would be in chaos and everyone would be miserable. Aiding in so much unhappiness would not look good on her record, which might cause Zeus to determine that her time here was a failure.

And failure was something she could not—would not—accept.

Chapter 17

Matt slipped from Chloe's bed late that morning, and showered and dressed without waking her. They'd made love again sometime before dawn, and he thought it best she had a good night's sleep before today's event began. Telling himself he would spend the week looking for ways to show her how much he wanted her to stay, he ate breakfast and rushed to the Hall.

When he arrived, it was clear that Clark had been hard at work for several hours. The smart-ass caterer gave him a single glance before making the first of several wisecracks. "Nice to know that somebody had fun last night after the wedding. Poor Chloe is probably all worn-out."

Ignoring that and the know-it-all's continued wry comments, Matt went to work assisting the setup crew. He didn't have a clue how the smug chef had guessed about his involvement with Chloe, but it didn't matter. Keeping their trysts a secret from Belle and Ruby was the important thing.

Now, propped in a corner of one of the Hall's two mid-sized reception rooms, he scanned the crowd of close to a hundred adults chatting as they enjoyed a variety of tempting dishes. A sea of kids, most of them male, were eating, roughhousing, and screaming their way through the festivities as well. Since he hadn't read about a baby explosion while away, he figured he was simply more attuned than ever to children. Their shouts of laughter and cries of happiness rang sharper in his ears. And the many pitfalls awaiting them hung heavier in his heart.

Judging by the two huge tables piled high with presents, he figured the celebrating clan—made up of Depestos, Martinis, Farinas, and several other families of Italian descent—were holding more of a blowout than a typical baby shower. Guests ranged in age from the coming child's 103-year-old great-great-grandmother, Nona Farina, to Gregory Michael Martini, four-month-old second cousin to the much awaited new arrival.

Marilyn Depesto glowed with the knowledge that she would soon give birth to the first female born to the Depestos in several generations. After delivering three healthy sons, she was scheduled to welcome Rose Michelle in just over two weeks.

Matt gazed at the mother-to-be's enormous belly and decided the party planners had cut the timing of this gathering close. She looked radiant, as did many pregnant women, but every once in a while he caught a grimace in her expression that worried him. He'd heard rumors of a questionable due date, but the risky schedule didn't seem to bother anyone in attendance. After all, the expectant mother was an expert at delivering babies. Why should they worry about child number four, when Marilyn could probably give birth to Rose Michelle in the morning and make supper that very same night?

He spotted Chloe, incredibly beautiful as usual, as she finished making rounds at the head table. She'd stopped and shaken hands with each guest, then offered them a wish of eternal happiness. Now she stood to the side and nodded to a group of adolescent boys. A kid of about fourteen, wearing a smitten grin, offered her a plate of food, while another handed her a cup of punch. Several other young men hovered on the periphery, as if ready and willing to do her bidding. The smile on her face told him she was in her element, charming every man in the place while still managing to handle the details of a busy affair.

The three-piece ensemble playing standard Muzak from the bandstand broke into a rousing rendition of what he assumed was a favorite song. Generations of Italians began clapping rhythmically while they sang in their second language.

All eyes centered on the hallway that led from the kitchen. Clark appeared, pushing a dessert trolley laden with a three-tiered cake swathed in pale pink frosting and covered with fuchsia-colored roses and white lilies of the valley. Smiling like a crazed pastry chef bursting with pride over his finest creation, he rolled the cart to Marilyn's seat and bowed from the waist.

"*Tanti auguri com il bambino,*" he said in perfectly accented Italian. "From the Castleberry family to yours."

Matt pondered that last sentence. Clark made it sound as if the cake was a gift from Belle, but if he remembered the contract details correctly, the impressive confection had billed out at five hundred bucks. No small gift to the parents-to-be.

Various attendees snapped pictures and ran videocams as Clark cut and the wait staff served the cake. In the midst of the excitement, Chloe sauntered to Matt's side. "Having fun?" she asked, stopping next to him.

He took in her tailored black pants suit, white silk blouse, and his gift of pearls draped across the column of her alabaster neck. "That depends. Can you answer a question?"

"Sure. Shoot," she responded with a roll of her baby blues.

"Did Castleberry Hall donate the cake?"

She sighed. "I wouldn't exactly use the term 'donate.' It was more of a thank-you investment."

"Funny, but I don't recall a single Depesto, Farina, or Martini ever having held an event here before."

"They haven't, but—"

"Is the mother, father, or any of the relatives personal friends with Belle?"

"I don't think so."

"Then . . ."

"It was my idea."

He raised a brow.

Folding her arms, she glared. "Haven't you ever heard of customer relations?"

"You're telling me it's good business to give away something on which we usually make a sizable profit?"

"In this case, yes."

He stuffed his hands in his pockets. "Because . . ."

"I met Marilyn's mother, a Farina, by the way, when we hosted a friend's daughter's wedding about six months ago. We got to talking, and she confessed her family always held their gigantic celebrations in the basement of one of their churches. When she told me her only daughter, married to a Depesto, was expecting a girl and it was a big deal, I suggested a special party. We went over the calendar, worked around a couple of other planned events, and picked the date." She heaved a breath. "I only wish we'd won the bid for the wedding they'd held for her nephew last month."

"I still think that cake is a little over-the-top just because they chose us to host their first event in an outside facility."

"Take a look around. There are at least fourteen young men here who will more than likely get married in the next ten years. Yes, the bride's family usually pays for the wedding, but it's only fair the groom and his side make recommendations. There are also a dozen couples of child-bearing age, which means upcoming showers, birthdays, and graduation parties." She smiled. "It's a fortune in future bookings for the Hall. Which translates to a fortune in Belle's retirement fund and, down the line, your pocket."

To Matt, beauty and brains were the ultimate turn-on. He rested his back against the wall to keep from kissing her. "When you put it that way . . ." Shrugging, he gave her a teasing grin. "I should have known better than to doubt your judgment. I don't suppose there's a chance you'll return to us after your father sets you free?"

Before Chloe could answer, a commotion at the head table caught their attention. One of the guests shouted, and Matt glanced over to see Marilyn, her hands cupping her belly, standing in a puddle of what he felt certain was amniotic fluid.

Immediately, he moved toward her. "Call 911," he ordered her husband when he made his way through the milling crowd, and managed to catch

Marilyn as she fell into his arms. "You're going to be fine," he told her. "I'm a doctor."

She shuddered and gripped his fingers. "That's good, because this baby's coming."

"Of course she is. The ambulance will be here soon. Just hang tight."

"Hang tight?" Marilyn shrieked. "Easy for you to say, Doc." She doubled over, then dropped to a squat. "I don't have a couple of minutes. Rose is coming right now-oow-oow!"

"Imagine, a baby born right here in Castleberry Hall." Miss Belle hobbled to the dinner table, hung her cane on the back of her chair, and took a seat. "It still hasn't sunk in. I can't believe I missed the big event."

"Me neither," said Ruby, pouring a glass of water from the pitcher in front of her. "By the time I heard the sirens and got dressed, the excitement was over. What I don't understand is why *someone*"—she gave Chloe a pointed glare— "didn't call or come get us when it happened."

"As I've already said, there wasn't time." Chloe helped herself to a bowl of soup from the tureen warming on the sideboard. "Things moved so quickly. Two women spread a tablecloth on the floor, Marilyn laid down, and boom, Rose Michelle practically slid into Matt's hands. It was that fast."

And that amazing. She sighed at the memory of

Dr. Studly, his eyes serious, his manner competent, as he'd delivered the precious baby girl. The tender expression on his face when he held the child in his arms was still etched in her mind.

"I'm proud of the boy, taking charge and seeing to things," mused Belle. "If only his mother and father were here to—"

"I just did my job," Matt said as he entered from the foyer. "It wasn't a big deal."

"Maybe not to you," Belle huffed. "But the Depestos and their extended family agree with me. They even videotaped the birth. I'll be surprised if it doesn't make the local news channels tonight."

Matt opened and closed his mouth, looking appalled, and Chloe bit back a grin. "No more hiding from your old colleagues. By tomorrow morning everyone will know you've returned home."

"I haven't been hiding," he grumped. "Just unavailable."

"Whatever. What's important is that they'll know you're here. I'm sure you'll be swamped with calls from doctors who want you to continue where you left off before going to Africa."

"And guess what else?" Belle announced. "A few of the Depestos and Farinas confided that Castleberry Hall is going to be the first choice for all their upcoming get-togethers. I'll need to hire extra help, maybe add on to the Hall, just to keep up with the business they send our way."

"You'll do no such thing," Matt chided. "Remember what Dr. Kellam said."

"He said I could do everything I've been doing, provided I took it easy," she shot back. "Which I plan to do." After spearing a chicken breast from a platter on the table, Miss Belle passed the dish to Chloe. "Besides, you need to get your own house in order instead of worrying about me."

Frowning, Matt accepted the platter after Chloe had taken a portion, helped himself, and passed the main course to Ruby. "What, exactly, is that supposed to mean?"

"It means just what Chloe said. You should get your practice up and running. If you don't want to join the doctors Suzanne wooed for you, find another group looking to add a pediatric surgeon to their repertoire. If that doesn't work, find a suite of offices and go into business for yourself."

"Gram, how many times do I have to explain the system to you? Joining a successful up-and-running group isn't easy or cheap," he argued. "As for going out on my own, well, that would take more money than buying into a practice. Besides, I'm still not sure medicine is—"

"What you want?" Belle snorted. "Stop fooling yourself, young man, and get busy doing what the good Lord planned for you. I'll loan you whatever amount you need to buy into an already flourishing group, or lease space in a medical building, purchase the needed equipment, and other start-up expenses. I'll even let you sign a promissory note for the advance to keep everything strictly business."

Ruby nodded. "Belle's got the right idea. Don't you think so, Chloe?"

The conversation was going just as Chloe had hoped. If Dr. Studly was involved in restarting his career, he'd get off her case and she could disappear as quickly as she'd come. From the way Matt had handled himself that afternoon, it was obvious he belonged in medicine, especially if it involved children. He'd played games with the grade school set, and actually gotten down on all fours to tickle and tease the toddlers. And when he'd held Rose Michelle in his arms . . .

"I think Matt is old enough to decide what he wants for himself," she muttered, picking at her food. Suddenly swamped by a wave of exhaustion, she set her fork on the tablecloth. "If you don't mind, I think I'll say good-night. It's been a long weekend."

"But you didn't finish supper," noted Ruby. "You're not coming down with something, are you?"

Chloe shook her head. "I'm fine, but tomorrow's going to be a busy day. Don't forget, Miss Belle, you and I have a lunch appointment."

Belle puckered her lips as if tasting something sour. "I say we get that Jadwin person to take us to the most expensive restaurant in town. In fact, I insist on it."

"Then I'm coming with," said Ruby. "I always love going to the Executive House."

"The Executive House isn't nearly as posh as the Palmer Club," Belle corrected.

"Is so. And they serve the best filet mignon in town."

"Who said anything about filet mignon?" asked Belle. "I thought Italian would be nice, or French, which means Le Petit Chat."

"I need food that sticks to my ribs," argued Ruby. "French cuisine is nothin' but frog's legs and cream sauce, and that stuff gives me gas."

Hands on her hips, Chloe cleared her throat to keep from laughing. "We'll eat wherever Jeremy Jadwin wants to take us, ladies. And Ruby, you have to promise to wear your dentures if you want to come along."

Matt grinned at Chloe as she walked backward into the foyer. "As far as I'm concerned," he said, "you've lived long enough to do whatever you want with your dentures, Ruby, but you'll definitely need teeth if you plan on eating beef."

"Well, of course," Ruby answered, flashing a toothless grin. "I never go without 'em in public." She waggled her fingers in Chloe's direction. "You have a good night. We'll see you for breakfast in the morning."

With notions of taking a hot bubble bath, Chloe mounted the stairs to the second floor. She planned to lay out her clothes for tomorrow's lunch date, then soak in the tub and crawl into bed. Even though Matt had let her sleep the morning away, it was obvious the baby shower had sapped her energy. She needed a full night's rest to keep Jeremy Jadwin from getting the upper hand, in order to negotiate a sales contract for Miss Belle with the most advantageous of terms.

After starting the water in the tub, she added a good-sized splash of gardenia-scented bubble bath. While the water flowed, she went to her closet and pulled out sweaters, slacks, skirts, and dresses in a rainbow of colors. Unable to decide between a dark gray power suit and a figure-flattering dress of sea green silk with long sleeves and pearl buttons running from neck to hem, she slipped out of her clothes and returned to the bathroom.

She shut off the taps, ready to enter the tub, then froze when a pair of muscled arms encircled her from behind.

"You look good enough to eat," Matt whispered, nuzzling the back of her ear.

"You just finished a hearty meal," she reminded him, trying to unlock his forearms from around her middle.

"I need dessert." He nibbled on her earlobe. "Mmm. Delicious."

She smiled in spite of his maneuvering. "Haven't you had enough pumpkin pie?"

"Never. But I'm thinking of switching my allegiance to angel food cake with strawberries and whipped cream."

"Because . . ."

"That's exactly what you taste like." He turned her in place and drew her to his bare chest, cupped her bottom in his palms, and tipped his head toward the bubble-filled water. "You think that tub is big enough for two?"

She ignored the fact that he was naked. "We can't. Miss Belle or Ruby might hear and—"

"Gram and Ruby are in the kitchen doing the dishes, and I have it on good authority that when they're through they plan to sit in the sun room and watch television, which, by the way, will keep them at the opposite end of the house for the next two hours." He stroked up her back and curved his fingers around her jaw. "I skipped dessert, and you didn't eat enough to fill a bird, so I think we owe ourselves a bonus."

Chloe sighed. Matt's heated erection pressed against her belly, searing her with his desire. At this rate she would never be able to forget him, as Eros had promised. How could she, when it seemed she was continually hungry for his touch, starved for his affection, and aching for his presence every moment of every day?

Moving to face him, she clasped his wrists in her trembling hands. "This has to stop."

"Sure it does." He kissed the tip of her nose. "But not tonight."

"Can't you see? The longer we continue sleeping

together, the harder it's going to be to say good-bye."

He wrapped his arms around her and held her close. "I don't plan on *saying* good-bye."

She sighed. "When are you going to accept the fact that I'm leaving?"

Feathering her cheek with his lips, he said, "Never. I've decided to use the power of positive thinking instead. If I believe with all my heart that you'll stay, you will. And if you don't, then you'll come back as soon as you're able."

She pulled away and shook her head. "It doesn't work like that. Sometimes, things can't be changed."

He bent and gave her another tender kiss. "I don't want to talk about it." He nodded toward the tub a second time. "Come on, let's get in and see how fast we can make those bubbles disappear."

With a roguish grin, he stepped into the frothy water, slid down, and stretched open his legs in silent invitation. Chloe told herself to walk away, but her feet were glued in place, her eyes focused on Matt and only Matt. His expression was so full of hope and longing, she couldn't let him down, not when they had but a few more nights to share.

She did as he asked and entered the water, then settled her back against his taut abdomen and lower chest; and rested her head on his shoulder.

Steaming water lapped at her breasts and belly. His clever hands traced the bubbles on her thighs.

"Mmm. This is nice," she murmured, finally able to relax.

He drizzled sweetly scented water over her breasts with a sponge, then ran it over her stomach and between her legs. "Ever done it in a bathtub before?"

She smiled at the thought. "Maybe. What about you?"

"Truth?"

"Of course."

"It pains me to say this, but I haven't had much experience with women."

"Really? A well-traveled man of the world like you?"

"Change that to a man who spent the last twelve years of his life in either a classroom, a hospital, or a jungle, and you'd be more on target."

Uh-oh. She recalled all the gods and mortals with whom she'd dallied, in a bed, on the grass, in the ocean, on a slab of marble, in a tree, on top of a cloud . . . Thinking on it now, the sheer number of encounters boggled her mind; she could never tell him about the reality of her life, and not just that she was a true goddess. In fact, that bit of information probably wouldn't upset him half as much as the number of partners that would forever lurk in her past.

"I don't believe you," she said, half teasing.

"You seemed an extremely accomplished lover to me."

"Thanks for the compliment, but there were only a handful of women before you."

"Describe a handful," she continued to tease.

His sigh ruffled her ear, sending a tingle down her spine. "Besides Suzanne, one girl in my senior year in high school, two in college, and a single long-term lover in med school. But that ended when we went our separate ways for residency. And there was no one while I was in Ituri."

Oh, dear. It was worse than she'd thought. "What really happened between you and Suzanne?"

"She and I dated off and on during my residency. Getting engaged after that just seemed the expected thing to do. Once I went to Africa, I had a chance to examine my feelings and knew we weren't meant to be together." He stroked her rib cage, then palmed her breasts. "It's—different between the two of us."

"What makes you say that?"

His fingertips found her nipples and plied them with attention. "Being with Suzanne was almost a chore. Since I've met you, I look forward to starting each day as if it's going to be an adventure, yet I'm at peace, as if everything in my world is finally right." He kissed the back of her neck. "It's an added bonus that I haven't had a single nightmare since we began sleeping together."

She swallowed a sob. "Nothing will be right

unless you return to medical practice," she advised. "You don't need sappy emotion for me cluttering your true purpose in life."

Matt covered her mouth with a soapy hand. "I don't want to hear any more. Not tonight, and not before you leave."

Enveloping her in his arms, he turned her to face him and pulled her up his chest. Then he joined their lips and kissed her long and deep. Before Chloe knew it, she'd slid down and impaled herself on his throbbing penis. Matt's tongue took charge of the kiss, sucking, tasting, demanding, until there was nothing she could do but obey.

Rocking together, they crested on wave after wave of desire, until her shudders gave way to tears of joy. Of completion. Of sadness for what could never be.

Chapter 18

Chloe pushed the last few bites of shrimp and pasta from one side of her plate to the other. So far, this business lunch with Jeremy Jadwin had consisted of little more than grumpy and terse comments from Miss Belle and polite chitchat from the salesman, while Ruby did nothing more than concentrate on her humongous meal. If someone didn't start a conversation regarding the sale of Castleberry Hall soon, the entire afternoon would be a waste.

"I believe we've passed enough time talking about the frigid weather here in Chicago, Jeremy," she began, taking charge of the discussion. "I'm sure Miss Belle would rather hear about Party Palace's plans for her family's endeavor."

Jeremy sat up straight, as if he too was ready

to arrive at the point of their meeting. Moving his plate to the right, he set his briefcase on the table and brought out a manila folder. After closing the lid, he opened the file and placed it on the briefcase.

"I'm very grateful you're going to allow me the opportunity to present Party Palace's side, Mrs. Castleberry." He grinned at Ruby. "You too, Mrs. Simpson."

Ruby, who had said no more than three words since receiving her lunch, gave a noncommittal shrug and continued eating her filet mignon, baked potato smothered in butter, sour cream, chives, and bacon, and side of asparagus.

Belle sniffed, her expression one of disapproval. "I still don't understand why your company thinks they need my business to open a Party Palace in the Chicago area. I wouldn't mind a bit of healthy competition."

"As I've said before, we do our homework. We scoured the city all the way past Skokie searching for the perfect property. Your stretch of land has an unencumbered view of Lake Michigan, something that's unheard of in this day and age. If we open in a less attractive location, we wouldn't be any competition."

"My husband's father purchased those ten acres more than a hundred years ago." Pride rang in Belle's voice. "He was a forward thinking man of . . ."

Chloe sat back in her chair and let Miss Belle ramble on about her past. It was only fitting that she enjoy a moment of glory. Her family had built Castleberry Hall from the ground up, and Belle had taken the company from a gracious meeting site to a place of grandeur and beauty.

Yes, Castleberry Hall had flourished since she'd arrived, but Chloe sometimes thought that had been pure luck. She'd come at a time when a few of the bigger venues had closed, which opened opportunities in the market. Though positive she'd gone over and above the expectations Zeus had set for her, she was willing to concede her job had been made easier because of the Castleberry name and reputation.

"I brought the contract for your perusal," Jeremy said, tapping the folder. "I'd be happy to go over it with you now. Or maybe you'd like to take it to your attorney, and get back with me in a day or two."

Belle glanced at Chloe, as if seeking guidance.

"I think we'd like to hear what you have to say today. That way, Mrs. Castleberry can think on it before deciding if the offer is worth her lawyer's time and attention." She took the menu their waiter offered and gave it a quick study. "While you explain, Miss Belle could have a serving of her favorite dessert, chocolate mousse."

"I could use a bit of chocolate right about now," Ruby cut in, scraping up a last bite of potato.

Belle heaved a sigh, as if her patience had worn thin. "Oh, all right, if you insist."

Chloe raised the menu to her nose, intent on hiding her smile. Ruby had eaten every bite of her lunch, and Miss Belle had done an admirable job with her salad, lobster Newburg, and vegetable, as well. If Clark were there, he'd be rolling on the floor with laughter at the older women and their in-your-face attitude toward the too charming salesman.

"I'd like coffee with cream," Chloe said to the waiter. "And these ladies will have chocolate mousse."

"And a glass of your best sweet sherry," added Ruby. "None of that cheap stuff, you hear?"

Jadwin handed the waiter his menu. "Just coffee for me, black."

Conversation came to a standstill while the table was bussed. Hoping to have a private word with the PPC rep, Chloe said to Miss Belle, "Perhaps you and Ruby would like to powder your noses? It will be a few minutes before dessert arrives, and a short walk might do you both good."

"That's a fine idea," said Belle, pushing from the table.

"I'll say," echoed Ruby. "I ate so much I need to loosen my girdle."

Straight-faced, Jeremy stood and pulled out Belle's chair, then assisted Ruby. Together the women tottered toward the restroom. Sitting down, he waited until they disappeared before saying, "They certainly are a pair."

Chloe folded her napkin and set it beside her plate. "I think they're wonderful."

"Of course, that's what I meant." He adjusted his navy and white striped tie. "So, how do you think things are going? Will your boss be receptive to our offer?"

"I'm sure that will depend on the offer," she answered. "If it's fair with good terms, I imagine Mrs. Castleberry will give it careful consideration."

Jadwin's smile stretched wide. "Then you've had a chance to talk over the deal with her, as I suggested?"

"I haven't given her any opinion on a sale to Party Palaces. I've merely advised Mrs. Castleberry to partake of a free lunch while she listens to what you have to say."

"But you'd be willing to encourage the transaction for, say, a percentage of the offer?"

Annoyed by his renewed mention of a bribe, she gave him a stony glare. "I'll be leaving the Hall in a week, so I doubt my opinion will matter one way or another. Isabelle is intelligent enough to make up her own mind."

"I get it. You don't want her to know we've had this discussion." He leaned back and folded his arms. "You can depend on me."

Chloe opened and closed her mouth, prepared to read him the riot act, when she saw Belle and

Ruby returning from the restroom. "Except for explaining whatever Miss Belle might not understand, I think my part in this discussion is over."

"Gotcha," he said. Giving her a wink, he stood and held out Belle's chair, then Ruby's. "Mrs. Castleberry, Mrs. Simpson." The server approached with a full tray, and he continued to play the charming host. "Ah, here's your dessert."

Chloe added cream to her coffee as Belle and Ruby were served their mousse. After making certain Miss Belle was comfortable, Jadwin flipped through the contract, found what he was looking for, and passed the papers to her.

"Our offer is on the top line. I believe you'll find it more generous than our first three, with excellent terms for a payout."

Belle quickly scanned the page, then focused on the line he indicated. In moments her face paled to the same shade as the paper, and she put a hand on her chest.

"Are you all right?" Chloe half rose from her chair at the same time Ruby inched forward. "Shall I call your doctor?"

Belle simply stared, then gave the contract to Ruby with a shaking hand.

Ruby's eyes grew round as saucers. "Holymoly." Gazing at Chloe, she offered her the document.

Chloe knew things were costly in the modern world, but she'd never needed to worry about money. Her tip-to-toe wardrobe, furnished apartment, and cellular phone had been provided by Zeus. She'd never purchased so much as a pair of stockings or a container of milk, let alone property. Still, she sometimes perused the newspaper just to learn the way of things in the twenty-first century.

Even so, she blinked when she spotted the figure typed in the first line of the first paragraph. Were numbers meant to contain that many zeroes?

"So, what do you say, Mrs. Castleberry? Do we have a deal?" Jadwin prodded.

"I think Isabelle needs to go over a few of the finer points with you first," said Chloe, handing him the contract. "And she'll definitely want to take this to her attorney."

"Finer points?"

"Yes. Number one, I believe Mrs. Castleberry would like the site to retain the name Castleberry Hall."

Jadwin made a note on the inside of the file. "Not a problem."

"And she and Mrs. Simpson will need to stay in the manor house until they find the perfect place to relocate."

The salesman cleared his throat. "And how long might that take, do you think?"

Chloe eyed Miss Belle as she answered. "I believe Mrs. Castleberry mentioned six months. Is that correct, Miss Belle?"

"Y-Yes," Belle stammered. "That should be enough time."

"I'll have to pass both of your requests on to my superiors at headquarters, but I don't anticipate a problem." Jadwin glanced at his watch. "Today is Monday. If we agree to your terms within twenty-four hours, can I assume I'll have your answer by Wednesday, Thursday at the latest?"

Miss Belle waggled a finger in Chloe's direction, then leaned near. "Can I take the entire week, do you think?" she whispered.

"I don't see why not," Chloe responded in a quiet tone.

Belle's eyes gleamed with tears. "All right, then. Tell him—"

Chloe laid a hand on Belle's arm. "You need to tell him. It's your future, so it's your decision."

"You're correct." She dabbed at her nose with her napkin, then sat back and said, "I want to give my attorney plenty of time to look this over and enter the changes. I'll give you my answer one week from today, and not a moment sooner. Now, I think it's time we ladies went home."

After hanging her coat in the front hall closet, Ruby turned to her lunch companions. "Don't know about you two, but I'm bushed. I gotta lie down and give my food time to digest."

"Go right ahead," said Belle. Slipping out of her coat, she handed it to Chloe. "We'll see you at supper."

When Ruby disappeared through dining room, Belle peered into the office, took note of the vacant desk, and said to her assistant, "Where do you suppose Matthew is?"

"I don't have a clue," Chloe answered, wondering the same thing. "Maybe he had walk-in customers and he's giving them a tour, or he's helping Clark in the Hall."

"Well, whatever he's doing, I'm glad he's gone, because you and I need to talk privately. I'll start the water for tea."

Chloe took care of their coats while Miss Belle tottered into the dining room. Though she thought Belle should join Ruby in a nap, she knew it was useless to nag when Belle appeared determined to have her way. When she arrived in the kitchen, the kettle was steaming and Belle was setting cups and saucers on the table. Chloe guessed she was puttering in order to gather her thoughts, so she took a seat in the breakfast nook and waited while Belle added tea to a china pot, poured in boiling water, and covered the container with a cozy.

After adding cookies to a plate while the tea brewed, Belle carried everything to the table. "I swear," she said, sitting down with a thump. "I've never had a more stressful lunch. That Jadwin fellow was quite a handsome devil, but there was something about him . . ."

"I feel the same. That's why I wanted you to

meet him in person. If you don't think he's someone you'd be comfortable dealing with, just say
no to the offer."

"It really doesn't matter if I'm comfortable with
him or not. It's the company's reputation that
counts. I'm going to call Saul Bernstein and have
him do a profile study on Party Palaces as well as
look over the contract. If he thinks there's anything fishy, I simply won't sign the paperwork."

Chloe added milk to her tea. "I could tell by
the expression on his face that your determination and requirements took him back a bit."

"Do you think so? I mean, he didn't seem flus-
tered when I asked for those changes."

"I have an idea he's adept at hiding his true feelings. I'm sure he was on the phone to headquarters the moment he returned to his hotel room."
Chloe snagged a chocolate chip cookie from the
plate. "Personally, I'm glad you threw him a challenge. He should have to wear himself out to get
this wonderful place."

Sighing, Miss Belle took a sip of tea. "What do
you think they'll say about my requests?"

"Yes, of course. Without the Castleberry name,
its chapel and ready-made reception halls, they'd
have to double their efforts to get things up and
running. And I can't imagine anyone wanting to
live here, except maybe the new manager. And if
they're being relocated, they'll have to invest time
moving themselves and possibly a family. Six

months isn't so long in the grand scheme of things."

Hunching forward, Belle peered at the kitchen door. "I have to ask you for another favor."

"Anything."

"I don't want you to say a word to Matthew until the attorney has read the contract and added the clauses, and Party Palace has signed on the dotted line."

"Do you really think that's a wise idea?"

"Matt is at a crossroad in his career right now, and he's already worried about my health. I don't want to cause him any added stress."

Chloe swallowed her first thought. If Matt found out she knew about the deal his grandmother was making, he could take it several ways. He might accuse her of influencing Belle when it was none of her business, or he might be thrilled that she'd convinced his grandmother to sell and make enough profit to retire in style. Either way, she doubted he would appreciate her help.

"I'm sure he'll be happy you decided to give up the business and take it easy. And I doubt he cares about my opinion one way or the other."

Belle smiled as she covered Chloe's hand with her own. "Don't you think it's time to stop playing games?"

"Playing games?"

"Remember, I've seen those pearls."

A wave of heat flared from Chloe's chest to

her face. "The pearls were just his way of saying thank you."

"Come now. I'm old, not stupid. I know all about the two of you."

"Know? What do you know?"

"Everything."

"I—I'm—" She blew out a breath. "How?"

"My eyesight and my hearing are still in proper working order. I looked for you and Matthew the night of that noisy party on the beach, and you were nowhere to be found, which I thought was strange. Then I heard a taxi pull up, and I watched you walk to the Hall. When you didn't return, it was obvious you and my grandson had found something to do together." Belle's smile grew to a full-blown grin. "Besides his lovely gift, I've seen the way he looks at you."

"Looks at me? How does he look at me?"

As if soothing a child, Belle patted her hand. "Like you're a bowl of cream and he's a hungry tomcat searching for a meal."

"Ah—I—um—"

"Close your mouth, dear, and remember what I told you when you first started work here. You have to taste the bounty from a lot of orchards before you find the sweetest fruit. My boy is as sweet as they come, as I'm sure you've discovered."

Too shocked to speak, Chloe merely nodded.

"So, what are you two going to do about it?"

"Do about it? I don't know what you mean."

"Let me be blunt. Do you love my grandson?"

Sometimes, Chloe told herself, it was kinder to be cruel. If she could convince her friend that the time she'd spent with Matt had been no more than a fling—a sort of "fruit" taste test—Belle would be hurt but understand. At least, Chloe hoped she would.

"Matt is a wonderful man, but no. He and I went into the affair with our eyes wide open. He knew from the start I'd be leaving, and he accepted it. We've agreed that when I go, I won't be coming back."

Belle's lower lip quivered, and Chloe thought that either she or Belle, or the both of them, would burst into tears.

"I see." Belle heaved a shuddering breath. "Well, that certainly proves what a silly old woman I am, doesn't it? More wishing and hoping for things that simply won't come true." She took a long drink of tea, then set her empty cup on the saucer and folded her hands. "I'm sorry if I embarrassed you or made you uncomfortable just now."

"You haven't told Matt about you suspicions, have you?"

"Told Matt? Hah! I know better. And it's a good thing I didn't, now isn't it? It would only be one more thing he'd use to prove me a fool."

Before Chloe could tell Belle she was wrong, Matt strolled into the kitchen. "Hey, what are you two doing holed up in here?"

"Having tea," said Belle, then blew her nose in a tissue. "Where have you been?"

"I'll tell you in a minute." He propped his hip against the center island. "How was lunch?"

"Fine."

"Fine," muttered Chloe at the same time.

"Did you decide on anything in particular?"

"Decide?" asked Belle.

"On the remodeling. Is Jadwin's company going to get the job? What's the name of his business, by the way? I don't believe either of you ever said."

"Name?"

"Of his business?" Chloe echoed.

"Uh, yeah. The company does have a name, doesn't it?"

"It's the Remodeler's Palace," Belle shot out. "Or something like that."

"Remodeler's Palace? Now there's a weird name for a renovation firm if I ever heard one."

"If they do good work, the name isn't important," Chloe added. "Right, Miss Belle?"

"Absolutely," Belle agreed.

Matt smiled. "Is Ruby around?"

"She's resting," said Belle.

"Well, go get her. I picked up my new car, and I want to take my three favorite ladies for a ride."

Belle pushed from the table and tottered off as if her tail were on fire, leaving Chloe to answer further questions. Deciding on a plan of attack, she smiled at Matt as she asked, "Where are you taking us?"

"For a ride along the lake, then out to dinner. It's our first free night together since I've been home, so I thought Gram and Ruby would appreciate it. And you."

"We had a rather large lunch."

"I hope you made that Jadwin guy pay big-time."

"Ruby and your grandmother certainly did. I don't think I've ever seen either of them eat so much." She folded her napkin and set it on the place mat. "It was impressive."

"I'm just happy Gram is satisfied with Jadwin's company. It's important she's content." He moved closer to the table. "What about you? Are you planning to see the guy alone again?"

Chloe stood and carried the teapot and cups to the sink, while he collected the cookies and other odds and ends and brought them to the counter. "I doubt it."

Turning her to face him, Matt cupped her jaw with his fingers and bent to kiss her nose. "That's what I like to hear."

She pulled back and he rested his hands on the curve of her hips. "I'm counting the days until I'm at my father's house."

"Then you're still intent on leaving?"

"I have to see my sisters and the rest of my family."

"Ah, the great family reunion. What city did you say it was in again?"

"City?" Chloe touched his forearms. "Why is that important?"

"Because I was thinking I'd take Gram and Ruby on a trip while the remodeling is being done. I don't think she's ever been to Greece, and I know Ruby hasn't. It might be fun to take a tour. Since it sounds as if you know the country, maybe you'd do a little sightseeing with us."

She turned to gaze out the window over the sink. "I thought we agreed to make the break clean and simple."

"Maybe you agreed, but I didn't," he said as he stepped into her side. "I'm not giving up on us, Chloe. Not until you tell me you don't care about me."

Preparing to lie, she took a deep breath, but female voices kept her in check.

"About time you got that new car," said Ruby as she and Belle entered the kitchen. "Give us a minute to get our coats and we'll be ready to roll."

Chapter 19

TO: Cdegodessa@CastleberryHall.com
FROM: Topgod@mounto.org
SUBJECT: Return to Olympus

In preparation for your journey home, it is imperative I remind you of the rules. Plan for retrieval anywhere from 6 p.m. until midnight, earth time, Sunday next. Attire: Chiton and sandals only. No property acquired on earth will be allowed on Olympus, including clothing, jewelry, and documentation of your successes or failures. Avoid transporting the following contaminants: chewing gum, breath mints, cosmetics, and baklava.

I look forward to your arrival,

> Your father
> And still Top God,
> Zeus

Chloe stared at the imperial summons with tears pooling in her eyes. Because the missive served as both a warning and a reminder, it needed no response. Her father's meaning was clear: return to Mount Olympus and meet your fate, O Muse of Happiness, and be prepared for whatever blessing or censure I deem it proper to bestow.

Since the afternoon of Rose Michelle Depesto's birth, she'd spent her waking hours concentrating on her job, intent on leaving Castleberry Hall in better shape than when she arrived. She'd fielded daily phone calls from Jeremy Jadwin, checked with Miss Belle's attorney on the status of the Party Palace contract, and taken part in several discussions with Belle that were meant to put her employer's mind at ease about the sale. In between those chores, she'd handled negotiations for upcoming events, kept appointments, and hosted a surprise engagement party given for an elderly couple by their grown children.

Now that she'd taken stock of her accomplishments, she realized everything she'd done over the past year had centered around Castleberry Hall. Not her position as a muse. Since when had she become so . . . so . . . mortal?

And so involved with Matt Castleberry?

She knew Dr. Studly had made an effort to stay busy as well. He'd taken his grandmother and Ruby to Dr. Kellam, brought Belle to the hospital for something called an EKG, and, when necessary, made himself useful around the office.

But their lives revolved in the opposite direction when darkness fell, because they spent their evening hours together in bed, pretending their idyllic affair would continue forever.

She decided she deserved every bit of heartache she experienced during her waking hours; she'd been both reckless and stupid for allowing Matt to ply her with sweet words, passionate kisses, and amazing sex. It was obvious he had serious feelings for her, even if he never voiced the exact sentiment, and she both longed for and feared the words.

It was useless trying to convince herself that she'd been smart to keep their relationship uncomplicated and logical, because the exact oposite always happened when she was in his presence. She lost all common sense when she slipped into his room, fell into his comforting warmth, and took solace in his arms.

All she could count on was the promise Eros had given her: once she returned to Olympus, Matt Castleberry would be nothing more than a pleasant memory of her time spent on earth.

Startled by the sound of the front door opening and closing, she sniffed back tears. A second later Matt entered from the foyer.

"Mail's here."

Chloe deleted Zeus's e-mail, then dabbed at her cheeks and forced a smile, but the moment he saw her face, Matt's own grin disappeared.

"You okay?" he asked.

"I had something in my eye." She tossed her mangled tissue in the trash. "Did the postman bring anything interesting?"

Shuffling through the envelopes, he stacked them on a corner of the desk. "Bill, bill, advertisement, advertisement, flyer for a new drugstore, bill." He studied a business envelope before handing it to her. "This one's addressed to you. It's from something called Party Palaces Corporation."

Keeping her hand steady, she reached out and took the envelope. So far, she and Belle had been able to keep the exact name of Jadwin's company out of their conversations, and she'd promised her employer she would continue to do so until Miss Belle was ready to confess everything. The letter was probably from Jeremy, asking her to do whatever she could to speed the paperwork along, just as he had in his last few phone calls.

She tucked the envelope in the top drawer of her desk without reading it. "Thank you."

Matt sat in the chair across from her. "Aren't you going to open it?"

"Maybe later."

He raised a brow but didn't comment. Then he said, "I've been meaning to ask, which airline are you flying?"

"Airline?"

"To Greece. And what time is your flight?"

"My flight?"

He grinned. "I never realized what a great echo this room had."

Chloe *tsked*. "I just didn't— Why do you want to know?"

"Because I thought I'd drive you to O'Hare."

"Drive me?" She picked up a letter opener and began checking the rest of the mail. "Why would you want to do that?"

Matt leaned backward and crossed his legs, his attitude casual. "Because I want to give you a send-off that will make you hurry home."

"I'm already going home, remember?"

"You're going to visit your family. Your home is here."

Engulfed by a wave of guilt, she frowned. "You don't know when to quit, do you?"

"Not where you're concerned I don't." He stood, rounded the desk, and squatted so they were at eye level. "No one wants you to go. Gram is beside herself, though she refuses to interfere with your decision. Ruby, on the other hand, is mad as a wet cat. Says she's tried to talk to you, but you walk away whenever she brings it up."

She hadn't been rude to Ruby, but she had made an excuse every time the older woman began to lecture. "I've been busy getting things in order so there won't be any confusion after I'm gone."

Matt stood and took her hands, pulling her to her feet. "We'll manage the confusion. Not having you here will be the hard part."

She drew back and shook her head. "Please stop. I don't want our last days together to be like this."

"Like what?"

"Arguing. I don't want to defend my reasons for doing something I'm honor bound to do."

Stern-faced, he propped his rear on the desk. "It's okay for you to sleep with me, but I'm not allowed to ask questions or try to convince you to stay?"

"Right."

Taking her hands again, he met her toe-to-toe. "What if I said I was in love with you?"

Even though he'd danced around the sentiment in each of their conversations, Chloe knew he was serious. "But you're not," she answered, hoping to convince him differently.

"How do you know what I'm feeling?"

"I know you have a dozen things on your mind that are clouding your judgment. You're unsure of your future, you've broken it off with your fiancée and you're on the rebound, you're worried about your grandmother. Pick any of the above."

"Or none of them. I know what I want, Chloe."

She set her mouth in a scowl. "Hah!"

Instead of answering, he wrapped his arms around her back and captured her mouth in a kiss. After a halfhearted struggle, she melted into his chest. The touch of his lips sent a jolt of desire zinging through her veins, filling her with longing, and aching for his touch in a more intimate place on her body.

Only three more days, she told herself. Three more days and Zeus would bring her home. Until then she would stay the course, enjoy her dalliance with Matt, and continue to tell him they had no hope for a future.

But oh, how she wished she was wrong.

Saturday morning dawned bright and clear. Matt awakened to sunlight streaming across his bed, realized he'd spent another night free of his bad dream, and smiled as he gathered Chloe to his side. After last evening's enthusiastic bout of sex, she had to know how much she meant to him, how much he needed her in his life.

Short of coming right out and saying "I love you," as he'd almost done the other afternoon, he'd used the word in a dozen different sentences. While there was no misconstruing his meaning, it was obvious he had to find a more compelling way to make her understand how he felt about her than gifting her with a string of pearls. He had so many things to thank her for: taking care of his grandmother, nurturing the success of his family's business, driving away his torturous nightmare, and giving advice on what he should do about his life, to name a few.

But gratitude wasn't the only thing he felt for

Chloe Degodessa. He'd fallen in love with her upbeat and practical view of the world, and he enjoyed the way she turned every problem into a possibility. Yes, she was beautiful, but even if she'd been the plainest woman on earth, he'd still love her for all her other positive traits. She was smart, sexy, funny, and caring. In fact, he couldn't think of a single thing he didn't like about her.

Nuzzling her sleep-tussled hair, he inhaled her tantalizing scent, honey and flowers and another elusive aroma he couldn't put his finger on. But, damn, it was nice.

And tempting as hell.

He positioned his knee between her thighs and snuggled against her, cupping her curvy bottom in his hands.

"Hmm," she muttered.

"This is your alarm clock speaking. It's time to rise and shine."

After another muffled groan, she chuckled into his chest. "A talking alarm clock? What a novel idea."

"It comes with a manual wake-up too." He ground his erection against her belly. "*Man* being the operative word."

Trailing his lips to her breast, he found a budded nipple and began to lave it with attention. Chloe moaned and spread her legs wide in welcome. He stroked her dewy cleft with his penis, then entered and held still inside of her. She wriggled encouragement, and he grinned.

"Patience, woman. I'm savoring the moment."

"You'd savor it more if you expended a little energy," she advised, squeezing her honeyed walls around his pulsing member.

Lost in the feel of her, he began pumping his hips, Chloe's pleasure his sole intent. Since she wouldn't accept the fact that he had true feelings for her, he would drive home the power of their sexual attraction and show her what she'd be missing when she left. That way, she was sure to return home.

In seconds she writhed beneath him while she hummed with satisfaction. She stroked his back, clutched his hips, and arched to meet him. Matching him thrust for thrust, she rasped his name, then stiffened with her orgasm, and he reached a crescendo of fulfillment in her arms.

Moments passed before Chloe said, "I bet a clock manufacturer would make a fortune if he found a way to install that as a regular feature on his product."

Matt propped himself on his elbows and smiled. "Maybe I should get a patent on the process."

"I think you're a little too late for that," she answered with a giggle. Then she furrowed her brow and traced his marred cheek with her thumb. "Promise me something?"

"Anything."

"Promise you'll see a plastic surgeon when I'm gone, and get this taken care of."

Damn. He'd become so used to the scar, he

almost forgot it existed. Rolling from on top of her, he inched off the mattress and stood at the side of the bed. "Why should I?"

"Because you're a great guy. When you find the right girl, she'll be all the happier it's taken care of."

What would it take to make her understand that he didn't want another girl? At a loss for words, he opened his dresser drawer, removed underwear and socks, and shrugged into his robe. "I'm taking a shower. Care to join me?"

She pulled the covers over her head. "Not this morning."

The door closed and Chloe sighed. Matt Castleberry was the most stubborn and frustrating man she'd ever met, be they god or mortal. But he was also the most kind and the most honorable, which made it difficult to dismiss him from her mind and her heart.

How many ways could she tell him she was leaving before he got the message? How long would it take for him to get over her and move on with his life?

Not long, she assured herself. Dr. Studly had everything a smart woman would want: intelligence, a brilliant future, a great body, kindness, and integrity. She knew it annoyed him when she talked about his scar, but she did it for his own good. If he dealt with his past, he had a much better chance of finding a woman who was capable of a future, to love him and bear his children.

And she was *not* that woman.

She raised the sheet, peered at the clock on the bedside table, and rolled her eyes. The Blackman-Blevins wedding was scheduled for two o'clock, just a few hours away. Besides tomorrow's Birthday Party, it was her last official event for Castleberry Hall. She had to shower, dress, and get to the chapel, then go over things with Clark in the reception hall. In between, the supplies they were hauling to the hospital had to be counted. And in between all of that, she had to prepare for her trip to Mount Olympus, because tomorrow evening she'd be going home . . . forever.

Keeping busy was good, she told herself. Any excuse to take her mind off Matt. Even though she knew it would never heal her aching heart.

"I wish you every happiness." Chloe clasped Lucinda Blevins's—now Blackman's—hand in her own and gave it a shake, then did the same to the groom.

The bride, a petite brunette with big brown eyes and a turned-up nose, smiled through her tears. "Thank you, Chloe, for everything. Scott and I are thrilled with the wedding. I just know the reception will be perfect."

"My pleasure," Chloe answered. "And speaking of receptions, I'd better get to the hall. Take your time with the photographer. We'll herd the guests into a happy hour filled with drinks and yummy hors d'oeuvres. That should keep them busy until dinner."

She tunneled through the crowd milling in the entry foyer, edged past the guests standing on the steps of the chapel, and headed toward the reception. Clark had been at work in the kitchen for the past four hours, seeing to his menu of roasted quail, mushroom and corn bread stuffing, and fresh string beans. She was certain the salad course, julienned beets and baby carrots over romaine, was ready to be served, as was the three-tiered cake covered with orange-flavored white icing and filled with a tempting mix of chocolate and Grand Marnier. She couldn't remember which of the twelve different hors d'ouevres tasted best, but she was positive the flavor and variety would be delightful.

Entering the reception foyer, she handed her coat to one of the staff and stood in the doorway of the dining hall. The color scheme of black, white, and red, complemented by Castleberry's elegant polished silver and delicate shining crystal, was even more stunning than she'd imagined. She was confident her floor-length sheath of black silk edged with red satin trim would allow her to blend into the background, yet still be fashionable.

Fashionable. The word was one of Zoë's favorites, ingrained in the demigoddess from birth. True, it was the reason she'd been created, but

Chloe wondered if her sister muse had been able to use the gift to her advantage over the past year. And how had Kyra fared with her wish of good fortune? They'd sounded positive and upbeat in every phone conference but the last two. She hated not knowing for certain all was well with her sisters.

As for her own gift of happiness? She had no idea whether she'd done enough to please Zeus. Did the joy she inspired last for a month, a year, or a lifetime? And did that happiness mean the same to the mortals she wished it upon as it did to her?

Propping herself in the doorway, she gazed at the opulent room. She would definitely miss the feeling of accomplishment this job gave her. Marriages, baby showers, christenings, graduations, and a dozen other celebrations had taken place here. All were a part of the life cycle of a human. Mortals had so many things to look forward to; so many joys and sorrows. And if they shared those joys and sorrows with a kind and caring mate, they thought it all worthwhile.

Miss Belle's own philosophy, spoken a few weeks earlier, rang in her brain. "You can say the words die and death in front of me. I know I'm not immortal. I've had a wonderful life with a darling husband, God rest his soul, surrounded by my family and those who love me, and there's nothing more rewarding in this entire world than that."

Was Belle's statement true? Could a life spent with someone you loved more than the life you lived be enough?

She pushed the question to the back of her mind. It did no good worrying about something she would never find out. Her eternity was on Mount Olympus, in the company of gods, doing little more than eating, drinking, and lazing away her days and nights. There were no highs or lows, and definitely no sorrows. Just endless hours of frivolity and . . . boredom.

And worse than the bordeom, she would never share that time with someone who loved her more than life itself.

Sniffing, she realized she was crying again. What in Hades was wrong with her? She'd shed more tears this past year—this past few weeks, actually—than she'd shed in the several thousand years she'd lived on Olympus. The sooner she went home, the better.

Squaring her shoulders, she waved at the band leader as she marched through the dining room. After scanning the guest book and gift table, she checked the seating chart and inspected the cake. As usual, Clark had concocted a masterpiece crowned with dark red butter-cream roses and decorated with red candy hearts and edible seed pearls.

As she neared the kitchen, she smelled a delicious aroma wafting from it. The sound of clinking china and sedate chatter grew louder. Pushing through the door marked IN, she passed two bartenders carrying trays holding sliced lemons, orange peel, cherries, and a few other mixed drink garnishes. "Hey, Ms. Degodessa," they said as one.

"Everything ready for happy hour?" she asked.

"We're doing the final check right now," one of them answered as he sailed past.

She went through the holding zone, an area fixed with stainless steel shelves and food warming capability. The salads were aligned on the cool side, waiting to be served. Waitresses bustled in and began loading the plated greens on large trays. Chloe nodded as she hurried by.

Clark was hard at work in the main body of the kitchen. As if sensing her presence, he raised his head and blew her a kiss. She laughed and walked to his side.

"Everything looks wonderful." She sniffed the air. "Smells even better. You need any help from me?"

"My, but we look elegant tonight," the caterer responded. "Has Matt seen you in that dress?"

"Not yet."

"Goody, because I want to be the one to put his eyes back in their sockets when he gets a gander at the total package." He glanced at her three-inch, sling-back, red leather pumps. "Looks like you could do some damage with those heels, girl. Be careful where you step."

"You're outrageous," Chloe answered, grinning.

"And you love me for it. Now, shoo. The guests will be arriving in the cocktail room any minute, and I have to finish decorating the munchie trays."

"Sure you don't need any help?"

"Not me. Why don't you go to the storage room and check out the stuff we set aside for the Birthday Party? The boys already brought the leftover bubble bottles from the chapel, and I had a couple dozen of those net bags filled with almonds from last weekend. I may have some more after today."

"That reminds me, I have to call the hospital and get the head count. I'll use the back hall phone. See you in a few minutes."

Chloe arrived in the storage area, called her contact at the hospital, and got the estimated number of attendees for tomorrow's party. It wasn't especially important they know how many adults would be there, but the count for the children had to be accurate.

The moment she disconnected the call, the air around her began to rustle, then swirl, forming a gently wafting vortex. Goose bumps paraded up her arms as the air shimmered and heart-shaped rose petals whirled, engulfing her in a snow globe-like reality. Pulsating colors joined the mix, covering her in a cloud of fluttering pink, yellow, aqua, and white.

The scent of musk, rose, and patchouli, mixed

with a hint of sandalwood, overpowered the aromas of the kitchen. Then the storm of petals ebbed and Eros appeared, morphing from cherub to lad to a fully formed deity, as was his usual entrance. Still in his flowing white chiton, his blond ringlets waved in the imaginary breeze as he again posed in magazine-model fashion. Smiling through sensuous lips, he bowed, and, as he raised his head, inspected her from head to toe.

"Love the gown, *chérie,* but that color! Who are you in mourning for?"

Chloe steeled herself for bad news. She hadn't summoned the love god, as she had a few weeks ago, so he could only be here for one purpose. And she doubted it was a good one.

"This color is always in style on earth. Just ask Zoë."

"I plan to, tomorrow night, after the three of you are home. Trouble is, I'm worried you won't be staying."

Now what? "What makes you think that?"

"For one thing, Zeus is annoyed because you didn't answer his latest e-mail. He doesn't like to be ignored."

"I wasn't ignoring him. I just didn't have anything constructive to say."

"And Hera has been flitting in and out like a gnat at a picnic, whispering secrets to her handmaidens and humming whenever she think's she's alone. We all know something's up, because she's been avoiding her husband like the plague."

Chloe's stomach took a bungee jump. "Any clue why?"

"Not a one. But she's entirely too happy."

When Hera was happy, it was a sure bet someone somewhere was in trouble. "Why do you think it has to do with me, Zoë, and Kyra?"

"Who else?" He set his hands on his hips. "How's that little problem of yours working out?"

"Problem?"

"You and your mortal and—"

"Oh."

"Oh? That's all you have to say? Oh?"

"I meant 'oh' as in 'it's nothing.' "

"If it's nothing, then why do you look so queasy?" He raised a brow. "You're not going to bring the flu or one of those other contagious diseases to our mountain paradise, are you?"

"Don't be silly. We can't get sick, remember?"

"Maybe not, but there's always a first time." Folding his arms, he heaved a sigh. "All right then, if you're sure things are going well and you're ready to leave, I guess we'll see you tomorrow evening."

"Tomorrow evening," Chloe agreed as he disappeared from sight in a swirl of petals.

"Who were you talking to," said Matt.

She jumped at the sound of his voice. "Um, the hospital. I told them I'd see them tomorrow."

"I thought I heard the word evening."

"Evening? No, I'm sure I said afternoon."

"Okay, whatever." He ran his gaze to her toes

and back, then stepped forward and took her in his arms. "You look fantastic." He nuzzled her neck. "Hmm. You smell even better."

"Thank you," she answered, relaxing in his embrace.

"My pleasure." He held her as if they were about to dance a waltz. Spinning her in his arms, he finished the impromptu twirl with an impressive glide and dip. "I can't wait to hit the floor with you again. You through back here?"

"I'm done until tomorrow morning."

"Great. That means I have plenty of time to ply you with my wiles. Be prepared."

Chloe smiled, but inside, her heart was breaking. The only thing she was prepared for was a final night in Matt's bed . . . and in his life.

Chapter 20

Chloe scanned the hospital's spacious community room filled with floating balloons, festive streamers, and a swag of brightly colored paper letters hanging over a large rectangular table that proclaimed HAPPY BIRTHDAY. The table, covered in gaily wrapped presents donated by members of the Optimists Club, also held three dozen bottles of bubble mix and a box with the party favors Clark had gleaned from the past month's events at Castleberry Hall.

The centerpiece of the display, a tiered cake frosted in snowy white, was topped by nine candles, one for each child celebrating a January birthday. Colored balloons had been piped onto the sides of the cake, with the birthday guests' names written inside to acknowledge their special day.

Clark spoke to a group of parents and children

in a far corner, while Miss Belle, Ruby, and Maurice Plummer held court at the door, welcoming each attendee as they entered the room. Matt stood against the back wall, his face so pale his scar stood out like a banner, and Chloe guessed he was trying to adjust to the sight and sound of so many seriously ill yet boisterous children.

Maurice finished his conversation with Belle and Ruby, and strode to her side, his smile hesitant. "Ms. Degodessa. Did I hear correctly? Today is your last day with Castleberry Hall?"

Chloe forced a grin. There would be talk when she left, it couldn't be helped. But the fewer people aware of the fact here at the party, the better. "It is, but please don't broadcast the news. I don't want to ruin anyone's good time."

"Of course. I understand you're going to see your father. Is he in poor health?"

"It's more of a family reunion," she answered.

"Ah. Then you'll be back with us soon, I imagine."

"I can't commit to anything at the moment, but I do hope your organization will continue to sponsor this event. It's such a worthwhile endeavor."

"I agree," Maurice concurred. His gaze traveled to the back of the room. "Too bad young Castleberry doesn't see it the same way."

Chloe glanced in Matt's direction, where he was now speaking with one of the doctors. "Dr. Castleberry is behind this project one hundred percent. It's just taking some time for him to adjust to his new surroundings."

"It would be better if he had that surgery to repair his cheek, don't you think? You never know how the children will react when they look at him."

Holding back a snippy retort, she inhaled a breath. "I don't think any of the children will give a second thought to his scars. I believe they're able to see past a facade, be it harsh or pleasant, and recognize what's in a person's heart." She batted her lashes. "Don't you agree?"

Maurice's face turned ruddy. "Right. Of course. It's what's inside a person that counts most, after all." He cleared his throat. "If you'll excuse me, there's someone I must talk to before we begin."

Satisfied that she'd defended Matt, as well as taken Mo Plummer down a peg, she spotted Mary Kinney wheeling her daughter Lyssa through the entrance. After giving Belle and Ruby a hug, Mary continued into the room along with her other children, Tricia and David. As a single mother of three, the woman had little to call her own, but she was devoted to her kids. Though her factory job was taxing, it provided the insurance coverage needed for Lyssa's astronomical medical bills.

For that reason alone, Chloe had seen to it Mary would receive every penny she'd saved from the wages she'd earned at Castleberry Hall, including her designer duds. The woman could either keep the clothes for herself or sell them to a thrift store and use the money to help her family.

Sighing, she fingered the pearls she'd tucked underneath the collar of her sweater. She should give Mary the necklace too, though she couldn't bring herself to let go just yet. Zeus's e-mail had been clear. She'd been ordered to return to Mount Olympus with nothing she'd collected while residing on earth, but the pearls were so beautiful . . . and they'd come from Matt. Perhaps, if she tucked them inside her chiton, she could slip them by her father . . .

Reeling her mind to the present, she made certain the envelope detailing her gifts to Mary was in her coat pocket. Then she slid the mink from her shoulders and walked to the Kinney family, who greeted her with a smile.

"Chloe, everything looks wonderful, as usual," Mary said. "Thanks so much for doing this for the kids."

"Nonsense," Chloe admonished. "We enjoy it." She draped her coat over the birthday girl's lap. "Hang onto this for me, will you, Lyssa? You can use it to keep warm."

Lyssa, who, on earlier visits had touched Chloe's coat and commented on how soft and cuddly it felt, snuggled into the fur. "Thanks. I'll take good care of it, I promise."

"I know you will. I hear you turned ten this month."

"Tomorrow. And since I can't have a party at home, I'm really glad I'm having one here."

"I think I saw a couple of packages with your name on them at the table. Why don't you go check it out?"

The family did as Chloe suggested. Just as she heaved a sigh at the thought of not knowing the outcome of Lyssa's treatments, a hand touched her shoulder.

"Hey, you okay?" asked Matt.

"I'm fine," she answered as she faced him. "I see you've been talking to Dr. Jones."

"Yeah. And I want you to be the first to know. I'm going back on staff here. They need doctors, and since I haven't opened an official practice . . ."

Tears clogged her throat, but she managed a smile. "I'm so happy for you, and the hospital. They're lucky to get you."

"That remains to be seen. I'm going to take it one day at a time, so keep your fingers crossed, okay?"

"When will you tell Belle?"

"Probably tomorrow, when we have some time alone. I heard this shindig often lasts until late."

"It can."

"So, when is your flight?"

"I—I'm taking a cab from here," she answered, sidestepping his question.

"A cab? You're packed? I didn't see any luggage."

"Clark brought my things in his catering van,"

she lied. "I'm storing them there until I have to go."

"I see." He frowned. "Do you have that phone number you promised? The one I can call to reach you?"

She crossed mental fingers, then said, "I'll make sure to give it to you before I leave."

"When will that be?"

"After six."

He stared at the neckline of her pale pink sweater. "You're not wearing the pearls."

Chloe ran her fingers over the rounded ridge below her collarbone. "They're here, but I didn't think this was the right place to display them." She raised a brow. "For some reason, Belle and Ruby are of the opinion they mean more than a thank-you. How do you think they got the wrong idea about them?"

"I haven't a clue, but it doesn't matter what Belle or Ruby or anyone else thinks. It's how you and I think that matters. When you come back home for good—"

"Matt, no. Please. I can't argue about this any-more—"

"Then don't." He grasped her hand and held it in both of his. "Look, maybe I haven't been as clear as I should have, but you have to realize by now how I feel. I love you, Chloe. I want us to share a future."

Chloe opened and closed her mouth. Then tugging her hand free, she turned and walked away.

Matt blinked in surprise. He'd had an inkling the day wasn't going to progress the way he wanted the moment he woke up and found Chloe gone from his bed. Last night's love play had been intense, almost frantic. She'd taken the lead and done everything imaginable that a woman might do to please a man. The experience had been thrilling, the best sex he'd ever had, but it always was with Chloe. He should have realized what she was trying to tell him then. What she told him just now.

She was leaving and she wasn't coming back.

He muttered a curse as he furrowed his fingers through his hair. He'd be damned if he was going to let that happen.

Chloe glanced at the clock on the wall for about the hundredth time that afternoon. Matt had stayed glued to her side for most of the party, holding her elbow, touching her hand or shoulder, or simply hovering. He'd made it so obvious they were a couple that Miss Belle and Ruby grinned like benign fairy godmothers whenever she caught them glancing her way. Now, at just past six, she had to make herself scarce or the day would end in a catastrophe.

She had no idea exactly how she would be retrieved, but Zeus was sure to send an escort. If anyone witnessed the godlike minion, things could get difficult.

"Please excuse me for a few moments," she

said to the group they had joined. Then she headed for the exit.

Matt followed close on her heels. "I'll keep you company. Have you called for that cab?"

Stopping in her tracks, she said, "Why do you insist on following me? I'm just going to the restroom."

He caught her hand in his, his smile cocky. "I plan to stick to you like white on rice. Moment to moment, hour after hour, day after day, until you promise to share your life with me. I've never been to Greece, but I've heard it's beautiful, so I was thinking—"

"You are not coming to my family reunion."

"Why not?"

"You're impossible," she said, grinning to hide her sorrow.

Then she walked backward a few steps and gazed intently, hoping to capture his expression and the emotion it held. At the end of the hall, she escaped to another bank of restrooms. Once inside, she waited for two nurses to leave before she opened her handbag and took out her chiton. Stepping into a stall, she slipped off her slacks, sweater, shoes, and undergarments, and slid the chiton over her head. Unclasping the pearls, she tucked them into a pouch hidden in the garment's full skirt.

Her stomach pitched and she plopped onto the commode. Heaving a breath, she placed her elbows on her knees, rested her chin in her palms, and concentrated on Olympus, envisioning the brilliant sunshine and fleecy clouds floating in an azure sky.

Every day was beautiful, perfect . . . and exactly the same as the one before. No marriages, no graduations, and definitely no baby or wedding showers. No senior citizens who made outrageous comments and failed to wear their dentures. No chefs who worried about her welfare or complimented her on her looks or clothes. No mother figure to confide in or ask for guidance either.

Chloe sniffed and sat up straight, running her fingers through her hair. She was a clever girl, and she'd done everything her father had asked her to do. Surely Zeus would acknowledge her success and grant her a special wish. If she worded the request properly, there was no way he could refuse.

Fisting her hands, she rubbed her eyes, then tore a string of tissue from the roll on the stall wall and blew her nose. In moments a door opened. She peered out from under the compartment and saw a pair of feet encased in winged sandals.

Hermes! The messenger god hadn't been off Olympus for at least a century. If Zeus had sent him to guide her, the old poop really did mean business.

"Chloe? It's time," Hermes said, his voice echoing in the tiled chamber.

She stood and opened the stall door. "I know. I'm ready."

"You've obeyed the rules? Zeus will be angry if you try to pull a fast one."

"I've done my best," she said, ignoring the weight of the pearls brushing her thigh. Now that she knew what she needed to do, she had to believe with all her heart that she'd be victorious in her quest.

He held out his hand and she took it. Air swirled around her, creating a vortex that carried her upward alongside the messenger. In moments they were in the sky, climbing higher and higher toward her homeland.

"I simply do not understand it," said Miss Belle, her voice quivering as she slowly paced the Castleberry Hall business office. "Why would Chloe leave without saying good-bye?"

Why, indeed? thought Matt. When Chloe hadn't returned from the restroom, he'd searched for her throughout the hospital. Two nurses remembered seeing her in one of the restrooms, but that was all. Then he discovered that Clark didn't know a thing about her luggage or her flight. When Mary Kinney showed him the letter she'd found in Chloe's mink coat outlining all that she'd been given, the sinking sensation he felt in the pit of his stomach blossomed into the terror he'd experienced in the jungles of Ituri.

He, Belle, and Ruby had arrived at the manor

house a few moments ago, where he'd raced upstairs to make a cursory check of her room. As Chloe had advised in her note to Mrs. Kinney, her closet full of designer duds and shoes stood waiting to be collected. Her dresser drawers were full, and the few cosmetics she used still sat on the bathroom counter alongside her bubble bath and soap. It was then he'd asked Ruby to give the suite a more thorough search, not because he wouldn't allow Mary to retrieve what she owned, but because Ruby might be better at finding a clue.

Now, sitting in the downstairs office, he made ready to inspect the desk. Though Chloe had promised to give him a phone number, that hadn't happened, but she might have left some personal information behind. More important, she might have written a letter for his grandmother, or given her some small token of farewell.

He glanced at Belle as she continued to hobble back and forth on her cane. "Gram, think of your heart and sit down. I'll do my best to find something in here that will give us more information."

Belle rapped her cane on the office floor. "Do not tell me what to do, young man. That girl was like a daughter to me. I'll walk, or worry, or shout if I want to."

"Okay, okay," he answered, though he stared until she took a seat. "Other than this desk, did she do work anywhere else?"

"Not that I'm aware of," said Belle in a quavering tone. "But what do I know? She didn't even care enough about me to say good-bye."

He kept mum, afraid if he opened his mouth he'd be a lot more vocal about Chloe's disappearance than his grandmother. Then he opened the top drawer and shuffled through a few notepads, an empty date book, a couple of bills . . . and the letter Chloe had received the other day from a company called Party Palaces.

"What are you doing?" asked Belle as he slit the envelope with a letter opener.

"Looking for something, anything to explain why the woman I love—"

"What did you do to the girl?"

Giving himself a mental kick in the head, Matt grimaced. "Not a damn thing."

"I'll just bet. Did you tell her how you felt about her? Did she know she was the woman of your heart?"

"Of course she knew."

"How?"

"Because I showed her about a thousand times over the past couple of weeks. And I gave her the pearls—"

"Knowing Chloe the way I do, giving her *things* wouldn't mean as much as telling her with words," she said with a humph.

"I did use words . . . today. In the middle of the party."

"Did you get down on bended knee and propose? Tell her she meant the world to you or was as important as the air you breathed?"

He shook his head.

"I didn't think so." Belle snorted in disgust. "You deserve exactly what you've been given. Now it's up to you to find her and rectify your idiocy."

Instead of commenting, he plucked the single sheet from the envelope and blinked as a check fluttered to the desk. When he picked it up, bile lodged in his throat. The check, written to Chloe Degodessa, was for an impressive six figures.

Glancing at the letter, he read the few lines of content. Then he locked eyes with his grandmother "This note is from Party Palaces, thanking Chloe for her help with the sale of Castleberry Hall to their company."

Belle turned as white as the paper the letter was written on. "Oh, dear."

"What in the hell's been going on around here?"

His grandmother sighed, then she began a tale that left Matt mystified. "I guess they thought Chloe had somehow influenced me to sell," she finished.

"Did she?"

"Only in a roundabout manner. Remember, you advised me to sell too."

"But I didn't have an ulterior motive." He held up the check. "Some people might consider money like this a kick-back or a bribe."

"But Chloe left the check, which means she either didn't know it was in the envelope or she never had any intention of taking it."

Matt had to admit Belle was correct. If Chloe had used his grandmother in hopes of obtaining money, this check would be with her and neither of them would be the wiser. Questions flooded his mind. How could she attend a family reunion—go anywhere at all—without her clothing? Why hadn't she told him exactly where she was going? Why did she refuse to return?

Did the nights they'd spent together mean anything to her?

Ruby walked in, her expression dour. "I looked through her closets, searched everywhere in her room, but I didn't find a darn thing. It's as if she just walked away without a thought to what she'd left behind."

"Did you try the airport?" Belle asked him "Call a few of the airlines and see if they could find her name on a passenger list or have her paged?"

Matt hunched over the desk blotter and put his head in his hands. "I doubt that's possible. The airlines never give up passenger names, unless there's proof of a terrorist threat. And seeing as how she covered her tracks, there's a good chance she didn't take a plane." He didn't say it out loud, but it stood to reason that Chloe's entire time here had been a lie.

But why?

Her eyes bright with unshed tears, Belle stood. "I'm tired, and I—don't feel so good. I think I'll go to bed and try to sleep or—"

Matt rose to his feet as his grandmother staggered, but he didn't reach her in time to save her from collapsing on the floor.

Chapter 21

Hermes deposited Chloe in her suite of rooms and gave her a terse inspection. "Make yourself presentable. Zeus expects you in his office in a few moments."

"Aren't you supposed to take me there?"

"Gracious, no," he intoned. "All three of you are due back tonight, and I have yet to finish my task as a guide."

Chloe's heart danced in her chest. "Then you've already retrieved Kyra or Zoë? Which one? How did she do? Tell me—"

"Sorry." Hermes shook his regal head. "I've been given strict instructions to keep my lips zipped. I'm sure your father will reveal all in due time." Striding to the door, he bowed. "Best of luck to you, Muse of Happiness, and may Zeus keep his word."

He flew off in a flurry of feathers, leaving her confused and, dare she think it, frightened. Had she misunderstood, or had the winged messenger already brought either Kyra or Zoë back to Mount Olympus? And how had they fared? The messenger's last comment made it sound as if their father might go back on his promise, which would be a disaster, where she was concerned.

Trembling in determination, Chloe drew her shoulders back and mentally went over her plan. Zeus would honor his vow. He had to.

After smoothing her hair, she put on sandals and made a beeline to her father's throne-room-turned-office. It was imperative she stayed calm, acted demure, and told the truth as she wanted him to know it. If she failed, she might never see Dr. Studly again, which meant her life would truly be over, no matter how long her eternity.

The moment she entered the massive reception hall, conversation came to a halt. Gods and goddesses sitting at the edge of the bathing pool, resting on silk-covered couches, or lounging on the stairway, gazed at her with a detached sort of curiosity, as if they had nothing better to do. As she began her march up the marble steps, they started to murmur until their voices grew to a torrent of sound.

Xenon, a minor god with a smarmy attitude and a jealous streak a mile wide, sneered as she passed him. "What's wrong, little muse? Are you not prepared to muck out the stables or wash our laundry for the rest of your pathetic existence?"

"Bite me," she muttered, continuing her climb.

Not a single one of her cousins had a kind word for her. Even Eros pretended to be occupied when she walked by. If she had the time, she would have stopped and informed him that his prediction had been in error. Instead of forgetting Matthew Castleberry, as he'd promised she would, her lover's face was etched clearly in her mind, his touch imprinted on her skin, his kiss still a burning presence on her lips, and his very essence an ache in her heart.

The moment she arrived at the top of the stairs, her father's deep voice thundered from his office.

"Enter, Chloe, Muse of Happiness, and make it pronto."

She straightened her shoulders and Matt's pearls pressed against her thigh. Prepared to tell Zeus the truth, she removed the gems from their hidden pocket and fastened them around her neck. She didn't belong here anymore, not really, but she would leave with her pride intact.

Zeus drummed his fingers on the blotter as he stared at her. Then his bushy brows met over the bridge of his hawklike nose. "You have done well, daughter, in fulfilling your destiny, but I expected you would."

Her spirits brightened. "I did my best, Father. I'm happy you are pleased."

"Happy, is it? Then what of the baubles around your neck?"

"They were a gift I couldn't leave behind."

"From the mortal who was your final dalliance, I assume?"

"Yes. But shouldn't we be discussing my work?"

"Your work." He tapped a folder on his desk. "I must admit, you performed admirably with those you met, but my wife tells me your presence made that single mortal miserable."

"Not intentionally," she began, ready to confess her feelings for Matt.

Hera skulked from behind a column at the rear of the office. Dressed in a diaphanous white chiton trimmed in gold, she glared with almost feral intensity as she said, "Come now, Chloe dear. Be honest. You had no intention of returning here for good. Tell my husband of your love for Matthew the healer, whom you've made so very sad."

Zeus stiffened. "Is it true? You love this human, and you no longer have a desire to live among us in eternal glory?"

"Yes! I mean no." She touched the pearls at her throat. "I did plan to return to Olympus, but something happened over which I had no control. I didn't mean to fall in love but—"

"Do you think me an idiot?" Zeus roared, his gaze resting on the necklace. "Not only did you intend to toss my generous offer back in my face, you defied me as well."

"I brought the pearls only to show you how much the mortal means to me. I deserve to be punished for my disobedience. I deserve to be banished to earth."

Hera placed a hand on her husband's shoulder. "See how clever she is. She found a way to disobey you and still get the best of the deal. I say you command her to stay here and work in the stables or the kitchens. Keep her from her precious mortal, and let her suffer the consequences of her foolishness."

Zeus arched a single imperial eyebrow. "Hera is correct. I could punish you, and make you stay here as a slave for eternity."

"Please understand, I desire a mortal life with the man of my heart," Chloe answered, her voice pleading yet respectful. "I'd willingly give up my immortality, surely punishment enough, if only you would grant me time on earth for the happiness I've inspired, as was my duty."

"Even if your life here included everlasting ease and comfort?"

"Even if it did."

"Hah!" Hera shouted, marching around the desk with her fist raised. " 'Tis but a ploy to get her own way, as usual."

"Hold, wife," Zeus ordered, freezing her in place. "Life on earth is no bargain. It's disappointment and toil and strife, no matter if you do so with the one you love. As it stands, I cannot go back on my word. Chloe did inspire happiness in enough mortals to fulfill my orders. I owe her a joyous life in return. And if she chooses to live that joy in a mortal's eternity instead of a god's, who am I to quibble?"

Hera's complexion mottled to a brilliant red. "So again, a daughter of Mnemosyne will be allowed to win."

"Nay, not win, for this was not a battle. Chloe did what I required she do. I would be a poor imitation of a top god if I denied her request." He stroked his snowy beard as he regarded Hera through hooded eyes. "I wonder, wife, how it is that you know so much about this muse's business? Were you not warned only a short while ago about the dangers of meddling? Perhaps it is you who need to be punished."

"What does it matter if I meddled?" Hera asked with a toss of her head. "She still disobeyed you."

"And because she ignored my order and fell in love, she shall be forced to remain on earth and live a mortal's short and tedious life. Though a bit askew from my original decree, it is a proper and just punishment."

Chloe swiped at the tears in her eyes. "Thank you, Father, and wish me a successful journey, for I must make amends to those I've left and inspire anew the happiness I can give them."

"But—But—" Hera sputtered.

"Say no more, for it is done."

Zeus waved a craggy hand, and Chloe found herself falling at an alarming rate of speed. She only hoped she would land somewhere near Castleberry Hall so she could ask Matt's forgiveness and tell him how much she cared.

Matt sat at his grandmother's bedside, staring through the window into the darkness. Dr. Kellam had left just moments ago, after giving his usual uplifting speech and sage advice. "Your grandmother is eighty-three, son. Setbacks like this are to be expected. I'll do my best to make sure she recovers, but that's all I can do. The rest is in the hands of the Man upstairs."

He hadn't put any technical name to Belle's condition, but Matt knew the score. Her age, her delicate heart, and the stress she'd been under regarding the sale of Castleberry Hall, coupled with Chloe giving notice, and now her odd disappearance, had weighed on her spirit and taken their toll, until she'd simply dropped.

He planned to spend the night here, and if possible, bring Belle home in the morning. Then he was going to start a search for the perfect senior care home, where he would install both his grandmother and Ruby. And in between that and starting practice at the Children's Hospital, he'd work at ridding his mind of Chloe Degodessa, though he doubted it would be easy.

If he knew where she'd gone, knew she was

safe, he might be able to forget her, but right now he couldn't imagine a life without her. He'd heard that time healed all wounds; would it be magnanimous enough to repair the hole she'd left in his own aching heart?

Hoping to sleep, he rubbed his eyes, leaned back in the lumpy vinyl chair and rested his head against the high back, but his mind kept running in place. As angry as he was with Chloe, he had to admit it had been kind of her to donate her things to Mary Kinney. What he didn't understand was how she planned to live without clothing or money . . .

A whisper of footsteps caught his attention, and he focused on a figure in the doorway. Nearing hesitantly, the vision walked as if unsure of its welcome. Matt half rose from his chair, then plopped back down.

"Chloe?"

When she arrived at Belle's bedside, she touched the frail hand. Even though the light was dim, he saw her expression soften, read the concern in her eyes. At that moment there was no doubt in his mind. She loved Isabelle Castleberry as if the woman were her own grandmother. And she would never do anything to hurt her again.

Chloe took a deep breath. "Will she be all right?"

Matt fought to remain calm and in control. If this was a dream, he didn't want to awaken. If it was reality, he prayed it would last forever. "Physically, it's almost identical to the last episode.

She's here for observation and a chance to decompress. If the tests are negative, I'll bring her home in the morning."

"I'm glad." She raised her head and their gazes locked. "How about you?"

"I'm hanging in there." He rose to his feet, but stood rooted in place. "Did you miss your flight?"

She shook her head. "I didn't go anywhere, not really, though I guess you've already figured that out."

"But you planned to leave without a word." Torn between fury and relief, he kept his expression neutral. "Why?"

She walked around the bed and stopped in front of him. "You have every right to be angry. I did a stupid thing, and I'm sorry."

He stuffed his hands in his pockets to keep from grabbing her, even though it was all he wanted to do. "We found the check, you know."

"The check?" She blinked. "What check?"

"The one Party Palaces sent you for a job well done. It threw me for a loop, until Belle convinced me you didn't encourage the sale for the money. Right after that, she collapsed."

Chloe sucked in a breath. Either Jeremy Jadwin had ignored her wishes or the check had been Hera's way of making sure Matt hated her. She had to hope her studly doctor was a kinder and more understanding man, a better man, than the harridan thought.

"At one point the company did promise me money, but I told them no. When I get home, we'll burn the check and the letter. I never want to see Jeremy Jadwin or anyone employed by Party Palaces again."

"I didn't want to believe you'd sell my grandmother out, or help to dupe her."

"Did you see the offer?" she asked with a tiny grin. "The sale would have made her a very wealthy woman. When I realized you weren't the one to run the Hall, I advised her to take the money and live out the rest of her days in luxury. But I didn't want anything for myself."

"She knew that, and I did too. Unfortunately, with her recent health problems . . ." He took a step toward her. "If she rejects the offer, someone will have to run the business for her, especially now that I'll be returning to private practice."

"You are? Oh, Matt, that's wonderful. It's where you belong, where you'll be happy."

"You and Gram told me so, and you were right." He nodded toward Belle. "She's definitely going to need help."

Chloe gazed at the bed over her shoulder, then back at him. "You're in luck, because Miss Belle once made me an offer I found difficult to refuse. Now I'm thinking I should be a smart woman and accept."

"Then you're going to stay?"

She brushed away the tears that had gathered in her eyes. "If you'll have me."

He cocked his head and gave her a cheeky grin. "And if I say I won't?"

Shrugging, she spouted the words he'd said to her earlier. "Then I guess I'll have to be on you like white on rice, moment after moment, hour after hour, day after day, until you relent and promise you'll take me back."

"Uh-oh," he said, his smile wide. "Sounds as if you mean business."

"I love you, Matt Castleberry. I want to share your future, whatever it may be."

Matt closed the gap between them and drew her into his arms. Gazing into her eyes, he said, "I was afraid I'd lost you. Why did you leave the way you did? And why did you give Mary Kinney all your possessions?"

Chloe rested her head on his chest and absorbed his warmth, his comfort, his love. "I thought it was the right thing to do. Dumb, I know, but I never renege on my word. Mary and her family can have everything I own. If I have you and Belle and Ruby, that's all I'll ever need."

His sigh was filled with relief. "I never thought I'd hear you say the words. And speaking of words . . ." Holding her at arm's length, his gaze roamed her body from head to toe. "What in the heck are you wearing?"

"This old thing?"

"It might be old, but it definitely leaves nothing to the imagination."

She slipped her fingers under the rope of pearls.

"I can lose the silly gown, no problem, but these pearls are one thing I'll never get rid of. I have to have something to hand down to our daughter."

"Then maybe we should have a wedding first, so you can wear them with your gown."

"Is that a proposal?" she asked, again swiping at her damp cheeks.

"No, but this is." Clasping her hands, he got down on one knee. "Will you marry me, Chloe Degodessa, and live with me forever? Will you share my joys and my sorrows? Will you love me more than the air you breathe, and stay with me until eternity?"

"Is that all?" she asked with a shaky laugh.

He brought her hands to his lips and grazed her knuckles with a kiss. "I only hope it's enough."

Pulling him to his feet, Chloe stepped into the circle of his arms. "Then yes, I will marry you, and share your joys and your sorrows. I'll live with you forever through eternity, because I love you more than the air I breathe."

"Well, it's about time," said a soft voice from the bed.

Both she and Matt turned to see Belle watching them with open interest. Curling an arm around Chloe's shoulder, he led her to the bed and whispered, "Look who's back."

"Thought I was dreaming, for a minute there," Belle muttered through a yawn. "Does that mean you're here to stay?"

"I'm here for good, I promise."

"And you'll run Castleberry Hall, and Ruby and I can live there as your advisors?"

Chloe glanced at Matt, her eyebrow raised. When he nodded, she said, "I wouldn't have it any other way."

"Does that mean I can use the contract from Party Palaces for kindling?"

"You can use it for whatever you want. Just don't sign it," she advised.

"Now, how about you get some sleep?" said Matt. "Daybreak will be here before you know it, and I have a lot to do tomorrow."

"Only if the two of you tell me you're going home to celebrate."

"I owe you so much, Isabelle," Chloe began, clutching her mentor's hand. "How can I ever thank you?"

"Well, I would like a great-grandchild before I meet my maker, but if that doesn't happen, it'll be good enough if you take care of my grandson. He's going to need you for a long, long while." She closed her eyes. "Now get out of here, both of you. We'll talk more in the morning."

Matt leaned forward and pressed his lips to his grandmother's forehead, then he and Chloe walked to the door. "You ready to go home?" he asked as they stepped into the hospital corridor.

Chloe inhaled a breath. "I'm ready," she answered, "for eternity."